Lakebridge
Spring

by

Natasha Troop

Text copyright © 2010 by Natasha Troop

All rights reserved. No part of this publication may be reproduced, distributed, or transmitted in any form by any means, or stored in a database or retrieval system, without the prior written permission of the publisher.

Red Frog Publishing a division of Red Frog Media

Visit our website at www.redfrogpublishing.com

The characters and events portrayed in this book are fictitious. Any similarity to real persons, living or dead, is coincidental and not intended by the author.

ISBN 1-461-12250-3

2nd Edition

Printed in the United States of America

For Marni

$x^\infty + 1$

Acknowledgements

Marni – There would be no book without you. It would still be a thought somewhere in my mind of something I should do, but I never got around to. You are my heart, my soul and my greatest joy. I only know love because of you.

Becca – Aside from Marni, there is no one person who is as responsible for this book seeing the light of day. Thank you so much for pushing me and never letting me forget that this needed to get done.

Stephan – Thanks for doing what you do and being an amazing friend.

Sally & Harvey – Thanks for watching the kids while I wrote.

Eliot – You remind me that we should always ask what is possible rather than thinking about what is not.

Rebecca – Yours is my most special and treasured of all magics.

Gabi – Thanks for taking care of the things that needed taking care of while I was more focused on this. You are, indeed, privileged.

Greg Mose – Thanks for inspiring me to write, get my book out in the world and for your wise counsel on this.

Colin Dickey – Yours was a needed voice at a critical point. Thank you for your observations and advice.

Spring

"Everything is blooming most recklessly. If it were voices instead of colors, there would be an unbelievable shrieking into the heart of the night."
~Rainer Maria Rilke

I

The Silver Knight paused for a moment and listened for the tell-tale thumping that signaled the enemy had reached the bridge. It was hard to describe the enemy. It was simply Evil clad in pitch black armor. Light lost its way near the foul being and, in the darkness of the bridge, it was only the clatter of his horse's hooves that gave notice of his presence there. The sharp metallic ring that came when the steed's metal shoes collided with structure nails was not present, so the Silver Knight continued on through the morning mist of the forest towards the bridge.

He thought to himself that it was this time of year he loved best. Some preferred the autumn when the leaves turned to yellow and rust. But it was this new time, this green season that gave life to his worn-out soul. The very mist around him turned green from the light through the leaves and he did not mind that his view was limited to the few feet in front of him. It was the beauty of all that he stood for and all that the enemy despised. He no longer kept count of how many springs had passed since his first encounter with the dark knight, but with the turning of each passing year, it was only in this season that he felt everything might be right with the world.

Summer heated the mist to humid and slowed his quest with its lazy crawl towards darkness. Autumn seemed a fair time, but underneath the cool days and happy festivals it held death in its grasp and death was his enemy's accomplice. Winter was no time for war. It chilled his shining silver armor to a frozen shell and kept his thoughts unclear with its frigid blinding whiteness.

Unbuckling his great silver axe from his back, he saw that the green light even gave his weapon a pale aura of life that its purpose so often had denied. He had forged it himself in the workshop that was all his father had left behind before his own enemy, an eastern lord who wore the device of the burning red sun upon his shield, defeated him on the field of battle. There was nothing dishonorable in his death and the Silver Knight held no ill will for the man who had left him an orphan. It was an honorable battle and his father respected and admired his opponent for both his own bravery and that of his people who lived and fought with a passion born of fierce belief in their gods and mighty loyalty to their kings. His father always said he would gladly fight with such men if given the chance. The Silver Knight wished he had a few such men with him this day. His father always warned him to be careful of wishes. They were full of promise but held no prize. A good weapon, his father said, would serve him thousands of times before a wish happened to come true. He could not wish the enemy undone. But a blow from his great halberd, born of skill and longing, forged and sharpened hard in the cold of winter and imbued with a touch of magic, could grant him a victory long sought.

He hefted his weapon one last time to test its balance and, hoped that it would part Lord Stansbury as it did the thick fog. As he began again towards the bridge, he noticed a moose in the mist and thought it a good sign.

* * *

The moose watched the man with the axe walk by through the mist and thought it a good sign that he did not stop and stare or try to approach him. So long as the man did not come near the moose, the moose had no plans to come near the man. Having avoided yet another encounter, he turned and headed towards the large hill where it amused him to stand and watch the leaves sway in the breeze. Stopping for one last munch of a new maple growth, the maple having far too many growths for the moose's aesthetic sensibilities, the moose wandered back onto his path. He had made his path some years back when some man had ordered some stones on his trail. Not that the moose minded the ordering of stones, per se, but he did feel that it would not serve his image well to wander hither and yon upon well placed rocks when he could meander quite freely on dirt and foliage. Much of the foliage that grew in the moose's way needed a good trampling every now and again lest it get out of hand and disturb the general aesthetic of the forest. Some animals had no concern for how things looked. But not this moose. He had a good eye for detail and would not stand idly by when he could do his own small part to make the forest more livable for all.

One of the things the moose really couldn't stand, however, were the large beasts that often ate men and at other times spit them out. From the moose's perspective, if you were going to eat a man, which seemed an unsavory undertaking, you should have the good sense to kill him first and then keep him down. He had seen other meat eaters kill and eat their food and their food never came back out alive. He didn't understand the smoky beasts, however. They mostly traveled on the grey hard rock the men had crossed all his paths with and they moved too fast, quite often running into other animals. His cousin had been hit by one during a winter storm when most of them had the good sense not to be out on the grey rock. His cousin had never been the same since and often confided to the moose that he would rather have not been hit by the smoky beast. It seemed a good notion.

So what he found when approaching the grey rock, as he was right now, was that it was best to just walk right across it and not pause to reflect on the yellow lines and spots that made the grey rock such an appealing sight. They were so very uniform and seemed to serve no purpose other than decoration. The moose often wondered where the men had found such a wondrous grey rock with yellow striping. But he never wondered too long and had made it a point, if he were going to wonder about it, to do so from his high hill spot rather than from atop the yellow stripe in the middle of the grey rock.

So the moose wandered across the grey rock, pausing just briefly to reflect on the marvelous yellow line before moving back to his path. Just as he stepped onto a small shrub next to the rock that had attempted to encroach upon his well-maintained trail, one of the great smoky beasts let out its great roar as it rambled by. If there were any of the smoky beasts he could not abide, it was the very large ones. The moose would even go so far as to hate them.

* * *

Rick Gonzalez hated his brand new Winnebago Vectra. He couldn't think of anything in the world he possibly hated more.

"Look," his wife Marisol said as she excitedly pointed where he could not possibly look, which was behind this great stupid beast of a machine. "A moose."

It was about time, he thought, having seen a hundred road signs, which warned merely "Moose" without displaying one. The only moose he had actually seen in this state were the small stuffed variety that inevitably crowded around the bottles of maple syrup and jars of apple jelly or apple cider donuts that seemed to live next to every last cash register. He hated them too. He hated the moose and their marquee signs. But most of all, he hated the Vectra.

First, he hated the name Vectra. What is a Vectra? He spoke three languages and not one of them included the word vectra. He knew what a vector was and he knew a guy named Victor and he read a play about a Greek girl called Electra but he had never heard of a vectra. So he had to assume that much like Adam in the Garden of Eden, some guy at the Winnebago Corporation, or maybe some group of guys or a group of guys with one woman sat down in a room at Winnebago headquarters and had a meeting about what to call this monstrous sucker of gasoline. The talked it over and threw around names like "Starmobile" and "Galaxy Trekker" and everyone of them had a good laugh over their café mochas or latte frizzies or whatever the local coffee chain was charging four bucks a cup for these days. Rick liked coffee. He liked good coffee, but just coffee. He knew every last well-fed imbecile on that naming committee just loved their mochachinos and he hated them. They probably came up with Vectra because one of them, probably the man who had a degree in engineering but had been a crappy engineer but a good worker who had moved up the chain of command and ended up in the corporate naming room came up with the notion that anyone consigned to such a gargantuan monstrosity as the Vectra would be traveling with a destination in mind on a given day and might set a vector for a given destination and so maybe they should call it "Vector." But the woman with the frappalatte thought that Vector wasn't sexy enough. As if a Winnebago could ever be sexy without a bunch of sexy people inside and the only reason they would be inside is because they thought it would be a fun thing to rent when they traveled to some vacation spot where the girls could go wild or something. Then some guy who liked whipped cream on everything, including his iced guava tea, wondered if they could make the vector electric and came up with the word "Vectelectric." That's how these meetings go with people just making up words that kind of sound like other words until they finally end up with meaningless words like Vectra. After one too many coffeejambas, however, they start to break down and settle on the least stupid sounding made up word. Rick hated the word Vectra and all the coffee zombies who invented it.

It wasn't just the name he despised. It was the amenities. All the ridiculous things that some mobile home designer thought might just make the Vectra just a little more attractive than the next cumbersome dinosaur. Like the powered sunvisors. Now this vehicle was designed for people who didn't want to do much, but to actually think that someone with the sun in their eyes might not have the physical ability to lower a visor to correct a glare issue was a bit too much for Rick. Rick had worked for twenty years as a branch manager for a bank in North Miami Beach. He knew a little something about senior citizens and what they might or might not want. Seniors would spend hours telling you why it was important to have clean change. They didn't like dollar bills that were slightly crumpled. They felt it an affront to the sacrament of American currency. They complained that the toaster the bank was giving away didn't brown properly. Needless to say, Rick hated senior citizens. Even more so now that he was considered one of their ilk. He didn't feel that old, but he knew the problems with modern society when he saw them and he knew what seniors might possibly complain about and pulling down a visor when the sun got too bright was not something anyone in their right minds might take issue with. But some bright penny at Winnebago felt that it would be better to engineer a button which would spin a servo to lower a sun visor than to possibly fix the biggest problem with the machine which was it got five to seven diesel miles to the gallon. Downhill. With wind. Autovisors were particularly despised by Rick.

There were many other little touches that bothered him. Some decorating genius thought that it might make the Vectra feel more like home if they installed ceramic tile in the bath and kitchen areas. Now first, he wasn't supposed to call it a kitchen. His wife kept reminding him not to call it a kitchen. It was a galley. Like on a boat. Now he often agreed that the machine had boat-like qualities. It made him want to vomit. Much like a boat. It stank inside the bathroom. Much like a boat. If they wanted to call the kitchen a galley, by the way, why didn't they call the bathroom a head? Keep the nautical theme consistent. Rick hated inconsistency. Almost as much as he hated calling his kitchen-like space a galley. Even galleys on real boats, not land boats like this scow, didn't have ceramic tiling to delineate the area. You knew you were in the kitchen because that was where the refrigerator and oven were. It's where you cook. It's where you sneak a few scoops of ice cream in the middle of the night. It's where your wife makes the great dishes that she used to make much better in the house you lived in for thirty years and raised four kids in but had to sell because she wanted to spice life up by shaking off her roots. He had shaken off his roots with his family fifty years ago after Fidel ruined Cuba for the middle class. He liked Fidel for that. He liked Miami a lot more than Havana. He liked Miami a hell of a lot more than the Vectra. And he certainly liked the ceramic tile in his old kitchen that now belonged to Kerrick and Devon, a gay couple who just got back from their wedding in Toronto and wanted to settle down in a quieter area of Miami because South Beach had become too trendy. There was only one thing the ceramic tile in the Vectra did. It made Marisol think that this wretched carrier was in some way a proper replacement for their home.

Their home did not have a CB radio. Of everything he found abominable about the Vectra, it was the CB radio that topped the list. He talked on the radio. A lot. To whom he had no idea. There were people out there with handles. They called them handles. Handles are something that you hold on to or open things with. Names are what you are called. Aliases are what you are called when you don't want to be called what you are supposed to be called because someone who you might not want to know that you are you might be listening in to your important conversation about the traffic jam on the interstate or the approximate position of a police office, cleverly called Smokey or Five-Oh as if they didn't know that's what they were cleverly called. Instead of names, they call them handles. That's CB talk. Rick would always just call himself Rick because he never felt a need for a clever nickname like Hondo or Touthless Lou or Trogdor. Some guy would always call him Ricky or some other would come back that he needed a proper handle and because he still retained a slight accent, would inevitably call him Babaloo as if he had never heard that one before. The rest of the CB world would seem to chuckle about this in their own strange language which he despised. But sometimes he had to talk to the world because Marisol would spend hours working on her novel with her headphones on while he was driving and he needed to talk to someone sometimes. But he hated the CB because people wouldn't just talk without giving some kind of information. He had no information to give. He didn't have to get anywhere quickly so never bothered to speed so never cared about Smokey's location or if there was a traffic jam somewhere. These things didn't matter to him. Life mattered. The universe mattered. Marisol mattered. He wanted to talk about all of these things that he used to talk about at the bank or the bar or with his buddies at poker. They would always listen and talk about their own lives while he listened and that was what he needed. Hondo only wanted to tell him to shut up about Lucy always wanting to be in the show. He had many words with Hondo and had been threatened on many occasions. He had heard it wasn't a good idea to mess with truckers but was not terribly afraid of someone messing with the Vectra. With its Caterpillar seven point two liter turbo-charged diesel three hundred and thirty horsepower engine pulling its weight along, he figured he could outrun a semi if needed. He was more worried that no one with any kind of intelligence ever operated a CB radio and that merely by pressing the button on his receiver, he became associated with the refuse of the airwaves. He thought it a step down from internet chat rooms filled with international morons typing greetings for hours on end without ever really imparting anything useful. He tried for hours on end to send out his messages to whomever might be listening and he got Hondo's threats and Aquaman's instructions on how best to avoid Smokey outside Laverne's Tavern on Route 13 outside of Idaville somewhere in Ohio or Wisconsin. He hated the CB because it promised communication but never delivered.

As much as he hated the Vectra, he could never hate it completely because Marisol loved it. She loved the GPS computer that always had the right directions to the next place she had always wanted to see but had never heard of before. She loved the two televisions with the satellite on the roof that moved with the Vectra so that she could still watch all her shows no matter where they were. She loved the Portsmouth Oak cabinets and the Green Slate interiors because she loved green and she loved wood and more importantly she loved the two together. She loved that her galley had an icemaker and a dishwasher and she loved that she could still go online to the internet chat rooms and say hello to people all over the world. What she loved most about the Vectra was that they were both in it together and that where ever they slept at night, they had never slept there before and everything was always new. Even all of the old things they saw were new to them and she never failed to point that out. She loved the Vectra because she knew that Rick would never have left North Miami without it.

So Rick loved the Vectra too because he loved his wife more than anything in the world and anything she loved wasn't so bad after all. But he still hated the damned CB.

"Look," said Marisol, sensing her husband needed some fresh air. "They sell souvenir bridges at that store up ahead."

* * *

Gil looked thoughtfully at his neat display of souvenir bridges as the tourists pulled up in their super cruiser. The display was almost neat, anyway. Each had a slight defect. Kurtz always called them "scars of planning" when he dropped them off for sale. Kurtz bore many scars of planning himself, but Gil rarely commented. Gil tried not to comment about too many things, really. He always thought that if you opened your mouth too wide, someone else's words would fly out. He had a hard enough time being responsible for his own words. His father used to comment that if an inappropriate comment existed for a given situation, Gil was bound to say it. His father used to comment that, anyway. But that was some time ago and Gil had changed a bit. Bore a few scars of planning himself.

He tried to place the bridges in such a way as to hide their greatest defects. Each bridge was ostensibly identical. Exactly twenty-five inches long and ten inches high, scaled precisely to what Kurtz called "Lord Stansbury's Abomination." By that he meant the Lakebridge. Everyone else in Stansbury...everyone in Vermont for that matter called it the Lakebridge. Only covered bridge anyone had ever heard of that spanned a lake. Sure Stansbury Lake wasn't much of a lake. More of a large pond, really. But by whatever definition they use for these things, it was a lake and Lord Stansbury had thought it prudent to stick a covered bridge over it a few hundred years ago. And not any old crossing, either. Gil had seen a few covered bridges in his wanderings. They all had their peculiarities. Some had lost their coats of paint and no society had come along to maintain them so they were gradually losing themselves to the weather. Others were well built and well kept. He sometimes stopped to admire the craftsmanship that went into their creation. The way the planks had been fitted together, the individual designs that made each one special. But none ever seemed as special as the Lakebridge. For one, it never seemed to lose the luster of its coat of red paint. As each of Kurtz's replicas duplicated (some a bit blackened from scorching!), the rich red sheen never lost its glow. This was not due to some determined conservationist who spent hour upon hour traversing the countryside looking for small pieces of history to restore to birthing glory. This was not the product of a local councilwoman who held a pageant or a crusade to maintain the former glory of the creator's dream. For that matter, it was not the result of some deranged local hermit who lived in a forest shack somewhere in the vicinity of the bridge and ate venison when he could find it or his own stockpile of homemade maple syrup created from his great-grandfather's recipe which allowed for a bit of fermentation giving the syrup a little kick when applied to the buttermilk pancakes he would make from boxes of mix he stored in the shed next to the gallon upon gallon of red paint that he would secret out to the Lakebridge every spring just after the thaw and repaint it and coat it to protect it from the upcoming year's wear and weather. There was no such hermit as far as Gil knew and Gil knew pretty much everyone in the area, including the odd hermits who lived on syrup and pancakes and the occasional hunk of cheese that Gil would secret to them to check their sheds for the tell-tale paint cans. From what he could gather from local history and old timers and odd hermits, the red glossy bridge over the almost lake had a kind of magic about it that kept it whole and clean and undisturbed by time.

What kind of magic, they would not say, but Kurtz would. He knew it for the blackest as he often said upon delivering a dented facsimile. Gil asked him why he was so obsessed with the bridge but he already knew the answer and knew Kurtz tried not to think to long upon it. It was only a small part of his obsession that built the bridges and yet another that damaged them. Each defect was different, as unique as the original was from its cousins around the area. One was less a bottom where the underpinnings had been removed by some incendiary device. Another had felt the grave blow of some sharp instrument and was barely fit for sale due to its lack of side and top. How it continued to stand amazed Gil and it wasn't for lack of trying to knock it down on his part. Gil had built a small catapult, really a trebuchet, and used it to wage small wars against the damaged bridges that he would set at different parts of his small store. Sometimes he would use his assortment of small stuffed moose, dressed in red flannel and winter hats, as sentries on the tower he built from the cans of maple syrup that lined his cash register. The moose would signal to him that all was clear to begin his assault. The bridge would be set over a small model lake that Kurtz had provided for him when he learned of Gil's plan of attack. Kurtz had actually designed the trebuchet, but would only supervise Gil in the building of it. This was an incredibly difficult exercise for Gil as his prosthetic right arm was good for rough work and sometimes holding things in place, but he had not yet become truly proficient with his left arm and had to go through many incarnations of his battle device before he had created one with the proper power to potentially destroy his target. Once the moose's signal was received, he would let loose his first assault. At first, his ammunition consisted of the small stones he thought sufficient to pulverize his target. But Kurtz was a fine craftsman and his creation withstood most every rock that fell upon it. The moose would simply shake their stuffed heads in shame. What kind of commander was he that he could not take out such a weak and wounded target? To rally his troops, he sought out a better class of ammunition. Kurtz recommended fireballs, but that seemed imprudent inside the store. Kurtz recommended taking the bridge outside and using fireballs, but he did not seem to understand Gil's intention. After all, it would require some amount of work to move his entire castle of syrup and chocolate outside merely to stage an assault upon a broken down model. Of course, he didn't tell this to his friend. He simply said that his battlefield was confined to the store grounds and that was where victory must be achieved. Kurtz nodded sagely and handed him a small sack of metal ball bearings of various sizes and materials that he had cast in his workshop. He warned to be careful as some contained mercury and if the aim was off it could do untold damage to the souvenir jars of maple syrup that lined the shelves along with the other bridges. Thus far, Gil had destroyed twenty ten-ounce maple leaf shaped jars of syrup and, much to his surprise, a single one-gallon can that one of Kurtz's special loads had penetrated with ease. As it bled on his floor, Gil could only laugh at the power of his small device and that the wreck of a bridge had stood up to all of its firepower.

The moose reminded him that it would only take one well-placed shot to take out the bridge as he watched the elderly couple exit their vehicle and approach his front door. He thought of reminding the moose that he was their commanding officer, but he simply removed his plush watchman from his grade-A dark amber battlements and replaced him in his barracks next to the register. There was a time and a place for everything and civilians should never be placed in harm's way when one misplaced shot would ruin the funding for future fights. He told Shelley about the assaults one time and on his next birthday she gave him a Playstation. She told him that it was bad enough she had to put up with Kurtz but that she would not stand for his delusions of grandeur. He thought of reminding her that they had yet to make a one-handed video game for the Playstation, but gave the machine to Sheriff Tom instead. Sheriff Tom had been through a lot that year, what with being elected sheriff and all, and needed a distraction. Gil's father did not think much of the new sheriff playing video games while on duty...but whose fault was that?

He saw that the couple was from Florida. Dade County from the license plate. That probably meant Miami. He went to Miami once about two years ago. It was on his way to the Florida Keys. He had seen the shows on TV about it but never quite expected it to be so amazingly hot and humid and really boring. His therapist thought it might do him some good to go down to the beaches and see some pretty girls and maybe even go swimming in the warm Atlantic. But he wasn't a very good swimmer when he had two arms and he had heard there were lots of evil globulous jellyfish and sinister sharks in the waters near Florida. He preferred to spend his time drinking rum concoctions in a local bar. He got hit on a few times by a few guys and this older lady who might have been a guy for all he knew but he preferred to think she was an older lady because he preferred to think that at least one woman found him attractive enough to hit on. One of the guys thought his prosthetic was a real turn on and wondered if Gil had any special attachments. Gil just started laughing and bought the guy a drink. Florida was fun for about a minute and then he wanted to be somewhere not so humid.

Come to think of it, Gil had worse times than Florida, but he still preferred Vermont. No matter where he went, he preferred Vermont. Something about there being really good food and not so many people on the road that appealed to him. Maybe it was all the trees or the occasional moose. But Vermont was just about the best place he had come across and he could tell just by looking at him that the old Hispanic gentleman who just grumped his way through the door behind what could only be his wife did not share his outlook on the Green Mountain State.

"Bit of a change from Miami, huh?"

The old man nodded. "We have a different type of tree. But I'll tell you what, we've still got you beat for French Canadians."

"You don't say?"

"I do say. They seem to skip this place altogether and make their way down to Miami like locusts. They like to fish. They like to fish a lot. I had one sorry snowbird come into my bank reeking of fish and he asked to rent out a safe deposit box. I had him fill out the necessary paperwork and give him the key and show him to the vault and you know what the sorry son of a bitch does?"

Gil smiled. He loved tourists. "I just can't think of it."

"He pulls out the ugliest looking catch you've ever seen, already starting to turn and tosses the thing into his box like it's gold. I ask him as nicely as I can why he's using my establishment as a fish locker and you know what the sorry son of a bitch says?

"I just can't think of it."

"He says, get this, 'Eets da beegest fish I eva dun cought and ee ain't never getting way from me.' Then the moron locks up his box and leaves, leaving his dirty fish stink all over my bank. My sister owns a little motel in Hollywood. That's Hollywood, Florida, mind you where our kind of freak isn't put on television. She says these dirty Frenchies come down and stay all summer long and use the little coolers she graciously provides in the room to store their fish in. What are they storing it there for? They don't have kitchens. It's not like they can cook it there. But they seem to love fish or at least love stinking up other people's rooms with their fish. I'm on my way to Montreal right now to see if the place stinks of fish as badly as my bank vault does because if it doesn't, I'm going down to the local store and buying up a bunch of fish and tossing it in their stinking houses."

Gil tried very hard not to fall down laughing as the man walked off to look at his assortment of souvenir candy and moose paraphernalia. He never thought much of French Canadians really. They came through on their way to somewhere else much like most people. But it did occur to him that they bore a strange fishy smell every now and again. He had never thought too much about it, though.

His thoughts were better spent elsewhere. Like with the man's wife who was carefully examining his target. It had been placed carefully on its spot and all of his calculations for its ultimate destruction rested with his ability to make adjustments, which he kept a careful log of in a small black leather notebook he had bought for the purpose of writing a diary of his days. He had written about two weeks worth of entries. Each entry seemed less and less interesting than the last and it finally depressed him too much to try to recount the same days over and again. Although, if he were still keeping a journal, he would definitely comment on the old man's problem with French Canadians. He might also comment upon his relief that the wife seemed interested in looking at the damnable bridge, but not touching it. While he did not have a "look but don't touch" policy in his store, because those that did were not friendly and his was, if anything, a friendly bric-a-brac store, he hoped people wouldn't touch that bridge in particular. Quite often he would focus a great amount of his psychic energy on the task. He believed if you thought something hard enough, the thoughts could make a slight impact upon the subject of your thinking. He spent a good few moments focusing hard on the old lady and it seemed to pay off. Once again, he contemplated keeping a journal of the effects of his concentrated focusing, but then he started remembering the total depression that always came with journaling and felt it better to leave that sort of thing to those who enjoyed their depressions.

The woman looked to him with smiling curiosity. "What happened to this one?"

"Every one is made differently."

"But it looks like this one was made and then intentionally destroyed."

Gil took some umbrage with that description. "It's not really destroyed now. Damaged to be sure, but if it were destroyed do you think it could stand there like that?"

The lady thought about his reply for a moment and did not seem wholly satisfied with his response. "I suppose not. Can I ask you the question differently?"

"I would welcome it."

"Why was this one made and then intentionally damaged?"

Gil had tried to explain to visitors in the past the many reasons why Kurtz took such care to mar his creations. He would often go into lengthy tales of an artist who felt it necessary to achieve total perfection with his bridge making. He would describe Kurtz as a master craftsman who would spend hours and sometimes days working with his models trying to get every last detail of the Lakebridge committed to scale. Gil had a great story about the time Kurtz had spent a month without food or drink living and sleeping on the bridge to absorb the essence of the construction before returning to his shop only to find that he could never make it just right. And with each passing attempt, his anger would grow and he would hurt each of his attempts in such a way to show that it was not the one true model before tossing it out on the fire pile for kindling. It was only because Gil respected the quality of the works that saved them from their fiery fates. But none of this was exactly true.

It always came down to one real reason, which the old Cuban gent was kind enough to get to before Gil had a chance to make it a more complicated issue, "The guy's loco, Marisol. Crazy-go-nuts making all these little models and then bashing them." The man picked up the one that bore burnt timbers. "Look at this one. It's been torched. This guy must hate this bridge something fierce to make all these models and do these things to them."

"Is that true?" Marisol asked.

"That's about it, really," said Gil, amazed by the man's insight.

"Weird. How much are they?"

"Twenty dollars a piece. But if you buy three, you get ten dollars off."

The man put down the bridge he had been scowling at. "Why would anyone in their right minds buy three of these things?"

Gil shrugged. No one ever had, but he always practiced the art of the up sell. He had once worked as a telemarketer and the words "UP SELL" were painted in day-glo colors across the wall of the basement where the phone bank was located. He had sold overpriced pens in Phoenix for a few months. He could never figure out which circle of hell Phoenix was, but it certainly seemed somewhere near the bottom. Yet it was a voluntary inferno. They paid to get in. People seemed to move there in ever growing numbers, making the place even more despicable. The desert was unfriendly enough without picking one of the hottest parts of it to build a city. But somehow Phoenix seemed worse than any of the small desert towns he had passed through simply because it was not small. It was sprawl. Massive ugly sprawl that kept on sprawling and one day would sprawl all the way from Tucson to Flagstaff if someone didn't come along and cauterize the bleeding wound of it. But no one would ever do such a thing because the land was cheap and wherever there was cheap land over priced houses could be built and sold to finance the next phase of sprawl. And he had been trapped in that ugly hell for three of the longest months of his life. He was actually in a small suburb of the sprawl called Goodyear that made the rest of Phoenix look beautiful by comparison. Goodyear was the armpit of the armpit. A stanky town that had one weird remnant of something cool and unique. It must have been a racetrack at some point but it was long shut down. It was this futuristic grand stand that remained standing, but slowly eroding from idiot graffiti and sand blown desert decay. Gil would go there after the sun went down and climb the fence that barely encased the place. Some local kids would be smoking pot or huffing gasoline, more likely huffing gasoline as it was just that much cheaper and more idiotic than marijuana. But he would ignore their psychotic death wish activity and focus on the architecture. Some weirdo had plotted this place out and sold his strange idea to people who constructed such things. The place should have been on Mars it was so out there and that was why it probably failed to draw the crowds to whatever race-like activity it was created to host. Either that or the insane heat of the Goodyear sun. Gil bet on the sun which beat into his brain to make enough money to get himself out of that lunatic town. So he sold pens and up sold pens. He was a mad pen selling freak and couldn't believe it when people would actually listen to his pitch much less buy his product. But after awhile he started to believe his own lies about how the quality of ink in his Bic pens was somehow of a higher grade than that which one might find at the local store. A pen bought among a gross of its companions for a slightly elevated price seemed a reasonable deal when one threw in a free camera. Did the camera work? Gil had never seen one and never knew. What he did know was that anyone who bought a box of pens from him would certainly be interested in knowing about his special deal on printer cartridges. And, strangely enough, he was right. What he really discovered is that most people are insanely lonely and will do just about anything to talk to a friendly voice. People say they hate telemarketers but they really don't. How many other people just call you out of the blue and tell you anything with a smile in their voice? Most of the time people dreaded picking up the phone because who ever was calling probably wanted something. The telemarketer really didn't want anything but to talk and maybe share a little information about a good product or service or survey they were conducting. But beyond that, they would listen to you too. They would never hang up on you and always be patient with your stories or concerns because they weren't selling you pens or bathing suits, they were selling their friendship. At least Gil was. And better yet, he was up selling his friendship at very little extra cost. He never hated the job and would have stayed had it been anywhere that wasn't Phoenix. But he had never forgotten the day-glo words on that basement wall that gave him all the reason in the world to try to sell three bridges when no one in their right mind needed more than one.

"You wouldn't be buying the three bridges for yourself."

"Who am I buying them for?"

"People who've never seen the Lakebridge. Like your kids. Wouldn't you like to share a little bit of your trip with your loved ones?"

"Not especially," the man gruffly replied. A tough sell. Gil knew his type. He had cracked them all the time when pens were on the line. But he could never quite get them to go for the three bridges. The most he had ever sold to a single person was two and that was to Vermont State Trooper Jennifer Julia Kennisaw. Trooper Kennisaw, she never let him call her Jennifer or Jenny or even Jen and especially not J.J., had a case involving the attempted destruction of the Lakebridge and needed the models for evidentiary proceedings. He was really not paying attention to what she was saying at the time as much as how she was saying it. He loved the way she talked and would have gladly just given her the bridges but she insisted on purchasing them because the state was footing the bill and there was no reason for her to accept them as gifts or for him to wrap them as nicely as he had. She just needed the bridges, thank you, and she was off to whatever she needed to do with them. She was a tough sell, but Gil wasn't trying to sell her bridges.

He was, however, trying to sell this man a few of them. "Why not?"

"Because they'd rather have the fifty bucks than a few bridges."

"But you aren't giving them a bridge. You're giving them a memory. You're giving them a piece of something you saw and thought to share and isn't that worth more than money?" Gil flashed his best salesman smile which he often flashed when he was telemarketing because he always felt that the people you were talking to over the phone could hear the smile in your voice. He also knew this Florida gentleman had never purchased a single thing from a telemarketer in his life and probably wouldn't even pick up the phone unless he recognized the number. Still and all, Gil tried for the sale because if he didn't sell bridges and the occasional stuffed moose, he would be living on settlement money alone and he never felt productive if his bills were paid with settlement money. It was a great shame to him that all too often he felt unproductive.

"But I've never seen your bridge," the man said. "I've only seen your models."

"Now I understand why you might hesitate in purchasing one, or many, of these items. If you've never seen the Lakebridge, then you can't share the memory of it with your loved ones back in Miami."

"Son, please stop trying to sell me your bridges. I know it's what you do, but I just don't want to buy one."

Gil knew when to back off. There were all kinds of people in the world and some would buy what you were selling just because you were selling it and they liked to buy. Those were the people who watched infomercials at 3am and discovered that they could wash their cars with the same compound that was used by NASA to build the International Space Station and wouldn't it be great to have that kind of protection in a car polish. Their homes were filled with everyday wonders that seemed to clog up drawers and closets and garages (Gil preferred to call them "car holes") and never quite worked for anything better than taking up space. Gil had made a vow never to buy anything directly from the television. Sure, he would buy things he had seen on television, but never from the people selling them there. It somehow seemed better if he got it in the store or from off of the internet. Somehow the purchase seemed a bit more contemplated. And besides, he avoided the opportunity to be up sold on some other fine product or attachment or warranty. Gil never believed in purchasing a warranty for any item under two hundred dollars. It just wasn't enough to bother.

Some people would never buy a thing they didn't need and hadn't thought about for sometime. Their worlds held no clutter. They researched appliances and did not feel that just because they lived in a modern world they had to have every modern convenience. Nor did they feel the desire to buy things for the sake of buying. It just depended on how people were wired. Heck, some people just don't like bridges, even the burnt ones.

"Look, Rick," said Marisol with a smile to Gil, the kind of smile that told him that she was the kind of saint that loved people she just met and would give them the world if it were in her pocketbook. "The sign says if you purchase three of these bridges and a stuffed moose, you get a guided tour of the Lakebridge. That sounds nice."

"I don't know," said a noncommittal but defeated Rick. Gil had seen many a wife turn his defeat into a victory for a single bridge. But none had ever bought the tour package.

Gil had never given the tour. Sure, Gil knew all there was to know about the Lakebridge, but he had never actually told anyone about it outside of a few of his friends in town who all seemed to think he was a bit nuts on the bridge. Not so nuts as Kurtz, but a bit crazy about the whole thing just the same. To tell the truth, he would have given the tour for free. He felt almost guilty taking money for it, even if he was selling stuff on the side. Almost guilty, but not quite.

"Would you like to sample any maple syrup or chocolate?" Gil up sold. He felt like he was pushing his luck a bit, but his luck was always begging for a shove and Gil was never one to walk by a playful child who wanted to touch the sky.

"What is it with you people and your syrup?" the old Cuban complained. Gil had heard the complaint before. "It seems like every shop or store or gas station I go into in this state tries to push some syrup on me. Did you know that, if I wanted to, I could go down to my local grocery store in Miami and buy genuine Vermont maple syrup? From what I can tell, it tastes just the same, costs a little bit extra, but doesn't require that I travel a couple of thousand miles to get some. Sure the variety may be a bit better up here, but if you really want to know the truth of it, I can't tell the difference between the grades of syrup. Maybe I've smoked a few too many cigars or something, but it all just tastes sweet to me. Heck, I didn't come here for the syrup. I don't even like syrup."

"What do you put on your waffles?" Gil honestly wondered.

"Nothing. I don't eat waffles. I don't think I've ever ordered a waffle. I don't like the word so I avoid the food."

It seemed like a good enough reason to Gil. He had heard far stranger excuses for not eating a thing. He was slightly disturbed by the lack of enthusiasm for syrup, however. Some people had a thing for fine wines or cigars. For Gil it was syrup. You give Gil a taste and he could tell you where it was from, when it had been tapped (give or take a decade) and what color and grade it was. He had made a study of it over the years. Shelley had encouraged him to write about it for some local magazine. Shelley still did not understand about the whole arm thing.

He never liked writing much to begin with and now that he could only write with his off hand, he thought even less of the practice. He tried explaining it to her, but she walked over to his computer and asked him if he could type with one hand. It was one of those questions that answered itself that she was always posing to him. She would even come by occasionally and show him some weird prosthetic catalogue that featured some new type of arm that could perform more functions than ever before. Gil often thought that if there was a television channel for amputees, they would have infomercials on for the most modern of devices that acted like an arm and, perhaps, a fishing rod. He often thought that if he were to replace his current arm, it would be with one that doubled for a fishing rod. They had them. It was an interesting notion. But he had never been very good at separating the fish from the hook when he had two hands and thought that with just the one, it might prove somewhat more difficult. He had grown rather fond of his present arm, however, and really didn't contemplate replacing it. He spent a few hundred hours with a different local artists having it decorated. Some people mistook his decorations for tattooing, and, in their own way, they were right. But unlike tattoos, Gil could replace the skin without any pain. A guy with a tattoo sleeve on his real arm was rather stuck with it. In any case, Gil was not going to get some Swiss Army device installed on his body just to appease someone else's notion of the amazing things he could accomplish if he would just allow for the future to creep in on his present. Gil had no problem with the future, though. He told Shelley that until he could get a bionic arm that could give him some kind of super strength and dexterity, he would stick with what he had.

His new friend, Marisol, had selected the three bridges that seemed the least damaged and a stuffed moose with a fishing pole. Why the moose was fishing, Gil had no idea…Gil often wondered about the designer of the stuffed moose in the hunting suit…it just didn't seem right. He carefully packaged each model in its own souvenir box, bagged them up and placed the moose carefully on top. She paid him in cash, which was rare these days but appreciated. Every time he had to do a credit card transaction, the bank made him pay through the teeth for it. It seemed sometimes like they didn't want him to take credit cards. It was one of the few things he agreed with the bank about as credit cards were a pain in the ass and it seemed some of his less savory tourists had a nasty habit of claiming that he had overcharged them or that they had never shopped at his store at all and, in such cases, the card company always agreed with the customer despite his signature proofs and hysterical protestations. Gil only ever got really hysterical with the credit card company…they were the devil. He asked John Kingsley over at the bank about it once when he was in making a deposit and John told him that processing little credit card transactions was not something the bank liked to do. The bank apparently felt it somewhat insulting to deal in small amounts of money. Gil wondered aloud as to who exactly it was in Stansbury who was transacting in anything over small amounts. John replied that the bank rarely felt anything but insulted these days. Gil said he knew how the bank felt, especially when dealing with the bank.

When Rick looked away, he slipped in a small tin of grade A dark amber syrup that was packaged to look like a small cabin in winter with a spout where the chimney should be and winked at Marisol.

"For pancakes, then."

"Thank you," she said, taking the bag from him. "Now how about that tour."

"Sure. Let me just lock up here and I'll take you right over."

The couple exited the store and went over to their Winnebago to put their purchases away. Gil could hear the old man complaining about the thousands of things he'd rather be doing in Miami but the woman had a way about her which suggested that her husband would always capitulate. It was something Gil had come to respect in the older married women who had come through his store. They seemed to have this gift for letting their husbands think that they were in charge, that their opinion really mattered. But the women still always managed to get what they wanted. This woman was no different. She knew her husband and, more than anything, she loved her husband. But she also knew what she wanted to do and that she would get her way and she didn't need to raise her voice or whine. Her simple, few words and beatific manner would always defeat her husband's grump and bluster. And somehow, Gil imagined, the old man wouldn't have it any other way.

As Gil secured away the few valuables that needed securing before he left with the couple, he looked over to his stalwart watch moose who reminded him that the trebuchet was locked and loaded. The moose was right. The machine sat ready, waiting for a simple adjustment in aim to fire off at the standing wreck of a model. The troops were cheering for him to attack. Just one volley, they pleaded. It wouldn't take too long and victory was, perhaps, finally at hand. He had planned this attack very carefully for some time and finally felt that he had the right combination to win this day. Checking to make sure the couple was a safe distance away, he lined up his shot. It was really about hitting the one small piece of timber that held the whole wreck together. He managed to hit the small expanse of air around the spot, but never a bull's eye. Gil checked with his lieutenant who gave him a curt nod with his antlers in salute for the glory that would come of the victorious attack. Satisfied that the conditions were optimal, he let his shot fly. He watched as the steel pinball sized load he had fired arced perfectly towards the bridge. Its destruction imminent, he could not help but to give a small cheer. Not loud enough to let all in on his confidence. Only his compatriot had heard him and shook his hoary head in sadness as the shot just barely missed. Gil watched in horror as the ball destroyed his display of maple-horseradish mustard jars which had been carefully stacked in the likeness of a castle keep. He had sent a picture of the display off to the small farm that produced the condiment and they had rewarded him with a t-shirt, a stuffed moose and a bottle of some of their premium grade-A medium amber which, as far as he was concerned, was the optimal flavor for use in his maple-oatmeal cookie recipe. As the jars crashed down around the bridge, most survived the fall. Only one or two were casualties of the attack and, as much as he would have liked to give them a proper burial, reconstruct his display and perhaps make a sandwich, he had customers waiting outside and needed to get them to the Lakebridge.

Gil left the scene of battle behind him and stepped outside. It would have been a perfect morning for victory. Even without it, however, it was pretty spectacular. Of the many things about he missed about Vermont in his travels, it was mornings like this early spring one that really made him all misty for his green mountains. He hadn't been everywhere in his thirty-three years, but he had been enough places to know that there was no spot like this one that was really home.

He locked up the store and went over to the extraordinary recreational vehicle. It was probably the most amazing one he had seen to date. If he wasn't mistaken, it had a satellite dish. He didn't even have a satellite dish. Not that he missed having one too much, but it would be nice to think that his house was better equipped than an RV. But this Winnebago was something else. As the couple climbed down to join him, he was able to sneak a peak inside. No doubt about it, his house was running a distant second to the thing.

Gil couldn't help but to comment, "Nice truck," with a slight amount of jealousy in his voice.

The old man shrugged. "It gets us from here to there. Bitch to park though and it drinks gas like an Irishman drinks beer."

Gil smiled as he realized that satisfaction was hard to come by. You could have everything that someone else could ever want but it would never be what you needed. Gil often thought it would all make sense if everyone could simply shift lives with the people directly next door to them. It always seemed like they had a better house or car or boat and if you could only have their house or car or boat you wouldn't have so many problems of your own. But that just wasn't true. If you had everything that your neighbor had, you still wouldn't have everything he wanted and you'd eventually be unhappy unless you shifted another door down. Most of the time, Gil was pretty happy with what he had. But sometimes he wouldn't mind trying to park a giant RV like this one just to see if it was that much of a bitch.

Gil chuckled a bit and pointed to a small path across the highway. "The Lakebridge is about a ten minute walk down that way. They never did build a good road in." Gil checked the empty road before leading the couple across.

Rick seemed a bit perplexed and asked, "If there has never been a good road in, why is there a bridge over a lake? For that matter, why *is* there a bridge over a lake? Couldn't they have just gone around or something? How big a lake is it, anyway?"

"Well, there's no real consensus about why the Lakebridge was built except to say that Lord Francis Charles Stansbury was something of an eccentric and was known to do certain things because they had never been done before." This was Gil's pat answer to the question of the Lakebridge. It always kind of spilled out of him the way a gumball will come out of the machine when you feed it a quarter. But as he led the couple down the path towards the bridge, he somehow felt obliged to give more than the rote response he would pass along to the look-but-don't-buy crowd that usually frequented his store. This old guy from Florida needed more than the random theory of the bridge to justify this excursion. As Gil led them along towards the lake, he broke the calm quiet of the morning in the woods, "That's what most people in Stansbury believe in anyway."

Marisol took the bait and probed, "And what do you believe?"

"It's not what I believe so much as what I know to be true. I've done quite a bit of research into the Lakebridge and into the history of Stansbury."

"Why?" Rick huffed out. The walk itself wasn't strenuous, but it was a distance for people who didn't see nature very often.

"There isn't a whole lot to do around here, sir, besides enjoy the scenery and find out things. As much as I enjoy the scenery, and I do very much…it's really the best this country's got going for it and I've seen most of this country so I know this to be true…but as much as the trees sooth the mind, sometimes you need to do something. Anything, really. For many years my father was the elected sheriff of this town and I used to spend a lot of time going through all of the old records looking at history. Stansbury is a strange town for the area. Most don't have their own elected sheriff or mayor like we do. I could never find out why this was the case. But I have learned a lot. Just in arrest records you learn a lot about a place. Did you know that it was illegal not to shoot an Indian if you saw one on your property? One man, Kenneth Bixby, absolutely refused to kill an Indian. Apparently, he refused to kill anything, even a moose which was also, apparently, a crime. A noble disagreement with the law, but a law broken is always in need of repair. Mr. Bixby was arrested fifteen times for not killing Indians. It seems his neighbor would watch the natives walk across Bixby's land and then kill them as they crossed over onto his own. This neighbor was the sheriff at the time and would quickly put Bixby in chains on each occasion."

"What was the punishment?" asked Rick.

"Mr. Bixby would be covered in maple syrup and buried up to his neck for two days."

"You're kidding!"

"Yes. I am," Gil laughed. "About the punishment anyway."

"So what was the sentence?"

"It was a five dollar fine, which was a lot at the time. It seems that the constable would receive a five dollar reward for each Indian he killed, but the town did not have the funds to pay him. So he would arrest Bixby, fine him and get his reward."

"That's kind of sick if you ask me," Marisol interjected. "It just doesn't seem right."

"History's not always pretty. Take the bridge, for instance. It was actually the reason that the town of Stansbury was founded to begin with. It was some years before the Revolution. Not the Cuban Revolution, mind you, but the American."

"Thanks for clarifying that," laughed Rick.

"No problem. There've been so many revolutions and my friends are always accusing me of being too general. Please let me know if you need clarification."

"We will."

"Excellent. Anyway, it was some time before the American Revolution when Lord Stansbury came over from England with his wife and daughter, Penelope."

"What was his wife's name?" inquired Marisol.

Gil figured that, being a wife and all, she was interested in wives or something. Gil had never been interested in wives. Not that he wasn't interested in having a wife someday, but the histories of wives just didn't intrigue him so much as their husbands did. He wondered if this made him a chauvinist. He had always tried to be fair, but he didn't feel he should be taken to task for not being inclusive in his research. It just didn't seem important at the time. Stansbury's wife's name was not important to the history. If it was, he would probably know it. She must not have done anything other than marry Stansbury and bear his children, specifically Penelope, who was an important woman. Or girl. At least a female, so Gil wasn't excluding woman. Just unimportant women. Gil didn't know the name of Stansbury's slaves either…did that make him a racist?

"Lady Stansbury. I'm fairly sure her name was Lady Stansbury." Gil watched the couple stare at him incredulously before chuckling. "Anyway, Lord Stansbury and family were traveling through the then colony looking for a place to set up shop. The nobleman had left England under a dark cloud. It was suspected that he was involved in the black arts and rather than risk a hanging from some reactionary Christian group, he packed up his shop and brought it here."

"Was he a witch?" Marisol asked.

"Aren't they're called warlocks." Rick replied.

"Actually the correct term was sorcerer. He was a sorcerer. If you believe in that kind of thing. Which I do. There are records from England that verify that his former place of residence had been a regular meeting place for strange rituals and sacrifices. Many locals went missing and there are reports that strange creatures would arrive through faerie mounds that shone with an eerie unnatural light."

Rick did not seem inclined to believe, "You're kidding us again, right?"

"Not at all," Gil replied in his most serious of tones. "Belief is a strange magic. The stronger people have faith in something, the more likely it is to be true…to happen. There is magic in the world. It's not as great as it once was, but it's still there. You'll see when we get to the Lakebridge. Once you know what it is, you can't help but to recognize it. It's not a good thing at the bridge, though. It's an evil thing. Stansbury practiced the dark arts and his creation was born of the blackest he could muster."

The couple was hooked. "Why did he do that?" asked Marisol. She seemed generally concerned and maybe a bit scared. Gil knew that the people of the Caribbean understood about dark magic. He could tell that Marisol, at least, knew enough to worry.

"When the family arrived in the colonies, it was late in the fall. Not so late that winter had set in, but late enough that the nights were colder than you see in South Florida on the coldest day of the year."

"That's about seventy-eight degrees," Rick said, trying to break the mood which had turned decidedly morose.

"A lot colder than that, Rick. Cold enough, in fact, to freeze over the water in the lake just enough to hold up the fallen leaves. You really ought to come back around to see the leaves change, by the way. It's about as pretty as nature can get."

"I've always wanted to see the leaves change," Marisol replied enthusiastically. "Everything in Miami is always the same all the time. I know it's natural for Miami but it just seems unnatural when you compare it to a place like this."

Rick seemed annoyed by this. "Miami is consistent. There's nothing wrong with consistent. At least there you only have to have one set of clothes. How many sets of clothes have you got, fella?"

"I haven't really thought about it. Not too many, really. I know there's some that dress for each season. I'm not much for it. I pretty much go in layers. If it gets colder, I add a layer. I guess you could call each layer a set. And if I never get beyond three layers, then I must only have three sets."

Rick seemed neither pleased nor displeased with Gil's answer. Gil knew better than to press the issue. He liked these people as much as he liked anyone he had just met and wanted them to think fondly not only of Stansbury, but of himself. A long time ago he really didn't care much about what people thought of him. He tried to ignore his ego and just be himself, whatever that was. Of course, he later realized that this was just an extension of his ego and he had only wanted people, including himself, to think he didn't care what they thought of him. Now that he understood that about himself, he made a real effort to ensure that people thought well of him. It wasn't that he was insecure, it was simply that he enjoyed the process of being thought well of, which always included pleasing people. These people, at least Marisol, were interested in the Lakebridge.

"I can guarantee you that Lord Stansbury and his family were not in possession of too many sets of clothing."

"Did he have a cloak or robe or something," asked Rick.

Gil was stumped. "I don't know. Why would he have a robe?"

"Didn't you say he was a sorcerer?"

"I did."

"Sorcerers wear robes, or so I've heard," Rick said, seemingly teasing Gil.

"So they would seem to do. I can't say for certain whether or not Lord Stansbury was in possession of a robe. He might have been. It would not be outside of the range of possibilities. But I doubt he was wearing a robe when he and his family came to this area of the country. Like I was saying, it was an extremely cold late autumn day."

"You just said it was cold," Rick interrupted. "Was it any colder than normal? Because if it's normally extremely cold or even cold enough that the ponds freeze over, I don't think I want to come back around for your fancy leaf show."

"You can see the leaves change in early September sometimes when it's not so cold as it was for Lord Stansbury and his family who were, I would imagine, not terribly interested in the leaves either. At least not interested enough for there to be record of any kind of foliage worship. What they were interested in was finding a place to settle down away from other colonists. The thing about Vermont, even today, is that if you want to find a spot away from prying eyes, it's really not that hard to do. It was much easier way back then. The Stansburys were definitely interested in avoiding other people. At least, it would seem Lord Stansbury was. From what I could gather, he had purchased a great many slaves before coming north and very little in the way of farming equipment."

Rick chuckled. "You've really spent a lot of time looking into this guy, haven't you?"

Gil had actually been accused of being somewhat obsessed with Lord Stansbury. It was really Gil's nature to be obsessed with things. But even more so, he was a completist. He never had more than three obsessions at any one point in time and would only take on a new one when he had thoroughly exhausted one of the current three. When he was ten, he had been overtaken with a need to collect every baseball card that contained a player who had played for the 1975 Cleveland Indians. It was an arbitrary choice as there was nothing terribly distinguishing about that team. But he went about methodically collecting not only the player roster from that year, but every other year any of those players played in the major leagues. Over the course of ten years, he tracked down every last card and placed it carefully into a binder he always carried with him. When he was confident that the collection was as complete to date as it could possibly be, he placed it on the shelf next to other projects including a diorama detailing the assassination of William McKinley by Leon Czolgosh that included working lights from the Buffalo exposition where the event occurred. If there was one thing that Gil was not obsessed with, it was his past obsessions. Once completed, they held no further value to him.

Gil was currently preoccupied with destroying the damaged bridge model, winning the heart of Vermont State Trooper Jennifer Julia Kennisaw and finding out how the Lakebridge had never suffered a single bit of recorded damage. The way things were going, he probably wasn't going to move on to another obsession for quite some time.

He had started looking into the history of Lord Stansbury and the Lakebridge around the time of Kurtz's accident. Until that point, he never gave the bridge much thought. It was the reason that tourists came through town year after year. It was always fun for he and his friends to watch the tourists drive in and ask the friendly locals where the bridge was. Whenever anyone would ask him, he would always break into his local yokel comedy routine, giving nonsensical directions such as telling an old couple from Ohio to turn left where the old church used to be. Sure it wasn't an original routine, but it was always funny to his friends who had to stifle their laughs nearby. Especially considering there had never been an old church in Stansbury. There had never been a new church, either. People looking for a bit of God had to seek him elsewhere. Sometimes this bothered Gil. But not for too long. During the years Gil had wandered around the country, he never gave much thought to the Lakebridge except when he would find himself asking directions from some local yokel and his snickering friends and then think back fondly to his own imaginary displaced house of worship. But Kurtz's accident brought him home. He remembered Shelley's call. Something about the way she described the Lakebridge had triggered his need to know why it was there. Although he left the area since then, he always did so with some degree of apprehension. He was afraid something might happen and he would miss it. He was fairly certain something was going to happen.

"So what happened when they got here?" Marisol interjected, tearing Gil away from his certain feeling something was going to happen.

"Well, for one thing," Gil replied, "Lord Stansbury found what some others might call a very large pond and named it Stansbury Lake. The English liked coming around here and naming things. The English are big on naming things."

"So are Spaniards," Rick said. "I think they thought if name it, you own it. They always assumed no one else had ever named anything that they were naming before them. When they were informed that their renamed lands had a name, they would just kill the guy who told them that. Most of the time, anyway."

"The English would just assure the locals that they were quite wrong," Gil said. "But when it came to this particular lake, there was no one around, no local natives, no moose...well, maybe a few moose, but they weren't interested in the naming of things...to tell Lord Stansbury that his little lake bore an ancient name. Nor was there anyone around to tell him that he couldn't settle the land and call it his own. There's really nothing around here but trees and mountains and unless you're going to produce syrup or cut wood, there's not much reason to lay claim to the land. At least there wasn't back then. Now the land is fairly valuable because it's just a nicer place to live than anywhere else. At least most of the time."

"When is it not a nicer place to live?" asked Marisol.

"When it's 20 below zero and the power lines freeze," laughed Gil. "Then I think fondly of the Florida Keys. Otherwise, I'm more than happy here. So was Lord Stansbury. He was as happy as an evil sorcerer was going to be. No one bothered him here except the occasional land surveyor who was quickly dissuaded from coming around with either threats or money, both of which Lord Stansbury had in great supply.

"So why did he build a bridge where there wasn't a road?" Rick asked, seemingly frustrated with his introductory lesson in the history of colonial Vermont.

Gil knew when to hurry things along. Actually, he thought he knew when to hurry things along, but was never very good at it. He tried on this occasion. "Most people build bridges from one side of a place, a body of water or a chasm or some kind, to the other side where it is otherwise inconvenient to cross. It doesn't take that much longer to get across the Lakebridge than to walk around the lake from one side to the other. The land isn't treacherous and there's no logical reason for it to be here. But sometimes logic and magic have nothing to do with one another. And sometimes bridges do more than help you get across a lake or river without a boat."

"What are you getting at?" the old Cuban demanded.

"Lord Stansbury wasn't interested in going across the lake," continued Gil. "When he was forced to leave England, he also had to leave behind his faerie mounds, portals or, if you like, bridges to wherever it was that he spoke with the evil he needed for his conjuring. He needed a way here in the new world to revisit the old world. But it didn't come without a cost." Gil paused for a moment here because he had a feeling that something wasn't quite right in the woods.

* * *

The Silver Knight always had a feeling that something wasn't right in the woods. In his many encounters with the Evil, he could not shake the feeling that he would never triumph. It wasn't a fear, for he feared nothing. It was, however, becoming a certainty. The dark lord had powers that the knight had no offense to counter. Ancient evils imbued into his very skin that prevented even the most fearsome strikes from drawing blood. But the knight would not give into his doubts. His past failures were in the past. Lord Stansbury's power could not hold against his assaults forever.

His current attack had been meticulously planned. Every detail had been accounted for. He knew that Lord Stansbury's center of power was the bridge itself and while his past attempts to bring it down had always ended poorly, this time it could not stand. He had destroyed too many models and damaged far more than that in his need to be certain…that chance could not intervene and once again keep him from his quest to rid his lands of this evil that had lingered far too long.

He approached Lord Stansbury's Abomination fearlessly. It stood as always, spanning the small placid lake and seeming to sit on the surface of the water without support. Red like nothing in nature and like no other bridge. It never faded and it had a glow that was intensified on days like these where the lake reflected it perfectly. From a distance, it bore some similarity to others of its type, but the Silver Knight had studied it and knew its construction was like no other. Its struts and braces bent in impossible angles and were inscribed with arcane symbols that had no known meaning. It was only open on the ends and what light might enter was blocked so that to look through it, one could only see darkness and nothing more.

It was from that darkness that the Evil called out to him. "You come again to battle. You come again to fail."

He once again held his ground as the Evil came forth. It was as if the darkness had become flesh and armor and extended its black essence from the shadows. Its eyes did not glow nor was it accompanied by flames or smoke. It simply was the dark come to life and even its words seemed to extinguish the light around it.

The Silver Knight had learned long ago that to bandy words with the foul creature upon the bridge was useless. With the grim determination that is only born of thwarted desire, he hefted his great axe and let loose a mighty swing and roared out his fiercest war cry.

* * *

Gil heard the echoes of Kurtz's roar and winced.

"What's that noise," worried Marisol.

The sound of axe against wood was enough for Gil to get a good idea what was happening. Kurtz was always supposed to tell him when he would be mounting an assault against the bridge. Kurtz knew that Gil's bad luck often extended to those around him and that Gil should be as far away as possible from any event that demanded success.

Gil's bad luck was legendary in Stansbury. Even when he was a kid, people somehow knew to stay away from him when they were attempting anything dangerous. Gil figured that old Mr. Bixby, the local carpenter, was the first to start telling folks about him. Gil's father had hired him to add a new room, an office for his father's special case file. It was one file, but a big one and it needed its own room. So the old guy came around with his tools and whatnot and Gil, then just about four years old, would often be nearby with his mother while the man worked. Gil always believed his mother was the only real cure for his bad luck because nothing bad ever seemed to happen while she was around. He was wrong about that. She couldn't always be around and occasionally, when she would leave him alone to play nearby the carpenter, bad things would happen. The first time, it was a simple slip of the hammer. Actually, the hammer slipped from the man's hand and sailed thought the air, eventually finding its home on Gil's hand. It was a clean break and no one blamed old Bixby but Bixby himself. But fairly soon, Bixby started telling people that it was the boy who kept bringing harm upon himself from flying splinters to the two-by-four that somehow put Gil into the hospital for a week with a concussion when it fell from a scaffolding and bounced a good twenty feet from its starting point. Bixby eventually demanded that Gil not be in the general vicinity of the project and Gil's parents agreed that it was probably for the best. Gil didn't know why he had been selected for bad things to happen to, but they did and quite often.

And quite often others suffered as a result of his misfortune. There was the guy he worked with in New Jersey at the chemical processing plant who loved to fish. Gil couldn't remember anyone who loved to fish as much as this guy. Gil couldn't remember the guy's name. He couldn't remember it when he was standing next to the guy. The guy was just one of those people who you couldn't interrupt long enough to ask his name when you forgot it. This guy used to brag about his fishing prowess though and said that he never failed to catch a fish. One day he invited Gil along and while Gil had tried to beg off, fearing for the man's track record which seemed all he had in the world, the guy would hear none of it. He seemed to think that Gil, from the mere fact that Gil was the only one who would listen to his fish stories, was his best friend and best friends fished together. Best friends also knew each other's names. While the guy certainly knew Gil's name because it was related to his beloved fish, Gil, stuck out in a river on a boat with the guy, still couldn't come up with a name. With Gil in the boat, the guy couldn't come up with a fish. He had never failed to catch a fish. Going back to his earliest childhood trip with his estranged father who had died of some exotic skin condition, he had never left the boat without something in his bucket. He couldn't understand why, on this day out with his best friend, Gil, he couldn't bring one out of the river. He told Gil it was his lucky spot. He told Gil it was his lucky reel. He told Gil it was his lucky lure. Gil believed him because Gil believed in luck. But Gil believed in the power of his bad luck more than all of the little tricks the guy had in his tackle box. Morning fell to night, the day having been eclipsed in the silence of the calm waters, and no fish bit. Gil had seen it before when people don't believe that their luck can change. He did kind of see the humor of the guy's denial being played out on a river, though. Actually, Gil always found the humor when things went wrong. Things weren't always supposed to go right. Fish weren't always supposed to bite. The guy didn't understand it, though. When he dropped Gil off at home, he was very quiet. Gil told him that he would be sure to get one the next time. The guy turned to Gil with a hollow look in his eyes and said there would be no next time. Fishing was the only thing he had ever been perfect at. It was his life and his pride and he didn't have it anymore. Gil never saw the guy again. Gil never knew the guy's name so he never found out if anything happened to him. Plus, he left Jersey shortly afterwards. The state had a weird smell he couldn't place but didn't like and he figured there had to be a reason that every tunnel and bridge leading into the state was free but they always charged you to get out. Gil never went fishing again. Well, not sport fishing anyway.

Even though Gil heard the chopping and knew that he was bound to upset any plans Kurtz might have made, he had the nice couple with him who were generous enough to buy three bridge models. He was also insanely curious as to how his friend planned to destroy the bridge. In the past, he had tried fire, a cannon and, Gil's favorite, the trebuchet. All had failed for one reason or another. None for lack of planning. All for lack of luck. All due to some supernatural force according to Kurtz. Still and all, Gil had warned Kurtz that his bad luck would most likely ruin even the best of plans. Recently, Kurtz told Gil that his newest plan was his best, but wouldn't share any details. So Gil led the couple on towards the bridge because he had promised them a tour and because he wanted to see it destroyed.

*　*　*

Rick had only agreed to go look at the bridge because Marisol wanted to see the bridge. Actually, he was a bit curious as well, but he'd never share that with his wife although she probably knew anyway...she had this weird psychic way of knowing everything he thought before he did. He did enjoy the occasional oddity. He had once driven five hours out of his way to see the world's largest gator. He had no idea how big the gator would be from the billboard, but for some reason he had to see the damned thing. It drove him a little crazy, actually. Hour after hour the size of the beast would grow exponentially until finally he expected to see a reptile the size of Godzilla. He couldn't imagine a cage or pen large enough to hold the creature. He thought they must have to feed the thing a few head of cattle a day in order to keep it from running amuck and attacking nearby Jacksonville. Some women would, of course, faint at the sight of such a demon. But Rick and Marisol were very much prepared for the sight of it. Rick even thought to keep his small pistol handy just in case it should free itself from its captors and charge at his wife. He was a pretty good shot and thought that, if given the chance, he could knock it down by a shot through its gigantic eye. One well-placed bullet could take out this ancient evil thing that had some how survived into the modern age. Rick might even get a medal. It wasn't that Rick really wanted to kill it. It was just that, after hour upon hour of driving towards it, towards his destiny, his imagination had built the creature and seeing it into a legendary event. Having no CB at the time to share his thoughts with, he could only entertain himself. He figured Marisol, with her special powers, could hear his fantasy just fine in her head, so he didn't bother to bore her with details she was aware of already. He just kept his mind movie running until they finally arrived at the roadside attraction that housed the creature from a lost age. He and Marisol braved the gift shop that sold stuffed alligators, alligator jerky, alligator skin belts, T-shirts that exclaimed "I SAW THE WORLD'S LARGEST ALLIGATOR AND DIDN'T GET EATEN!," and an assortment of snow globes that displayed scale model gators crushing miniature metropolises ranging from New York to Paris, all cities deserving of a giant gator attack. Finally, they paid their ten dollars a piece and went though the turnstile to the area behind the store. Rick expected, imagined and hoped to be amazed at the size of the world's largest gator. There was no amazement, though. There was just a very large alligator in a swampy little pool surrounded by rusty chain-link posted with signs that read "Please don't feed the gator!" and "Please don't taunt the gator!" It was, indeed, larger than normal. Rick couldn't really say if it was the largest in the world, but it was the largest he had seen. But it wasn't big enough and it didn't do anything out of the ordinary for a gator stuck in the muck. It made him feel stupid for thinking it could be anything more than it was. But, actually, he was glad to have seen it. He spent ten dollars to confirm that there were no prehistoric gators that might randomly crawl into his city and kill people. He also never needed to wonder about it when he saw the signs. He could tell others that it was nothing much. Most of all, he could complain about it.

 He was fairly certain he was going to be able to complain about the so-called Lakebridge. He didn't expect much more than your average covered bridge. Marisol had made him stop at every last one they had come near so far. She had read that book about all of the bridges in New York or someplace and decided that she had to see every last one in New England. He had no love of bridges, though. He had no dislike of them, but he had no love of them. They served a purpose. They got you from here to there. Roads also get people from here to there but Marisol wouldn't drive twenty miles out of their way to see some special road, would she? Well, perhaps she would. She also reminded him that there was no longer anything that was out of their way because their way was whatever way they went. He had to keep reminding himself of that. If he didn't go look at bridges, what would he look at?

So far, however, this one was different. First, this guy with the painted fake arm was just about the first person he had run into on this trip that he wanted to stick around and talk to for any length of time. Gil was friendly and interesting which seemed a bit rare these days. Most people who were too friendly were just plain stupid or wanted something from you. Gil seemed like all he wanted was to talk about his bridge, maybe sell a few and, most importantly, listen to what Rick had to say. But Rick was actually interested in this bridge after listen to his guide. While the history was the stuff of legends, Rick liked legends. But even more than that, when they had finally arrived at the lake, there was some crazy guy in what looked like armor made from old scrap metal chopping down a huge tree next to the bridge, which was surprisingly red. Not faded like some of the others he had seen, but bright red...almost new. And it was odd, but he felt a little uncomfortable standing near it. He visited the Coral Castle down south of Miami once and felt a weird energy there, too. This insane guy had managed to build this huge monument to his love for his wife, which was romantic, except that there was no way he could have been able to do it like they said he did. He didn't believe all that nonsense about pulleys and levers. There was something else and when you went there, you could feel it in the air and as amazing as I all was, it felt wrong. This bridge had the same effect. It should have been a beautiful bit of scenery, this calm little lake in the midst of all these trees, but it was wrong in a way that made him really uncomfortable. But not so much that the crazy guy didn't make him feel just a little better and he was able to shake off the weird energy from the bridge and focus on him.

"What's that guy doing?" asked Rick. Rick was more amused that interested, actually. "And what is he wearing?"

Gil tried to hide the smile from Rick, but Rick knew he was amused as well. "That's my friend, Kurtz. The one who makes the models. He's wearing some armor he made out of silver plates and serving sets he collected from the local antique stores. He's chopping down a tree. It looks like he's going to try and land it on the bridge."

Rick laughed at this. It was the last thing he expected to hear and certainly the last thing he expected to see. "Why's he doing that? And wearing that stuff?"

Gil turned serious for a moment on him. "Kurtz had a bad experience on the Lakebridge. He kind of blames it for the bad things that happen around here. He's been trying to destroy it for some time now."

"Isn't that against the law?" Marisol asked.

Gil chuckled. "It might be if he ever succeeded. This is probably his twentieth attempt on the bridge. Nothing seems to work."

"Why not?" Rick wondered, but somehow knew the answer. Rick actually found himself more interested in this than he had been in anything since he left Miami.

"That's what I've been trying to figure out," Gil confided. "But I haven't quite found the answer. Something tells that when I do, Kurtz will be able to take that thing down."

"Why do you want to destroy it?" Marisol seemed concerned. Rick knew she didn't like this kind of thing.

Gil's face grew very grim. It gave Rick a slight chill. "Because it's evil. Evil should be destroyed, don't you think?"

* * *

The Moose thought it a shame that the man with the axe chose to destroy that particular tree. It was a great and beautiful tree and deserved to keep its place beside the lake. It rounded out the area nicely and completed a lovely landscape as far as the Moose was concerned. But men had little regard for the way trees fit in with other trees to form a pleasant vantage. The Moose thought as the tree crashed down into the lake that he would miss it.

* * *

The Silver Knight cursed as his missile missed its intended target. He had planned this attack down to the last detail. Nothing had been left to chance. Every strike of his axe was placed precisely upon the great tree to guarantee that it would fall straight and true upon the Evil and his abomination. But the tree now lay in the lake beside the bridge, having only scraped it as it fell, and he could hear Lord Stansbury laugh as he rode away victorious from the field of battle.

The Silver Knight looked at Lord Stanley's Abomination where the tree had grazed it and smiled just a little. There it was. Just a scratch or two where there had never been one before. He picked up his axe and walked back into the misty woods. He had not won this day… but this was not the end of things.

II

Tod watched the tree fall and miss the bridge. He really hoped that Kurtz would do it this time. The poor guy tried so hard and just couldn't make the thing go away. Tod knew how to do it. To kill the bridge. To save the town. Tod knew how to do it. Tod had destroyed things before. He thought he had destroyed Kurtz. That was why he stopped destroying things. He promised he would stop and he stopped. He promised never to break his promise and he would not break it. Destroying the bridge, even to help Kurtz, would break his promise. He couldn't even tell Kurtz about how to do it. He did not regret his promise, though. Life was better this way. But Tod still protected the man as he could.

After Gil and the old couple left the bridge, Tod drove his truck down to the fallen tree and hooked it up to his winch. He thought that later he might come back and blow out the stump.

III

The motorist gave Vermont State Trooper Jennifer Julia Kennisaw his cell number after she helped him fix his blow out. He said that he felt an undying need to repay her help with dinner in Burlington. She smiled and reminded him to get a new spare for his Land Rover as soon as possible before returning to her squad car where she carefully deposited his number, Jerome's number, next to all of the rest in her notebook of possible sex offenders who had previously given her their numbers.

Most of the guys who rewarded her with their personal information in the hopes of a date or more were lawbreakers. She always thought it amusing that these guys, after being pulled over for doing eighty miles per hour, would ask her out after they asked her how fast they were going. Jennifer always knew how fast she was going. She didn't understand how anyone could not know how fast they were going. It didn't make sense. You always at least knew that you were going faster than the law would allow. Even if they weren't looking at the speedometer, they had to know that. And when she would pull out behind them, they had to look down and see their rate of speed before they tried in vain to slow down so that she might be kind hearted and forgive them the offense of endangering other drivers or the occasional wandering moose.

She remembered an instance where a 1969 VW Bug, powder blue where it hadn't gone to rust, had taken it upon itself to tangle with a full grown bull moose. She never understood the attraction people had to Bugs. They were hollow in front. Being hollow in front meant that there was nothing between the driver and whatever it was that might find its way into the so-called trunk area at 70 MPH, which was about as fast as those old beaters could go. Sure, some were sooped up so they could reach higher velocities, but most of them were just about able to make it up a small hill if the wind was in their favor. There just didn't seem to be much point in owning one unless you delivered pizza in a crowded city and needed to be able to parallel park in tight spots. So therefore there was absolutely no reason to own one in Vermont. So therefore Jennifer had no pity for the frat boys out of Bennington who thought it would be good fun to pile into the powder blue Bug owned by their newest pledge who was at the school on scholarship and worked for three summers to be able to afford the luxury of what some might call a car…but not her. They managed to get seven brothers and a sorority sister into the too tiny car one spring evening after too many kegs of beer. She never understood the attraction of squeezing into a small space with a bunch of other people. She liked air. She liked lots and lots of air. Being smushed into a small space, like the inside of a Bug, with a bunch of other people pretty much guaranteed that there would be too little air to go around. She was fairly certain that night when the six brothers of Rho Alpha Tau and their friendly little sister from Psi Phi were heading up the highway towards Montreal - as Vince Nickels, a survivor, recalled they were doing - that there was not nearly enough oxygen in the car for proper decisions to be made. Mix lack of oxygen, an abundance of alcohol, an idiotically unsafe small car and a randy bull moose and you are in for a long night of cleaning up the highway. Jennifer was still amazed at the resilience of that moose. He had been hurt some, but not as much as the septet in the spent pile of iron that was left of the Bug. The fire that erupted after the car flipped three times before hitting a large roadside tree didn't help matters any for those inside. While Vince Nickles spent a few months in a body cast and some months in physical therapy after being thrown through the front windshield of the vehicle at the moment of impact - he bounced off of the moose, apparently - at least he had to good fortune of reducing the body count by one. His father, some kind of important lawyer from somewhere where they thought it was a fine idea to pay way too much money to send their kids to a mid-level college in a quiet Northeast town to keep them out of trouble, thought there must be someone, anyone he could sue. So he sued everyone from the governor down to Mary Phillips, the researcher for the Department of Fish and Wildlife who had been tracking the moose and his brethren for some kind of study about how often moose cross highways - apparently a matter of some concern. In the end, Mary was the only one who lost her case, but as she had nothing but the clothes on her back, her backpack and a small collection of novels by French surrealists, Thomas Nickles Esq. settled for her novels and authentic Spanish boda bag in which she kept red wine when she could get it for quiet nights with the likes of Paul Eluard and Andre Breton. She complained a bit to the courts about the ruling, but Nickles was determined to have some kind of recompense for his son's stupidity and if it meant some dog-eared second hand library books and the remnants of a bottle of Chianti, he would have it. Mary petitioned the Department to be reimbursed for her losses and her superiors bought her a canteen and a Stephen King novel.

On a hunch, Jennifer pulled her squad car off the road at the next turn and waited patiently with her speed gun. Her hunches and patience were often rewarded. When she was ten years old, her mother told her there was nothing more powerful than patience. Her mother told her if she felt something in her bones to be true, then all she had to do was wait and not worry and things would turn out the way they should. If there was one thing Jennifer was certain about it was that her mother was never wrong. Never. Jennifer rarely made an important life decision without consulting her. Actually, Jennifer rarely made any decision without consulting her. Jennifer was madly in love with Shelley, who worked behind the counter at Osno's Drug Store in Stansbury. She had been since the day she went in for a bottle of aspirin for her then partner, Sergeant Kurt. Sergeant Kurt didn't like to leave the squad car during a patrol unless it was to eat. All other stops were Jennifer's responsibility. She got his coffee. She bought his Twinkies. She took care of all the stops. She really didn't mind. She had a hunch that if she worked with Sergeant Kurt, her service would be rewarded and so she was patient. She would be equally patient with Shelley because her mother told her that, given enough time, the girl would eventually find out that her prospects of finding a man as good as Jennifer in a town like Stansbury were slim because of the town's curse and all. Jennifer never thought much of the Stansbury curse until her mother verified it.

Jennifer's mother was sixteen years old the first time she realized that Stansbury was cursed. It was 1968 and every boy of draft age in town got drafted. Every last one that might have made a fine husband for her mother and even a few who would have been rather mediocre, but acceptable, given the options. But she had no options because the government pulled all of their draft cards over the course of a single month and each and every last one of them was set to be inducted on the very same day that Jennifer was conceived in an ill advised rendezvous with soon to be Private William Kennisaw - Billy to his friends and to all his girlfriends. Many of Billy's girlfriends shared the important trait with Jennifer's mother in that they found themselves pregnant sometime shortly after Billy, along with every last boy of draft age in Stansbury on a bus heading out to Basic Training at some far off exotic location in New Jersey or Alabama, ended up a casualty of a war he would never even fight in when his bus found its way into a ravine somewhere in the Catskill Mountains. The only survivor was the driver, Benjamin Hawthorne, a distant relative of both Benjamin Franklin and Nathaniel Hawthorne who shared little in common with his illustrious ancestors. He also shared little in common with the dead soon-to-be-soldiers in his care, including the fact that he was not a resident of Stansbury and, therefore, not subject to its nasty little curse. He was, however, subject to a long stint in a New York State Penitentiary for a number of cases of manslaughter that, strangely enough, had nothing to do with the bus accident and everything to do with a psychotic episode involving a 65 Chevy truck and a bus stop full of people that Benny claimed he was trying to save from the horrors of dying on a bus.

To this day, Jennifer still wasn't sure how many of her schoolmates were her brothers and sisters. Her mother told her not to try to find out. She said that there was no real point in it. She said it wouldn't make her life any better and it wouldn't make their lives any better. Jennifer always listened to what her mother said.

Jennifer looked up as the Jeep Wagoner went speeding by. She didn't need to use her speed gun to know that the SUV was going a little faster than the laws she enforced would allow. She flipped on the light bar on her cruiser and pulled out onto the highway. She recognized this one and would not be adding another name to her collection of sex offenders.

* * *

Ben recognized the familiar blue and red lights of the police cruiser flashing in his rear view mirror. He looked down at his speedometer and was hardly amazed to discover he was doing about 80 miles per hour. When he would take these long drives to think about things, he would often forget to watch his speed. The trouble was, he had recently taken a few too many drives to think about things. He had tallied up at least ten speeding tickets from Bangor to Buffalo. He did have to say that he had come to enjoy his conversations with the officers that pulled him over for roadside chats. Many times, as a matter of fact, he would leave such encounters without getting a ticket. He believed it was because he was exceedingly honest about his transgressions. For some reason, police felt it was necessary to ask the question:

"Do you know how fast you were going?"

He knew they didn't teach that in cop school. It must have been from all of the cop movies they watched. They all walked up to his window with the same studied swagger. He loved that swagger almost as much as he hated that question.

"Do you know how fast you were going?"

Yes. He knew how fast he was going. Anybody who said they didn't know how fast they were going was lying. When he saw the flashing lights, he reflexively looked at his speedometer to see how bad it was. He couldn't imagine anyone else doing otherwise. The only reason people said that they didn't know how fast they were going was because they somehow felt that they could get out of the ticket if they played dumb. This was just stupid. The only other person besides these drivers who knew how fast they were going was the cop who pulled them over. Cops really didn't make too many mistakes about this. The speed guns were fairly reliable but, even more than the gun, the experience of tracking speeders gave police a sixth sense about their rate of travel. But drivers somehow believed that if they either played dumb or denied their crime altogether, that the officer would stop and think:

"Hey, maybe this citizen wasn't going so fast after all. Maybe I'm wrong. I should apologize for the inconvenience, offer him a home baked cookie and send him on his way with an apology and a repentant smile."

Not so strangely, no officer had ever said such a thing. He did know of some cops who would give good-looking women - or men - a warning and a phone number. Ben thought that this was an abuse of the badge, but he didn't think it was a major one. After all, sitting by the side of the road next to a diamond yellow "Moose" sign for hours on end could be a pretty lonely affair. There were the very rare occasions that a moose wandered by to say hello. It was usually around daybreak at the end of a night's shift when the coffee was too cold and no driver had been by in hours. That was when the moose liked to come by. Ben was fairly certain it was the same moose. It would approach his cruiser and dip its head down for a moment before it would approach the highway. Without fail, it would pause at the side of the road as if it were waiting to see if a car was coming. Then, when all was clear, it would lope slowly to the center of the road and stop at the yellow line. Ben had no idea why, but it made those rare mornings somehow special to see that weirdo moose do his ritual.

So Ben looked down at his dashboard and, past the layer of dust that had begun to cover the protective glass over his instrument panel, he saw that his speed had, without his being aware, crept up to 80. It was always 80. He was fairly certain cars would, if given the opportunity, live at 80. When he was going 80, it never felt like 80. It felt comfortable. It felt safe and right and he never quite understood why it wasn't a legal speed. He would never pull someone over doing 80. 70? An unsafe speed. There was something somehow wrong with 70. 70 was ridiculous because 65 was legal. Why break the law for five extra miles per hour? 70 was like robbing a bank but only asking for a hundred dollars. 70 made people doing 65 uncomfortable and pissed off people doing 80. It was a no-win speed. And anyone going over 80? Well, they were just asking for trouble. You never knew what was going to be beyond the next blind curve or what might dart out into the road in front of you. Cars started to do strange things over 80. Unless they were high performance sports cars. Those he pulled over on general principal. The problem with high-speed sports cars, especially in Vermont, was that those people who generally tended to own such beasts also tended to feel the need to drive them in such a way as to prove that the cars could do everything they were advertised to do. The fact was, these cars were not made to occupy the highways and byways of the United States. Except, of course, Montana. They could drive as fast as they liked in Big Sky. Buy a Ferrari and keep it in a garage in Montana. Go there a few times a year and red line it. But not in Vermont. Certainly not in Vermont. Ben felt these cars were designed for Europe where they have really nothing better to do than to drive cars really really fast and build roads that are capable of handling cars that are going really really fast. Europeans have all sorts of time on their hands. Almost as much as the Japanese. But at least the Japanese make sensible cars. As a cop on the side of the road waiting for the dawn and the moose and whatever the new day might bring, Ben hardly ever gave the Japanese cars a second thought - unless, of course, they were glowing with some weird neon underlighting and spoilers where there ought not to be spoilers. A four speed Corolla should never suffer the indignity of a high performance spoiler or racing flames. There is no point in it and it just looks silly. He would pull a Lamborghini over just because. As a matter of fact, he did once. It was driven by Paul Sanderson of the Bennington Sandersons, as if Ben could give a good goddamn about what family the bored scions of the idiot wealthy came from. Paul Sanderson of the Bennington Sandersons seemed unusually irked that he should have to be pulled over by a local policeman like Ben. Paul Sanderson of the Bennington Sandersons seemed unusually sure that his prestigious position as the incredibly lucky genetic heir to the incredibly lucky genetic heirs of some long ago successful hard working industrialist guaranteed him some kind of free pass to behave like a monumental fuckwit and simply exert his idiot presence and will of non-personality in the way of a small town sheriff doing his job and that small town sheriff would, like some bygone constabulary dealing with the idiot offspring of a local land baron, simply bow his head in apology and wave the boy on his way. Paul Sanderson of the Bennington Sandersons was downright livid when Ben forced him, at gunpoint, to take a field sobriety test and, after being judged under the influence of some narcotic, placed in handcuffs and then not so gently forced into the back of the squad car like, as Paul Sanderson of the Bennington Sandersons said over and over again as he was taken to the station for booking, a commoner. Paul Sanderson of the Bennington Sandersons certainly didn't expect Ben to look in his red Lamborghini with spoilers in all of the right places but still, inexplicably, with that stupid pull-me-over neon underlighting, and find his too large stash of cocaine sitting quite out in the open on the passenger seat next to the bottle of Cristal. Ben actually started giggling at that point. As an adult, he never ever giggled except that one time. He just couldn't quite wrap his head around the idea that there was someone in the world that actually strived to be such a complete and utter stereotype down to the very smallest of details. There were still times - such as now…fortunately, Ben was being pulled over anyway - that Ben would stop and have to suppress a violent laughing spell at the thought of Paul Sanderson of the Bennington Sandersons as he sat in the jail cell whining that he would have all of his many teams of lawyers sue Ben and the whole town of Stansbury and maybe the whole State of Vermont for this offense. Oh, yes. Paul Sanderson of the Bennington Sandersons brought his lawsuit and it did not make the local district attorney, Daniel Warrington, of the Stansbury Warringtons as he would say every time the rich wretch would open his mouth about his lineage, very happy and when he wasn't happy, he was less likely to be nice and when he wasn't nice, he could be downright spiteful. So Paul Sanderson of the Bennington Sandersons was prosecuted on numerous felony counts of possession and treated very much like a commoner and found guilty despite the best efforts of his expensive team of lawyers to prove that somehow a wandering moose had dropped the illegal substances in through the window of the expensive red sports car that was doing 127 miles per hour on a two lane highway and that Paul Sanderson of the Bennington Sandersons was the victim of a vindictive small town sheriff who used wildlife to plant evidence on the local elite. They actually used that term quite often, which did not go over well with the jury of people who did not think of themselves as a part of the local elite. Nor Judge Randall Farnsworth, who positively hated those who thought of themselves as any kind of elite. So Paul Sanderson of the Bennington Sandersons ended up in the state penitentiary where, despite many appeals, he stayed for many years and learned that sometimes it is not such a good idea to bring up one's lineage at every given opportunity and that maybe just maybe it would be safer all around if he drove a nice efficient Japanese car... and laid off the coke.

Ben was certainly not of a mind to bring up his standing as Benjamin Hamilton of the Stansbury Hamiltons to the young trooper who was swaggering her way toward his window. She would probably just laugh. Probably.

"Do you know how fast you were going, sir?" she said before she even look at him. He liked her technique in this. He had told her so many times before.

"You know I do, Jenny. At least 80, but most likely no more than 80. It's usually 80, isn't it?" Ben thought he detected a slight grin at his response. But Jennifer had obviously been practicing stone faces in the mirror for some time, so she would give him no hint of familiarity.

"It's Officer Kennisaw, sir." He was amazed her face could move enough to speak. "You are aware that the speed limit on this road is 65 miles per hour, sir."

"You know I am, *Officer* Kennisaw."

"And you know your status as the former sheriff of Stansbury does not give you the right to break the law, do you not?"

"I would hope so. You've informed me of that every time you've pulled me over."

"Then why do you persist in breaking the law, Ben?"

She had a point. Ever since Ben had stopped being sheriff of Stansbury, he had taken up the strange habit of breaking the law. While he was sheriff and for many years before, he always toed the line. He never thought to do otherwise. He enjoyed being sheriff and deeply respected the rule of law if not all the rules that were codified. Sometimes he would bend in his interpretation of the laws as they pertained to those who he sometimes let off with a stern warning or not even که. But when it came to his own activity, he never drove over the speed limit or even crossed the street unless it was at a legal point of crossing. It just wasn't a part of who he was as a person. His father always told him, from the time he was five, that he would be a cop. Ben didn't know if it was because his father just really wanted him to be a cop or if it was something that was evident in a five year old boy who never played the robber. When his friends played Robin Hood out in the forest, Ben was always elected to be the Sheriff of Nottingham. He didn't mind it, either. He had always wondered why Robin of Locksley couldn't go about his helping of the poor without resorting to banditry. It just didn't seem right to constantly victimize government servants and upset the status quo just out of some sense that there was an injustice being done. Robin was a nobleman. He could have used his lands as a place of refuge for the peons and, perhaps, sought to change the system from within. But Robin resorted to criminal behavior and for that he needed to be punished. If it had been some poor peasant robbing and stealing for some righteous cause, he would have been shunned. But not the noble Robin. No. He was special because he was royalty. Ben never liked the idea of royalty so when he got to play the Sheriff of Nottingham Forest, he did so with relish. More often than not, his friends would complain because Ben and his group of deputies would usually succeed in bringing the so-called merry men to justice. They couldn't argue with him, though. He always played fair. He thought that if the historical Sheriff of Nottingham could have just played fair, he would not have been vilified and, perhaps, he and Robin could have worked things out. Ben understood that some lawmen were not entirely lawful, but he couldn't rightly disrespect the badge even by playing a cop as a bad guy.

Ben looked at Jennifer. She reminded him so much of himself when he was in her position. He knew that she would make a fine Sheriff of Nottingham.

He didn't really have a good answer for her question. "I don't know what it is. Lately, I've just been…distracted."

"If you're so distracted, Ben, then perhaps you should do your thinking at home. Maybe take a walk and think rather than get in the car. I'd hate to have to clean your remains from the side of some poor moose."

"I appreciate the sentiment. But I have a lot on my mind and a lot of time now to think about it."

"And whose fault is that?"

Some people were unhappy he had lost the last election. Jennifer was one of those people.

"My fault to be sure. There were more important things than being sheriff."

"Such as?"

He really didn't have a good answer for this because in his mind he had never really stopped being sheriff. What he was doing now that he was not sheriff was, in fact, an extension of being sheriff. He simply knew that he could no longer be sheriff and do the thing that he was doing now.

"Such as taking long drives and occasionally being saved from running into a moose by a concerned friend."

He wasn't ready to tell just yet. Soon. But not just yet.

"I know I should have it all committed to memory by now, but I need your license and registration."

Ben flipped down the visor and gave Jennifer the documents. He stopped keeping them in his wallet some time ago. It just seemed a waste of time.

* * *

Jennifer walked back to her cruiser to write Sheriff Ben up again and it just seemed a waste of time. It continued to trouble her that she had to write tickets for Sheriff Ben that he would dutifully pay the next day. Dutiful. That was Sheriff Ben.

For as long as she could remember, there had always been a Sheriff Ben in Stansbury. He wasn't the kind of cop who made you feel better when he wasn't around. Even when she had done something wrong, it did not seem so bad if he caught her. It seemed right…somehow fair. When she was thirteen, she declared to her one and only friend, Francis Townsend, that she would take a picture of Mr. Osno. No one had ever seen Mr. Osno, at least no one that would tell. Mr. Osno owned and operated the only pharmacy in Stansbury and no one had ever seen him, at least no one that would tell. Jennifer and Francis would go into Osno's Pharmacy to watch people interact with the mysterious proprietor. They would sit at the counter and pretend like they were back in the fifties and eat their ice cream and watch as, one after the next, people would bring their slips of paper from their doctors that said what they needed to help fix what ailed them. They would hand those slips off to whomever it was that worked behind the counter.

At the time, Mr. Osno's counter girl was Gertie Louise Lawrence who was a senior who planned on going to Vassar when she graduated. Gertie could do nothing at all but talk about going to Vassar when she graduated and so it surprised no one at all that Gertie did, indeed, go to Vassar when she graduated. The problem for Gertie was that once she got to Vassar, she lost all focus and direction. She really didn't know what she wanted to do once she got there. Her whole identity had been built around the wonderful time she would have studying art history and English literature and being a Vassar girl. The problem was that as much as she enjoyed talking about these things, she hated actually doing them. She found art history to be dull and she never really did like reading. For a time, she got by pretending that being a Vassar girl would change her in some deep and profound way and she would come to enjoy the things she always imagined she would enjoy. She would bore her roommate, endlessly going on about how much she loved being at Vassar, but beyond this surface veneer, her emptiness grew. Instead of going to class, she would only talk about how much fun she was going to have in class that day, as if imagining the outcome of the day would somehow make that day's events happen. If she imagined she was a perfect Vassar girl, then eventually she would become a perfect Vassar girl. But nobody at Vassar liked her because they were all perfect Vassar girls and they knew she was a faker. They started leaving notes under her pillow that advised her to leave, that she wasn't fit to be a Vassar girl. She ignored them at first. She had an uncanny ability to ignore reality in favor of her imagination. One of her professors told her she would make a fine author, but she hated actually writing. She imagined she would be a fine writer and all the other Vassar girls would love her and admire her for her stories and poems, but she hated actually writing and so she never gave them a chance to love her, which they decidedly did not. One of her professors told her that perhaps she and Vassar were not a good match. By this time, it was getting harder and harder for her to live in her fantasy. The reality that she was not, nor would she ever be, a perfect Vassar girl would persistently shatter her dream and try as she would to put the pieces back together again, there were always gaps where reality would seep through and the more she focused on plugging the gaps, the less she was able to maintain the fantasy world. Every so often, she would look out across the beautiful campus and watch all of the real Vassar girls and she would try to imagine she was one of them just the way she did when she was behind the counter at Mr. Osno's drug store. But it didn't work. She wasn't one of them. She would never be one of them. One day, quietly, she packed her bag and left the campus without a word. She didn't speak a word to the passengers who sat next to her on the bus back to Stansbury. She didn't speak a word to her parents when she came home. As she passed old friends on the way into town, she kept her eyes down. They thought that now she was a Vassar girl she was too good for them to spare a friendly word. That wasn't the case for Gertie. She only had but two words left and they were for her former employer. She calmly walked into the drug store and went to the slot where people left their prescriptions. She took a small note pad from her handbag and wrote her two words on it. She tore the paper off and slipped it into the slot and waited. A moment later, a small bottle of pills dropped through the exit slot. Without a word, Gertie took the bottle of pills home and took the bottle of pills with a glass of water and it did not take long for her to quietly fade away. Jennifer remembered being sixteen and watching from behind a tree across the street from Gertie's house as Sheriff Ben escorted the corpse to the coroner's station wagon.

For three years, Jennifer and Francis tried to catch a glimpse of Mr. Osno and all they ever saw were prescriptions going in and drugs coming out and never a sign that a human being existed behind the wall except for the day that Gertie came in and wrote her two words. For three years, Jennifer and Francis tried every trick in their very small book of tricks to discover the truth about the pharmacist. And they did discover some truths. Osno's Drug Store opened its doors at the beginning of the twentieth century. At the time, Stansbury never had a business that lasted more than a few years. As a matter of fact, Stansbury still never had a business that lasted more than a few years. Things would happen. While Jennifer was investigating Osno, she began to keep a notebook detailing every business that had failed since the pharmacy opened its doors. There had been 142 in all. Everything from dentists to dry goods. It wasn't because the people of Stansbury did not want to have these services. On the contrary, the locals were desperate for a successful business other than Osno's Drug Store. Stan Morrison, who made it through the Korean War mostly intact ("Only lost but the one leg," he would chuckle), kept trying to open a sporting goods store. Stan was responsible for 15 of the failed businesses. Stan loved Stansbury and the people of Stansbury and felt that it needed a sporting goods store because he loved sports and he loved sporting equipment and he wanted to share his loves with his loves. The first store he opened was called "Stan's Stansbury Sports." He opened it just after he returned from the war without his left leg. It seems he was teaching a young Korean boy the art of lacrosse with a stick he crafted himself when a grenade fell towards him with bad intent. Now Stan was an excellent lacrosse player and had no trouble fielding the explosive device in his net and flinging it back in the direction it came from. As he turned back to continue his lesson, the boy shot him in the leg - apparently the boy had no taste for lacrosse - and ran off. Normally, a bullet to the leg wouldn't have resulted in an amputation, but Stan believed in the power of prayer above all things and, after having been struck in the leg by a small caliber bullet, Stan prayed for guidance. For some time. Because the bullet was so small, the wound clotted and stopped bleeding while he prayed. Although it still pained him greatly, Stan believed that his prayer had been answered and that there was no reason to be concerned about the wound any further. Every day, the leg continued to feel worse and worse, but Stan was fully convinced that his prayer had been answered and that everything would be fine. Others around him, however, found that his horrible limp and the increasing stench from his untreated leg were cause for concern and, against his protestations that things would be fine, took him to the surgeon who wasted no time in removing the leg which at that point had become gangrenous. Stan took it all in stride - although he could no longer actually stride, believing that it was his fault in that he prayed for the bullet wound in his leg to be cured, but did not specifically ask to keep the leg. The lack of a leg did not get in the way of Stan's love of sports and sporting goods, although he was no longer able to participate in his passion, ice hockey. When he opened Stan's Stansbury Sports, he threw a big party for the whole town and the whole town came. Sadly for Stan and the whole town, a bottle rocket went off course and landed on the roof of the store. No one paid much attention to it as the rest of the fireworks continued to light the night sky for the next hour. It wasn't until the after-haze of the fireworks powder cloud began to dissipate that Billy Kennisaw noticed the smoke coming from Stan's Stansbury Sports. Unfortunately for Stan, Billy didn't care much for sports or Stan as much as he did for Linda Parker, unwed mother of John Parker. Stan, never one to let failure get in his way, rebuilt his store and reopened it, this time as Stansbury Stan's Sports. Over time, as more fires, floods, freezes and even the Forest Service in an unfortunate act of land reclamation that took The Sports Store of Stansbury along with Stan's home, never stopped the optimistic owner from trying to enrich the lives of the people of Stansbury with sports. Sadly, both Stan and Super Stan's Sports, his fifteenth and final attempt to bring joy to the town, met with disaster when a large truck delivering a shipment of baseballs and baseball bats went out of control and slammed into the storefront.

Jennifer discovered some other truths about Osno's Drugs. They mostly revolved around the fact that no one in the many years that the store had been open ever met, saw or spoke with the proprietor of the store. Orders were all placed by the girl who had been hired to work at the counter. The girl who had been hired to work at the counter had been hired by the girl who previously worked at the counter. No one remembers who hired the first girl who worked at the counter, Jane Carver, who disappeared shortly after she left Osno's employ to become a modernist. All supply orders were placed by the girl who worked at the counter. All supplies were delivered to the girl who worked at the counter. She would take all the pharmaceutical supplies and place them one by one into the slot. At the end of every shift, she would take all of the day's earnings and place them into the slot and then her pay would be returned to her via the same slot. There was always only one girl who worked at the counter and when she could not work, the store would be closed. These were the truths Jennifer discovered about Osno's Drug Store.

    Jennifer and Francis were determined to discover the ultimate truth about Mr. Osno. They became convinced that he was either a vampire or the evil Lord Stansbury. One way or another, all of the problems of the town, all of the bad luck, must be related in some way to the continuing presence of that unseen and unknown proprietor. Jennifer became convinced that the only way they could save the town was to expose Osno to the light of day. Francis became convinced that Jennifer was going to get them killed or worse when Jennifer told Francis of her plan. Jennifer tried to convince Francis to go along with her. All she did was convince Francis to go to Sheriff Ben and tell him everything. Jennifer was convinced it was when she told Francis that they were going to blow a hole in the back wall of the drug store with some dynamite that she was going to steal from the Matthews who used it to blow stumps when they cut down trees. Sheriff Ben listened patiently to Jennifer as she explained her evidence against the enigmatic pharmacist. She showed him her notebooks. She displayed her absolute certainty in the facts as she knew them.

    "Facts cannot be refuted, Sheriff Ben."

    "Indeed, Jenny. They cannot. You do seem to have accumulated a lot of them."

    "So you have to arrest him."

    "On what charge?"

    "Umm…"

    She looked at him and saw that he would gladly blow down walls for her if she gave him a reason to. But she had no reason. There was no crime. There was just evil and she knew that even though she had facts that indicated that

Osno was evil and she had facts that he was part of what was wrong with Stansbury, there was no crime. She looked at Sheriff Ben and saw that he understood her frustration and for the only time in her life she knew, if just for a moment, what it was like to have a father and she loved him for that.

"Jenny. Keep finding your facts."

"I will. I promise."

Jennifer amassed a library of facts, but never uncovered a crime. But she would and then, even though Sheriff Ben was no longer sheriff, he would do his duty and bust down that damned wall with her and destroy the evil bastard. Of course, that didn't stop her from doing her duty. She wrote Ben Hamilton yet another ticket for speeding.

"Just be more careful, would you, Ben?"

Ben almost smiled. "I'm real close, Jenny. Are you?"

She almost smiled back. "Still just the facts, Ben." She walked slowly back to her patrol car. She wished that Sheriff Ben could solve his crime and be Sheriff Ben again.

* * *

Ben watched Vermont Trooper Jennifer Julia Kennisaw walk back to her cruiser in his rear view mirror and wished he could put all his facts together and solve his case. He knew it would somehow solve everything that was wrong in Stansbury, including Jenny's case against the druggist. He had enough facts to fill a large room from wall to wall. He had a room built to hold all his facts and, when he wasn't accumulating speeding tickets, he was sitting on the threadbare couch in that room trying to put those facts together in some kind of meaningful way. He stopped sleeping in his bed years ago after his wife, Virginia, died. There were times that he thought he should move to a smaller place, just big enough for him and his facts.

However that would require moving those facts and that might upset the work and that might set him back and that would mean another girl would die when he could stop it if he could just figure it all out, so he stayed in his room on his couch with all his facts all around him.

Jennifer waved as she drove off.

Ben waved back at her. In a way, he was glad she stopped him. Not because he wanted another speeding ticket. His collection of those did not need company. He was just happy to stop for a moment and look at the world around him. He loved Vermont. He couldn't rightly think of a better place on the good green Earth to live. It was a perfect place as places go. The people were right in the head in a way that the people elsewhere just couldn't get. He heard that the people in New Zealand were cut from a similar cloth, but he didn't need to travel to the other end of the planet to have what he already had. Plus, Vermont had the best cheese, the best syrup and the best scenery. It was the people though, people like Jenny who thought people shouldn't speed because they were more than likely to hit a moose and she felt worse for the moose that got hit rather than the fool who hit it. The people here didn't care what the rest of the country thought because what happened to the people of Vermont was entirely different than what happened to the people in Oregon. And while the people out west were certainly sure to be nice enough, they could take care of themselves and make their own cheese, which Ben had heard was good quality, but not to match the local stuff. Ben loved America to be sure, but he loved Vermont most of all and sometimes, just sitting on the side of the road, he felt lucky to know this place and know these people.

Ben put his car in drive and headed on back to Stansbury. For all of its strange luck, he loved Stansbury.

He had been sheriff of the town for a good long time and it never occurred to him that he would do anything else. But he had to give it up. Sheriff Tom received just the three votes in the last election. Everyone else in town had voted for him. Including Sheriff Tom. But Ben had voted for Tom. So did Tom's mother, Danielle Hawkins, and his girlfriend, Mary Beth Ketchum. Everyone else in town voted for Ben. Including Sheriff Tom, who told Ben that he really did not want to be Sheriff. Ben felt sorry for the boy, but he could not be sheriff any longer. Just before the votes were counted, Ben withdrew from the election. The people of Stansbury were rightfully angry and confused by what he had done. Sheriff Tom was not quite as rightfully angry and confused by what he had done, but he still resented Ben just a little. Ben never felt too badly for Sheriff Tom because the boy *had* gone and filled out a form to run for the position. No one forced him to give up his promising career as a cartoonist. No one except, perhaps, his mother and girlfriend who were always after him to grow up and do something important with his life. Ben was certain that what angered people the most about his abdication of the post he had held for so long was that he refused to talk about it. The election was a thing of the past and yet no one would talk to him about anything else - especially Sheriff Tom - which is why he was often found driving 80 miles per hour rather than sitting at Charlie's Grill drinking a cup of coffee and doing the Sudoku. He used to do crosswords but the number puzzle was so much more compelling because it did not require him to have command of the increasingly esoteric knowledge that crossword writers inserted into the puzzles to show how wonderfully clever they were to all of the crossword aficionados… solving the Sudoku was about expanding his mind to the point that he could see the patterns and numbers in ways he had not seen them before...and he needed to see things differently these days...everything depended on it. Charlie used to keep a table for him. Charlie told him that a man of his stature needed his own table and no one else could sit at it, no matter how full the place was. To be fair, the place was rarely, if ever, full enough that people would have to stare at Ben's table and wonder why they could not sit there. Charlie even affixed a "Reserved" sign above the table next to a placard that read, "We proudly support our local law enforcement – and that means you, Ben Hamilton!" Ben was certain that Charlie was the angriest of all those who were angry about his abrupt retirement. Something about the way Ben could never get a table anymore or the way Charlie would snarl, "All full up," when there wasn't a customer that led him to avoid the place altogether. In fact, the only place in Stansbury that Ben could get the time of day was at the blasted pharmacy and that was only because Shelley, the current girl behind the counter, was like a daughter to him and old Osno, well, he only communicated with the pharmacist via notes through his slot and the answers had about as much character as a bar of white soap. He didn't imagine the strange recluse that Jenny was sure was the devil himself gave much thought to local politics or who wore the badge these days. Ben would occasionally drop by the place to get a soda and chat with Shelley. Those chats always seemed to turn to Gil and Ben really didn't want to spend too much time talking about Gil or to Gil. Not that he had any ill feelings towards his boy, but between Gil and that poor boy, Kurtz... Well, Ben had decided some time ago that there wasn't much he could do until he solved his case and these wasn't much use getting into the kinds of conversations with or about Gil that would inevitably lead back to his case and why he had stopped being sheriff. Gil had taken it worst of all. Ben loved Stansbury and he ached to tell every last body in the town why he up and abandoned the care of it to the very young Sheriff Tom who had never been anything but a doodler. Actually, there was one body in Stansbury who Ben wouldn't tell and that was the reason he couldn't tell anybody.

Ben looked at the road and decided it was time to hit it. There were still enough hours in the day that he could do something other than wander and think. Thus far, wandering and thinking hadn't done him a whole lot of good. It seemed a better idea to do the job he quit his last one to do. He had been just around this spot on the road into town when he had first realized that something was wrong in Stansbury and he needed to fix it. He had just come back to town from a stint working for the state as a member of the governor's personal guard. He mostly did the driving. The governor always said that Ben was the best driver he ever sat behind because Ben seemed to understand that driving was intuitive and Ben didn't over-think every turn. He just turned. The governor, Deane Chandler Davis, was one of the nicer people in power that Ben had come across. Sure, he was a Republican, but Vermont Republicans were not like other Republicans and were certainly nothing like the current crop of politicians who use that name for their political party. No modern Republican would push through something like Act 250, but Governor Davis did. Act 250 kept - and still goes on keeping - the Green Mountains green. Ben's favorite criteria that the act put on land developers was the eighth, which read, "Will not have an undue adverse effect on aesthetics, scenic beauty, historic sites or natural areas, and will not imperil necessary wildlife habitat or endangered species in the immediate area." Ben thought this should be part of the U.S. Constitution. Every place has its own beauty - although none as beautiful as Vermont of course - and none of it deserves to be spoiled by stupid development like Ben had seen and heard about in other places. These land developers build houses and business parks as if there are hordes of people who are waiting in line to buy a house and open a small business. The reality seemed to be that people couldn't afford the houses and there just weren't enough small businesses to fill up all the spaces. These places would stand empty and eventually looters and squatters would come in and leave the places even more ugly than they were when they were new. Gil told Ben that when he was working as a roofer in Sacramento, California - it was such a long way away to fix roofs…Gil always went such a long way to do such unimportant things…not to say that roofing was unimportant, it just seemed to Ben that he could have stayed in Stansbury to fix roofs or do any of the other hundred or so jobs he had done in other places before he lost his arm and had to come home - that these developers just kept on building long after the market demanded their buildings. They kept on building in every empty field and they kept on building through every grove of trees and other beautiful bit of nature the Golden State had to admire. Ben had heard that parts of California were amazingly beautiful and wondered how such a liberal state had gone so long without something like Act 250. Gil said it got so that he would drive around on the new empty roads that had been built to provide access to all the new empty buildings and he would pull into the empty parking lots and park for hours and just listen to the nothing of it all. Nature had been wiped away and there was nothing left but glass and concrete and emptiness. Gil said they were simply the most depressing places he ever came across because so much effort had gone into creating a void. Ben couldn't make any sense of it. He supposed it was because he was a human being. All those creatures that went around destroying the world by making empty buildings, they had no more connection to humanity than the buildings they made. They were all empty inside, waiting for some soul to fill them. But these places and these people were soul vacuums...they were vampires sucking the life from the earth. The world needed a global Act 250 to wear around its neck like a talisman against the life-sucking developers and miners and drillers and killers and then the human beings could survive in a world with more trees and fewer empty strip malls.

He remembered one time that he was escorting the governor and his wife, Marjorie, to dinner at the Dog Team Tavern outside of Middlebury. Ben was more than happy to sit in the car and wait for the governor to finish eating before heading out to grab a bite for himself. Governor Davis would have none of it and invited both Ben and his partner at the time, John Farrell, to sit at the next table over and enjoy what would become Ben's favorite restaurant. Ben actually loved Middlebury only slightly less than Stansbury. He had taken a few classes down at Middlebury College after his wife died. He had needed the company and Gil had gone off to do his odd jobs in odd places. He wanted to be with people who didn't call him Sheriff Ben all the time and ask him to do things for them all the time. He knew this was why the people of Stansbury were so angry at him. He just about never turned down a request and would do some of the oddest things a sheriff could be asked to do such a the time he had performed an exorcism of the cabin out back of Fred Merrick's house because, as Fred had complained, that damnable ghost was breaking all kinds of laws and it was Ben's job to deal with lawbreakers, both corporeal and spiritual. What Ben wanted was to eat at the Dog Team

Tavern as often a possible because he couldn't imagine a better restaurant in all of the world. Yes, it was kind of corny with all the bric-a-brac, including an old historic overcoat, a child's snowsuit, a huge collection of old political buttons, a dollhouse, an old sign for orange soda and the hide of a wallaby. He asked the owner at the time, Eben Joy, why there was a head of a wallaby on the wall and Joy had replied, "Why don't you have the head of a wallaby on your wall?" There was a head of a bear, some throw pillows with the face of a husky embroidered on them, some historical artifacts owned by or about the original owner, a missionary named Sir Wilfred Grenfell, a marble statue of snow drifts with a little dogsled and dogs and at least a dozen unique silk mats. Ben liked corny and he loved coming in and looking at all the stuff about Grenfell and his missionary work. Ben had often thought he would have liked to travel up to Newfoundland like Grenfell did before he retired to Vermont and bring some culture to the Newfies, but they would probably just try to cook him some fish and laugh at one of their damned stupid Newfie jokes. "Didja hear da one aboot the fish oot a da water? No? Oh, it were a good un. Too bad you missed it. hurr hurr." Of course, none of the bric-a-brac would mean a thing if the food wasn't so great - great not only in size, but in quantity… the portions were generous and you never left hungry. When you sat down, they gave you a sticky bun. The sticky buns at the Dog Team Tavern were like heaven. Ben was always going out of his way to get a sticky bun. Ben was always making other people go out of their way to get him sticky buns. Some things in life were unimportant to go without. Those sticky buns were not one of those things. Ben sometimes used his position as sheriff to commandeer those buns. The owners strictly rationed them, which forced Ben to abuse his power just a little. They would half-heartedly complain that they were not even in his jurisdiction, but Ben would throw his then considerable weight around – although he had lost a bit of his girth in recent years - and they would give in to his demands that the buns were needed as evidence in some minor case and turn them over to his care. Of course, the buns were just the first part of the meal. Ben's portions from the relish wheel, a kind of Ferris wheel of sides and condiments that the waitresses would roll up to your table, had, over time, decreased from when he would require the kitchen staff to refill the wheel after he had served himself. Ben was always partial to the horseradish cottage cheese and the apple butter, which he would slather all over the homemade bread. By the time they got around to bringing the prime rib he would just about always order, Ben would have little room left. The first time he went there with the governor, he just about filled up on corn relish and sauerkraut before the beef arrived. He knew he would have to finish the portion when the governor looked over at him with a smile and gave him a thumbs-up. After that evening, Ben learned to pace himself a bit and even saved room for dessert from time to time - no mean feat! Ben proposed to his Virginia there, arranging for the ring to be placed on the relish wheel. For Ben, there was no better place in all the world. But there would be no more desserts. There would be no more generous portions of prime rib. There would be no more relish wheel or homemade bread. There would be no more sticky buns. The Dog Team Tavern burned down one day with its owner and its relics and its memories. Ben remembered hearing about it from John Farrell. Ben had been sitting on the floor of his little room with all his files when John walked in looking like death. Ben hadn't seen John in years, but John knew this was the kind of news best delivered in person. Ben hadn't cried very often in his life, but he cried that day. When that place burned down, a part of him burned down with it that could never be replaced.

Ben thought about how fast he was going and decided to stay within the speed limit for the time. It wouldn't be beyond Jenny to drive a mile down the road and wait for him to go speeding by so she could give him another lecture and ticket. Plus, the closer he got to Stansbury, the slower he took the road. It just wasn't a good practice to go speeding through the town with the worst bit of luck in all of New England. He had been called out to about this spot in the road when he was a new deputy in these parts. He liked being a deputy in Stansbury a whole lot. He knew everyone in town and everyone knew and respected him. He wasn't a greenhorn like so many before him and his service to the governor gave him a bit of status in the small town he was from and, of course, he never took advantage of it because he wasn't in it for the status. He loved the law and he loved his town and people knew that about him, which made him even more popular. Sheriff Marsters, ol' Jim, used to tell him all the time that he would be the next sheriff of Stansbury and that he would be sheriff so long as he wanted. Ben couldn't have imagined at the time that he would ever not want to be sheriff of Stansbury. Of course, Ben still wanted to be sheriff of the town he loved, but he couldn't. It was a day in early November just after the leaves had fallen and the tourists had gone their way to warmer climes and he was just a deputy on duty, driving down this stretch of highway making sure that nothing was wrong and feeling in his gut that something was very wrong. Ol' Jim used to say that every good lawman had a gut he could trust like a Swiss watch. That day Deputy Ben knew that something was wrong in town. He went to bed the night before knowing it. He woke up knowing it. He told his wife over coffee and cider donuts - the same silly recipe Gil still used in his little store, God bless him - that something was wrong. Of course, Virginia said there was always something wrong in town and no one would speak about it. As if they did, that something would come crashing down on their heads. She didn't believe in jinxes, but she did believe in the bad luck that plagued their town and she was always after Ben to leave and he knew that if they had just left town when she wanted she wouldn't have died like she did. He still didn't leave town because curse or no, he still loved it and would never leave. Deputy Ben told Ol' Jim that something was wrong that day, really wrong and the sheriff agreed with him. They both just kind of sat in their office for a time waiting for a call and not talking about it but knowing it was really bad all the same. Finally, Ben couldn't take the sitting and waiting and told the sheriff he was going out for a drive to check in on the town. The sheriff just nodded. He didn't have to tell Ben that he would find something because they both knew that something was waiting out there to be found and neither of them had really wanted to be the first to come across it. But Ol' Jim knew that Ben was likelier than most to volunteer for such a thing and later told Ben that he was just kind of waiting for Ben to go rather than asking him. It was the kind of thing that was best volunteered for, that way there'd be no blame later on for the darkness that always followed the discovery of that kind of evil. Ben got in his cruiser and just kind of meandered around, not really knowing where he was going but knowing if he wandered enough, whatever it was would find him. He kind of expected that everyone in the town would know what he and the sheriff knew, but the day was like any other. No one seemed to be aware that their lives would all change that day. And, strangely, after all was said and done, the only life to really change that day was Ben's. Everyone else in town just kind of went on as before trying not to think about the horror of what happened and succeeding in not putting it together with the other horrors just like it that happened before and would continue to happen long after. They just didn't want to know because if they did, they wouldn't stay. There was a kind of communal amnesia that even Ben would occasionally cling to in order to just do the day-to-day work of keeping the town as safe as he could for as long as he could. The people of Stansbury did not want to acknowledge that there was nothing natural about the black luck that lingered in the heart of the place like an incurable slow moving cancer. Ben kept driving that day, looking for something out of place and, the longer he drove, the more he began to feel that maybe his gut was wrong about today. He began to hope he was wrong and his hope made his mind muddy. He stopped off and had a cup of coffee at Charlie's Grill. Charlie wouldn't take a dime from him that day or any other. Charlie stood by Ben while he drank his cup.

"What is it, Ben?" There was an unspeakable sadness in Charlie's question.

"I'm afraid I don't know, Charlie." Ben looked at the little bit of sugar and grounds that had not dissolved at the bottom of the cup as if he could tell the fortunes of the day from the remains. He wanted to see a sign that nothing was wrong but there was just the bottom of the cup. "I'm afraid to know."

"If anyone can make it stop, Ben…" Charlie suddenly stopped. He and Ben knew that what he had to say was unfair. "Coffee's on the house."

Ben left a dollar on the table anyway and went back to his cruiser. In this time in between autumn and winter, the town had a strange beauty. There was a clear blue that extended from the sky to the ground, the leaves no longer lingering to filter the light and the snow not yet there to color it all white. It was bluer that day than most and the blue held a coldness to it that chilled Ben more than any deep winter had ever done and Ben knew it was all about to come crashing down around him. He knew that he would find that thing that would change him fundamentally and instead of going home and climbing into bed and letting Ol' Jim find it, Ben volunteered. He made a promise to keep the town safe and he always thought he would keep that promise even if it destroyed him. But when he got back in the cruiser he balked. Something in his mind did not want him to be there and without even realizing it, he steered the car out onto the highway and started heading down towards Middlebury and sticky buns and relish wheels. He was just past the tourist shack that Gil now owned and ran when his trip to Dog Team Heaven was aborted. When he thought about it later, he realized that he never meant to leave town that day. It was that instinct inside him that set him on a course out of town and towards the darkness. He was just past the little path that led on down towards the Lakebridge when he saw Jack Bixby sitting there by the path with his old fishing rod leaning over his shoulder and a hand-rolled cigarette burning in the corner of his mouth. That wasn't an odd thing in and of its self. Jack was always out fishing some little place like Ewell Pond just north of Peacham, which was bigger than Stansbury Lake by a half. It could be the coldest day in the coldest winter on record and Jack would be out with a hole cut in some pond or lake with a hand-rolled cigarette burning in the corner of his mouth and he would have that old pole ready for a fish to come along and get itself cooked. Jack would even catch a fish sometimes, but never in Stansbury Lake, even though he was just about the only one who ever gave a thought to trying. For some reason, people didn't recreate there. It never felt right.

So it wasn't odd for Jack to be out by the lake. Ben pulled up in the shoulder next to Jack the same as normal because Ben had always done so before. There was nothing like routine.

"How they biting, Jack?" Routine question.

"Seen better days, Deputy." Routine answer.

Ben checked his watch and saw that it was somewhat early for Jack to have given up for the day. This was different and Ben knew.

"Calling it a day a bit early, eh?" Different.

Jack looked up at Ben and began to cry softly. "I won't be fishing the lake anymore, Deputy." Jack took the hand-rolled cigarette from his mouth and crushed the ember out on the ground and then put the stub in a little silver box. "You need to go and see. I stayed until you got here so you could go and see." Jack got up, leaving his pole on the ground. He wiped the tears away on his sleeve and looked at Ben. Later on, after Ben understood about the people of Stansbury, Ben sincerely hoped that Jack would be able to forget what he saw that day. "You have to go and see, Ben." But like Ben, Jack had never been able to let it go.

"What, Jack?" Let it go, Jack. Forget.

"Go and see."

Ben left Jack on the side of the road and headed towards the bridge. Jack never was able to forget. For awhile, he had tried to put it behind him and stopped fishing the lake. That wasn't enough. He knew what he knew and he had seen what he had seen and he couldn't stay. Much like anyone else who was from Stansbury, he loved the town and never thought of leaving it and when he told Sheriff Ben that he couldn't stay any longer, Ben knew why he was leaving. It was why Ben couldn't. Even though Jack left Stansbury, the town never did quite leave Jack. He moved out to Maine, thinking that maybe fishing the ocean would help cure him. He found a little place in Kennebunk and would spend his days out in a little boat beyond the breakers fishing for dinner. He wrote to Ben that he could fish the ocean because there weren't any damned bridges over the ocean to ruin things. Just the sea and the boat and the fish. Ben had always imagined that Jack was sitting in that little boat of his with his line in the water and a hand-rolled cigarette burning in the corner of his mouth when the storm took him. They never did find the boat or the fishing pole or the little silver box that held the makings of hand-rolled cigarettes and they never did find Jack either. They said it was the storm that took him, but Ben knew better.

Ben didn't look back at Jack as he headed down the path towards the Lakebridge. He rarely visited the town's lone attraction. He saw no charm in it. It was a stupid thing. There was no reason to build a bridge, let alone a covered bridge, over a lake that was no more than a pond. But it did bring the tourists by and that helped the town, so Ben just tried to live with the thing without giving it too much thought and without visiting it. He remembered going down to the lake with a bunch of friends when he was about eight. His friends said the bridge was haunted and he had heard that too and they all laughed about ghosts in that scared way that eight year olds laugh about things that terrify them so they don't cry and they all went down to the bridge that day to challenge the ghosts to come out and scare them away. The ghosts never came that day, but the boys didn't stay around that long either. There was just something wrong and they could all feel it, like when you walk through a cemetery and suddenly it gets hard to breathe and you know if you don't leave right away your throat will close up on you and then you'll be just another ghost haunting that old piece of ground. Ben and his friends rarely went back down by the lake after that day. No one encouraged them to and no one mocked them for their fear. Everyone in town had it and no one in town talked about it much in the same way that everyone in town knew they had the blackest of luck and with the exception of the few who made a habit of pissing in the wind, people like Gil, no one talked about it. Ben walked down the path to the bridge that day and he knew it would change him.

Now that Ben was no longer Sheriff, he rarely lingered by the path to the Lakebridge. Unless something happened, it held no interest for him. It was an evil thing. Normally, he wouldn't even slow down for it but today he saw his son and a pair of tourists standing by Gil's little shop talking to Jenny and thought there might be something to know.

* * *

"Do you want to know something, Officer?" Rick was finally enjoying himself on this trip.

"It is my goal in life to know things, sir." The attractive cop responded, obviously not amused.

"Vermont State Trooper Jennifer Julia Kennisaw lives to know things. I wish she's get to know me." Rick thought Gil was trying to hard with that one.

"You don't have to call me Vermont State Trooper Jennifer Julia Kennisaw, Gil."

Rick looked at his wife. "Young love."

"I'm not in love with-" The young officer was turning red. At first Rick thought it was with embarrassment but when she turned to him, he saw the anger there. Being married to a Latina, he knew female anger and was sorry he brought it on himself... or Gil. "I don't like men. He knows that."

"I can't call you Jenny or Jennifer or J.J. and since we've known each other for twenty years, calling you Officer Kennisaw just seems a bit formal." Rick wanted to warn Gil not to mess with angry women, but he could see from the smile on the young man's face that he was one of those thrill seekers who jump out of airplanes or tie bungee cords to their waists and jump off of bridges. Once Rick had thought to go to Spain and run with the bulls. Now the operative word for Rick in all of this was "thought." He thought about it and then thought he liked living without a bull's horn impaling his ass and tossing him twenty feet in the air before being trampled by other fools looking to be gored and trampled. Rick thought about jumping off or out of things and then thought he'd like living more than potentially feeling every bone in his body break before his skull caved in on his brain. Rick thought about all the crazy things people did and thought they were all ways to spell some kind of incredible boredom that must infuse their lives and that they all needed to learn to find pleasure in the little things like drinking a cup of really good coffee with your wife. Not some fluffed up coffee drink, but coffee...just coffee. Or, when the chance arrives, watching other people risk their lives for nothing more than a cheap thrill. Now that Rick was out of the line of officer's ire, he turned to his wife and smiled. "This is turning out to be a great trip, Marisol."

He saw Gil smile a little and thought the boy was playing with fire.

* * *

Jennifer saw that little smile on Gil's face and knew that he was just playing with her. Of course, she knew that he had a crush on her. He had that same crush for over twenty years. For at least ten of those, he knew she was a lesbian. He also knew that she was in love with his best friend, Shelley. Jennifer spent many hours by the side of the road watching the cars go by and lamenting that she was in her own personal bad romantic comedy. She even felt for Gil a little bit, knowing how unrequited love felt, especially when the person you were attracted to did not share your orientation. But that little bit wasn't enough to soften her to his advances or his flirts. Plus, he was making her look bad to the tourists and as a representative of the State of Vermont, if she looked bad, the state looked bad.

"When the business is official, you should address me as Officer Kennisaw."

"And when it's not official?" Gil smiled again. He was having too much fun. She looked over at the couple and they were kind of smirking, too. Vermont looked bad right now.

She smiled at the couple. "Anytime you see me, Mr. Hamilton. Anytime. It's official." Vermont was looking better.

She and Gil kept having this conversation. Sometimes it was fun having it in front of other people. He couldn't win it, so it was fun. Vermont was fun.

* * *

Rick thought that Vermont was really fun.

* * *

Gil thought that Vermont was fun. Where else could you stand by the side of the road hitting on a lesbian trooper in front of an affable pair of tourists who just witnessed a crazy man try to drop a tree on a bridge? Gil could hardly think of it.

Gil saw his father pull his old beater up next to the Winnebago. The fun was over. He put his smile away for later. For someone who deserved it.

* * *

Ben saw his son's smile disappear when he arrived. Virginia used to be able to get them to talk without all the stupid father-son tension. He remembered when Gil came back from Alaska after the accident up there. It wasn't easy for him to come back, either. Apparently he had been out on one of those damned dangerous fishing boats that everyone thinks are all romantic because they're so damned dangerous and what was even more damned dangerous was that Gil was on the damned thing so, of course, the damned thing went down and took everyone but Gil with it. Gil's bad luck generally wasn't as bad for Gil as it was for everyone else around him and it always seemed to get worse for people the farther away from Stansbury the boy got. People in town had enough of their own that his didn't seem to work on them as much. But for Gil to get work doing the most damned dangerous thing you could do…well, Ben always felt that Gil bore some amount of responsibility for that boat going down. Ben was sure that Gil felt it more. Ben was also sure that the capital "U" Universe had taken Gil's arm in a desperate attempt to keep everyone outside of Stansbury safe from him.

Ben turned the car off and made his way over to the group. The man in the guayabera was obviously enjoying himself more than anyone else there. Ben nodded to him and then looked to Jenny.

"Long time, no see, Jenny."

"Everything's under control here, Ben."

"Really? Really?" Gil had that frustrated look on his face that Ben had unfortunately seen way too many times.

The boy looked back and forth between Ben and Jenny. "He gets to call you Jenny?"

"Professional courtesy," she smirked.

"But he's not a professional anymore." Gil spat the words out at his father.

"We in the law enforcement community respect the service of all our brethren, on the job or retired." Jenny looked to Ben for his approval. Ben had a really hard time giving it to her in front of his son.

Ben regretted stopping. He hated being this close to the bridge. Nothing good ever came of it. He rarely stopped in at Gil's store and not just because the boy held him in such contempt. Gil never understood why Ben let Sheriff Tom win and he should have understood more than anyone. Gil knew more about that damned bridge and the history of the town and the darkness than anyone else and he knew why Ben had to stop being sheriff.

"Looks like Kurtz tried to drop a tree on the bridge." Jenny looked like she was enjoying herself a little. That made Ben smile.

"Did you call it in to Sheriff Tom?"

"He said he was otherwise occupied and asked if I could go down and see if there was any reason to pay the kook a visit."

"There's no reason to be mean, *Officer Kennisaw*."

Jenny didn't acknowledge Gil. "Do you care to come down and take a look with me?"

"I told you nothing happened to the bridge. Nothing ever happens to the bridge. A meteor could drop out of the sky and destroy all of New England and that thing would still be there." Gil turned to the tourists and managed to put on a smile. "The best part about Vermont is that so little happens here, our state troopers have to investigate every tree that falls in the woods."

Jenny didn't acknowledge Gil and headed down the path. "Coming, Ben?"

Ben didn't want to go. He looked at his son, though, and saw everything that the boy was feeling. There was so much locked up in there, but mostly frustration. This thing he had with Jenny would never be finished and, sadly for Gil, he always finished everything he started or just kept at it. Right now, for Gil, nothing he started this go around, from Jenny to the Lakebridge, would ever…could ever end well for him.

Ben looked over to the couple. "You folks enjoy your visit." The old man nodded back at him and the woman smiled. Nice folks. Ben hoped they would make it out of Stansbury without incident. But then again, they had stopped at Gil's so they were fair game to whatever force it was that the boy unintentionally inflicted on those around him.

For a moment he moved towards his car to leave, but something drew him to follow Jenny. For no good reason, he went along with her.

* * *

There was no good reason why his father chose to follow Jenny. His father rarely went by the lake. He always told Gil that he knew what was down there and there was no reason to pay it a casual visit. Gil was pretty sure he went to get away from Gil and that was fine. Ever since the election, they didn't have much to say to one another. Actually, Gil didn't have much to say to his father. His father had a lot to say to him, but had long since stopped trying to say it. If Gil could say anything about the man, he understood people better than anyone else Gil had ever met. He was also incredibly noble and that's what killed Gil about the damned election. Ben was supposed to be sheriff of Stansbury. It was his calling and he gave it up and now he just drove around racking up speeding tickets and sitting in his case room looking at his files and trying to figure out how to stop it all and not listening to Gil who knew that it couldn't be stopped so long as the bridge was there and since the bridge wasn't going anywhere anytime soon, Kurtz's efforts notwithstanding, there was no reason to stop being sheriff. The town needed Sheriff Ben to keep it all together and everyone knew it. Sheriff Tom knew it, which is why he just about never left his office. When his father sat him down to explain it all, Gil understood and he told him as much. Gil knew the deep pain his father felt about the case. But it wasn't enough to abandon the town to drive around like a maniac hoping something would come to him as the mile markers ticked by to the coast and back. Gil told his father that when he was ready to be sheriff again, Gil would be happy to help him with the case. His father told him that he couldn't be sheriff and work on the case and that Gil was never to even glance at the case files or step foot in the case room. It all had to stop. But Sheriff Ben did not have to stop being Sheriff Ben to make it all stop.

 Gil watched his father walk down the path after Vermont State Trooper Jennifer Julia Kennisaw. He had nothing better to do than work on her a little more. Of course he knew she was a lost cause. But at this point, his whole life was a lost cause. He turned to Rick and Marisol who had been watching the whole melodrama without comment.

 "Care to see Vermont's finest in action?"

 "You sure you want to do that, son?" Gil could see that Rick couldn't help grinning. Gil really liked Rick.

 "No. But I'll go and do it all the same."

Rick shrugged at Marisol. "We've got no place to be right now. Maybe someone else will try to do something crazy."

"Not outside of the range of possibilities." The couple again followed Gil as he made his way towards the bridge.

* * *

As Ben made his way towards the bridge, he heard Gil and the couple following after him. For a moment, he thought about turning around and leaving. He had only followed Jenny in the first place to put some distance between himself and his son. And now he was on this path again heading down towards the Lakebridge again. Even though he knew there was nothing more down there than a fallen tree sitting in that little lake. Even though he knew that tree ought to have rightfully fallen on that bridge, smashing it to kindling. Kurtz was as precise a lunatic as one would ever meet. If there was one person who didn't need his head scrambled any more than it came by naturally, it was Kurtz. Of course he was Gil's friend. Ben looked around at all the green, all the life of this place, all the beauty of this place and once again hoped that when he walked down the little embankment that led to the lake, the green - or the orange or the yellow or the blue or the white…so many beautiful colors in this place as the seasons went round - wouldn't be spoiled by that damned red.

When Ben left Jack Bixby behind, he knew that the thing was there, waiting for him. He knew what the thing was and he knew where the thing was and he knew that all he had to do was turn around and go back and he would be safe. But he was responsible for the town. He wasn't yet sheriff, but he knew he would be and so he was responsible for whatever came and he had to face it. When he finally came in view of the lake and the bridge, he thought about

Jane Simmons and John Macintyre. Jane and John had never been the subject of rumor. Everyone just knew that they were for each other. When they were in the first grade, they played together while the other boys and girls still believed in the existence of mythical creatures called cooties that lived on members of the opposite sex and laid in wait to attack you if you got too close. What cooties would actually do to you, no one knew. All they knew was that you could catch them and, once caught, you had them and, once you had them, you could never rid yourself of them and would forever be pariah, a carrier of cooties. To all the other boys and girls, Jane and John were cootie central. To even go near them while they played innocently, one day with Jane's dolls and the next with Jack's cars, was to risk certain doom. The teachers worried that it was too early for a girl and a boy to be so close, so much more than friends. But some, like Miss Lauren Farnsworth, believed in soul mates and that as much as people could be predestined for one another, Jane and John were and it was so wonderful for them that they could find each other so early in life and never know the kind of void that she felt having never met hers. Although Miss Farnsworth was quite jealous of Jane and John, it was only in that self-pitying sense that someone who has waited for fate to find her rather than finding her own fate feels towards those who they see as blessed by what curses them. She didn't allow her jealousy to twist her insides like others might. She was a romantic and saw that the joining of these two children was proof positive that the universe meant for people to be with specific people and she had been right all these years to wait. She would keep on waiting and, as far as Ben knew, she still waited. Ben asked her on a date one time, but she declined. She was polite in her explanation of soul mates and had even used Jane and John as examples before bursting into tears at the memory of the two. Ben shed a tear or two himself which made him think that perhaps Miss Farnsworth could be his soul mate, but did not mention this to her because she seemed quite sure of herself and had made it clear that she was quite certain that they were not soul mates. But Jane and John were. Everyone knew it as much as people believed in such things. For a while, their parents thought it wasn't healthy or proper for a girl and a boy to spend so much time together, their parents having never quite given up their belief in the efficacy of cooties. They sent them off to camps away from one another in the hopes that they would make friends with other girls or other boys and learn about cooties and why it was so important to avoid them. Even though the pair made friends with other girls and boys and had the kind of fun one has at summer camp, whenever they were reunited at the end of summer, they picked up as if they had never been apart and even their parents began to realize that somehow they produced a girl and a boy who were uniquely perfect for one another. Ben had only been deputy for two years when he went walking down the path to the bridge that day and he thought about Jane Simmons and John Macintyre. He had only come into contact with them in the way a small town deputy comes into contact with any twelve year old, which is to say in that friendly, but authoritative manner that policemen have with young children on the verge of considering whether or not to be law abiders or law breakers. Friendly, to show them that the police are your friends and will always be there to help you when you need it and, hopefully, protect you if you need protecting. Authoritative, to remind them that the police will be there to catch you if you do bad things. Ben only gave the two as much thought as one gives to a girl and a boy who are about to discover the only cure for cooties is kissing. Ben hoped when he saw them start holding hands as they walked out of Osno's that they could hold off awhile longer…that they could stay innocent even though what the two youngsters had was about as pure as one could imagine such a thing could be. Later on, when Ben started working on the case in earnest, he imagined other things about Jane and John. He imagined that someone had been thinking about Jane and John for a long time, for as long as they had been a couple. He imagined that someone had been watching the children grow and watching their bond deepen. He imagined that someone needed them for their purity and their innocence and needed them before they moved beyond purity and innocence. He imagined that someone had been preparing to do this thing for as long as that someone knew of the children and that someone could finally wait no longer, could not wait for the myth of the cooties to be dispelled with the onset of puberty and lust. Ben spent a long time imagining what made that someone use Jane and John that November day when he walked down towards the bridge. That someone had used them. *Used them.* Ben was already crying that day as he neared the bridge and saw what that someone had done to John Macintyre. That someone stripped the twelve year-old boy of his clothes. That someone placed the boy at the entrance to the bridge so he was facing the path. John Macintyre was there to greet any and all who came to see the bridge that day. John Macintyre stared with his lifeless eyes at any and all who came to see the bridge that day. That someone used five lengths of hand-made rope to tie John Macintyre in place. A piece of rope stretched each limb tight, making it seem as though the boy were floating. Another piece of rope kept the head upright, that someone had taken care to keep John Macintyre's body from leaving its precisely placed position. Roy Childers from the state coroner's office said that it looked like a pentagram the way the ends of the rope had ropes tied all around edges, completing the figure, like some kind of Satanist ritual. Roy was chiefly responsible for the theory that there were Satanists in Stansbury and that's why God had forsaken the town. Even confronted with the evil of John Macintyre's murder, Ben didn't cotton to that theory. He knew the people of Stansbury and knew there wasn't a coven of Satanists among them. He also knew that this was no black mass as people liked to attribute to Satanists. For one, the boy wasn't placed in a pentagram. Sure, it seemed that way when you looked at John Macintyre. That someone might even have wanted people to think such a thing. Ben was pretty sure that someone didn't much care what people thought, actually. The problem as Ben saw it was the way that someone had positioned Jane Simmons at the other end of the bridge. Ben had tried to point out to Roy and others that her body did not form an equivalent pentagram. Of course, Roy and the others had their easy theory and did not want to think why that someone might decapitate and dismember the girl, leaving only a torso with a left arm strung up at one end and right leg tied down at the other. They didn't even want to think about how no one had ever found the missing pieces that someone had removed. They certainly didn't want to look at the strange geometric figure that was created when Ben combined the forms as they appeared when he looked straight on through the bridge. It was a symbol that someone was trying to create, all right. It wasn't a pentagram or some tribute to an evil lord. That was too banal. Ben researched the figure over the years as he worked on the case both during his spare time and during official time. He even traveled to England to show it to some people over there that knew about ancient evils and no one could be quite sure of what that someone was trying to do that day. Ben could only come to the conclusion that the bridge needed Jane Simmons and John Macintyre and that someone was responsible for filling that need. What was worse, what Ben seemed to know that no one else, except perhaps Gil and Kurtz, is in his own way, understood was that this wasn't the act of some psychotic group of pseudo-Satanists. This had happened before and would happen again. Even Ol' Jim seemed to finally buy into the Satanist theory. It was easier than Ben's unfounded theories about that someone. Gil told him that someone was Lord Stansbury who had somehow survived all these years and would keep on surviving so long as the bridge was fed. Ben thought that it was a useful theory because that's exactly what that someone might think. What Ben finally discovered was that the longer he stuck around Stansbury and tried not to think about it all, the easier it was not to think about it all and just go about his business. There were times, some times long stretches, when Ben would just go about the business of being sheriff and there were times that Ben was okay with not thinking about that someone. But it was his duty. He would always come back to Jane and John and those who had been sacrificed to the bridge before them and know he had to do something to stop it. So he built his case room to house his research and he spent time in that room every day pouring over everything he found. Somehow that worked to keep it from fading from his mind. It had worked for awhile at least, but then he found that there were days at a time that he would not go into the room, that he would just go about being Sheriff Ben and then he would snap back and remember what he had to do, what that someone had done and what he couldn't let happen again. Gil never understood about the forgetting because Gil was immune to it. Gil didn't understand that he couldn't be Sheriff Ben and work on the case because he needed to leave Stansbury to think about it. When he was on his drives, when he was away from the town, he never forgot Jane Simmons and John Macintyre.

As Ben followed Jenny down to the bridge, he saw that the bright red was beginning to fade a little… just a little. He was sure that someone had seen it as well.

IV

I love Stansbury. I love Vermont. Heck, I love the United States of America. Great places, one and all. The people of the town, the state and the country all know that these are places that you can do just about anything you want. I know that I can do what I want even though I haven't always done what I wanted to do. There are times when I go down and sit by my bridge - and it's only my bridge in the way that it is my lake or my town or my state or my country... my ego isn't so large as to think that I am the owner of all these things, I possess them in the way that we all claim ownership of those things around us - and admire the craftsmanship of it.

It's not a normal bridge. Not that anything is normal, but there are standards of things that people come to think of as normal. Yes, it is a covered bridge in Vermont and these are not entirely uncommon. But Lord Stansbury's bridge is different. For one, it spans a small lake. A beautiful lake that glows with the seasons, green in spring and summer, gold, orange and red in fall - our season to be sure - and white in winter. The bridge crosses it. That's all it does. It doesn't join a broken road over a creek or span a river valley. It would seem to be there to get you from one side of the lake to the other a few minutes quicker than you would if you just walked around. It doesn't seem to make any sense at all. Of course, those of us that have been around it for some time know just exactly why it was built and it wasn't to bridge the beautiful little lake just outside of Stansbury. If you know the right things to say and do, it can take you other places. Places you might not want to go. And then, of course, there is its construction. Every plank was laid with care in endlessly complex designs. It can unsettle you a little to ponder just how long it took to place each board and peg. Some of the planks seem to bend at impossible angles and some of the corners inside do not seem to be corners at all, but seem to bend in dark curves. If you stand on the bridge too long, it can unsettle you some, like that choking feeling you get when you wander through a graveyard. And then, of course, there's the color. It's red. It's always red and doesn't ever seem to fade no matter the season. It's an unnatural red that tints the moonlit lake bloody. Gil, a local seller of all things Vermont and keeper of Stansbury lore, once told me there was no way anyone could be painting it. He would know. I'm sure he also knows that the bridge was made to keep itself. It's part of the design of the thing. If you're ever in Stansbury, I'm sure you'll go down and pay it a visit. You should. It is a beautiful thing to look at.

Have you ever really looked at the way things, like bridges, are put together? Every piece cut just so and sanded down and put into its perfect place to create a whole, perfect thing? Some people just don't get it. They look at the constructs of man and see…things. They see the whole thing and they look for flaws and sure, there are flaws. I see them, sure. But I try to look beyond them to see the whole of a thing. Even Lord Stansbury's bridge has flaws - that it was ever made, well, that could be considered a flaw of a kind. But those flaws are in the people looking at the things ever so much more than in the people who made the things. Everything they see is filtered through their prisms of imperfect thought and their negative worldview. They don't love their towns or states or countries. They don't love their mothers and sisters and neighbors. They don't really much love themselves. They can't see the love that the craftsmen and craftswomen - I've been trying to do better at recognizing the great works of women. I've even been reading great books by women recently because I read an article about the great works of women, how they were often neglected by a society that mostly promoted the great works of men. To tell you the truth, the great works of women are no better or worse than the great works of men. Some are greater than others and some are lesser than others. Ultimately what I think is great may be different than what you think is great. You know what? That's just fine for the both of us so long as we don't think less of one another for our opinions on great works. If you like something I don't, that's just fine, just so long as you like something and want to talk to me about it. If you don't like anything, then there's no use talking to you because you'll never understand why I like what I like. If you don't like anything, you might as well not exist. They can't see the love that the craftspeople put into their works because they have never made anything. All they can do is complain.

I was in a restaurant in Boston recently. It wasn't the greatest restaurant I had ever been to - that one burned down a few years back…I promise you I had nothing to do with that - but I was enjoying my meal just the same. I saw what the chef was trying to do with his flavor profiles. He was trying to be original in the way that chefs take a standard dish and put a twist on it. The way a chef might take macaroni and cheese and, instead of macaroni, use rigatoni. Then they put in a combination of cheeses, I really like it when they put in some Roquefort with a little bit of chevre, it's just a nice mix of that sharp blue taste and the creaminess of the goat. I love that. That is the kind of alteration of a classic that makes sense to me. They like to add little bits of meat like pancetta or venison sausage and then cook it in an individual crock-pot with a layer of Parmesan crust on top. It can be delicious. At this restaurant in Boston, it wasn't quite delicious and I didn't quite love it, but I loved the chef for trying it all out because he really wanted to make something sublime and had just missed the mark. I'm sure that, given time, he would realize the dish would be better served without the white truffles. Chefs have this weird attraction to truffles or truffle oil…these things go well in some dishes, but not all dishes… and they keep sticking them into everything.

So I was there enjoying my meal, because even though it wasn't perfect, I found things about it to enjoy. I always do this. It is the best way to live. I urge you to try it rather than finding things to complain about. You will live longer, I promise you. So I was there enjoying my meal and there was a gentleman at the next table over who was not. I was there, at that restaurant in Boston, when I heard this gentleman at the table next to mine ask the server if she could get the manager. The server very politely asked if there was something she could do. Her name was Felicity. She introduced herself to me as Felicity when she told me about the specials, including the chef's special macaroni and cheese which she said was the best she had ever eaten and, even though I disagreed with her, I told her I understood why she thought it was the best she ever had and that her passion for the dish was to be commended. She gave me the genuine smile of someone who knows how to love things. Felicity wasn't smiling as she walked away from the customer who had insulted her by telling her she was not qualified to do anything for him. He could have rephrased his remark. He could have been polite. You can ask to speak to a superior and be nice about it. You should always be nice. You never know who might take offense.

With his unfortunate dismissal of Felicity, I had to downgrade him from gentleman at that point to customer. A gentleman can resolve things without cruelty. This customer was the cruel sort who believed that he would be better served through belligerence and bullying. The manager was Mark, who had come by earlier and introduced himself to me when he checked in to see how I was enjoying my meal. Mark, who I learned a lot about over a glass or two of single malt scotch at a local tavern, the best drink in the best kind of establishment, had a degree in Hotel and Restaurant Management because all he ever wanted was to provide people with the best possible service. When he was young he had always seen people behind desks at hotels or behind podiums at restaurants or bringing him food or drinks or whatever he ordered and they were always smiling and seemed so glad to see him and so happy to be serving him. He told me he thought that it must be the greatest thing on earth to serve people what they wanted because that made the people being served happy. Mark wanted nothing more than to make people happy.

Mark, who made me happy with his rare ability to find pleasure in serving others, put on his best smile when he went to deal with the customer at the next table. He put on that smile even though Felicity came to him in tears because the customer made her feel that she couldn't be of service. Mark still wanted to make the customer happy. The customer did not want to be happy, though. The customer wanted a free meal and the customer wanted to make Mark miserable. The customer wouldn't even get any perverse pleasure out of this. He didn't even know what he was doing except that he could never be happy. He couldn't stand it when others were happy. He really couldn't stand it when others tried to make him happy. Mark could not help the customer. Mark was well trained in his craft and knew he could not satisfy this man, no matter what he offered him because Mark refused to be made miserable about his work. Mark refused to provide free meals when there was not a real reason for it. Mark wouldn't even offer a free dessert to customers like this one because Mark knew that it was a perverse game they were playing and Mark refused to play it. Mark loved his work and he loved making people happy through his service. He also knew that some people were simply incapable of being happy and he refused to play along with their attempts at dragging everyone around them into their miserable excuse for a life. As I watched the events, I knew I wanted to know more about Mark, of course. He was worth knowing. But I really wanted to know more about the customer.

I invited Mark and Felicity out for drinks afterwards and ended up treating the entire staff of the restaurant. It was my pleasure. I was fortunate in my birth as far as money is concerned. It has never been something I have worked for or worried about. I spend it as freely as it was given to me. I listened to the staff as they opened up to me about their lives. I was the friendly patron buying drinks and people open up with a scotch or two they don't have to pay for. As interested in them as I was, and I am always interested in good people, what I really wanted to know was how they dealt with the customer, who I decided was incapable of enjoying this life or loving anything. After Mark refused to give the customer a single concession, the man loudly announced that he would never eat at the restaurant again and that he would not be tipping Felicity. Mark smiled at the customer and said that was his right. As Mark passed by my table, I pulled a hundred dollar bill from my billfold and told him to give it to Felicity. Mark did not seem surprised by my generosity. He recognized that I was someone who was happy to be served and happy to serve others and I could see that my act had restored Mark's positive spirit somewhat.

It didn't take too much work to discover the customer's name and address. Dr. Dennis Covington was an economist who taught at Boston College. He wasn't a tenured faculty member. He was a lecturer who bounced from college to university to college and never really found his way into a tenured position. I was fairly certain it was because once people got to know him, and people in academia, while cloistered and self-aggrandizing, still had some insight into others, especially those whose jobs were to discover potential professors… once they got to know him, they recognized that he was not a very effective educator because he hated his subject in as much as he hated everything and the only reason he had drifted into teaching economics was because after years of studying the economy in the hopes that he could attain some measure of wealth, he discovered that he had no talent for acquiring wealth. In fact, he discovered that he had no talent for anything, which was probably a reason that he hated everyone else, especially those who were talented in whatever it was that they did. People like Mark, who were talented at serving others, for instance. Dr. Covington spent his nights hating everything he watched religiously on television and then going on the Internet to blog about just how much he hated the latest reality show or hour-long drama.

I took some time away from Stansbury to audit one of his courses that he hated teaching. I never felt one way or the other about the study of economics. I'm sure it was important in some way for the functioning of the world and that without experts in it, the world as we know it would end and people would go back to trading chickens for walls. After a few classes with Dr. Covington, however, I felt that the world just might be a much better place without Dr. Covington studying economics. I talked with the other students in the class, which was the primer on economics that all non-majors enrolled in when they decided to use economics as a means of satisfying some requirement in their degree program. To a person, they all felt that a world without Dr. Covington teaching economics would be a better one. They at least felt that their Boston College experience would be vastly improved if he were not their professor so early on - or, in the case of a few, so late in - their academic careers. He made people wish for anarchy. I found Internet chat groups and web pages solely devoted to the mutual hate of Dr. Dennis Covington. I forwarded them to my friends Mark and Felicity and they told me that they would circulate his picture to other restaurants in the area in the hopes that no one else would have to suffer him as a customer. I quietly encouraged students to start a petition to have him fired from his post at the college. I quietly encouraged his neighbors in his Back Bay apartment building to start a petition to have him evicted from the building.

Janie Danielson, a sophomore at BC, offered to go to the administration and claim that he sexually harassed her. I could not be responsible for adding any sins to Dr. Covington's resume. It was not allowed. He had to be the maker of his own despicable life. And, to be honest, I detest liars. Janie said that she didn't need my permission and she was right. She didn't. But I was doing a service in removing Dr. Covington from the lives of others. For him to serve the greater good of Stansbury, it was required for him to ultimately understand that it was entirely his own fault for what was happening to him. If he could point a finger at Janie Danielson and say that her lies were his undoing, it would give him a righteousness that he did not deserve and the spell would not work. The Dennis Covingtons are too rare and valuable to allow to spoil. When I cut Janie's throat, I wasn't especially gentle about it nor did I spend any real amount of time planning it. I didn't give her any explanations. She was a filthy liar and didn't deserve anything more than a cow at a slaughterhouse would get. Gil, who before selling stuffed moose and maple syrup to tourists had knocked around the country and worked for a time at a slaughterhouse, told me that they only cut the throats of the cows after they knocked them in the head with a hydraulic bolt... unless it was a Kosher place and then they cut their throats to kill them. I didn't even stick around to watch her bleed out, and normally I felt it my duty to watch the life leave a person. Her death would never be useful to me. I couldn't have her ruining my plans with Dr. Covington.

It only took me a few months to have Dr. Covington removed from the life he haphazardly built in Boston. The college chose not to renew his contract. His apartment manager, having found out about his termination by the college, used that as an excuse to terminate his lease. None of the restaurants in the area would serve him and he was banned from all the television Internet sites where he frequently posted his noxious opinions. Now here was the part I hoped for. Dr. Covington, for his many faults, wasn't an entirely stupid man. Regardless of what some government workers who are kept from promotion due to the lack of a Ph.D. think, most people with a doctorate to their credit have a modicum of intelligence. Dr. Covington figured out that he was the target of a campaign against him and became somewhat focused on finding his tormentor. I wasn't especially worried about any violent acts from him. It didn't fit his character. At the most, he might write some nasty things about me on his blog and then there would be things written about me on the Internet. I work very hard to make sure nothing is ever written about me on the Internet because then it will be there forever. Once it is on the Internet, it is there forever. I did, however, want Dr. Covington to find me.

You see, I need someone filled with a good, strong hatred of everything. These people aren't easy to find. Most of the time, they are in prison because they beat or killed someone. Or they just go and kill themselves. Most of the time, they find something that they like, even amongst all the hate. Maybe they do drugs and they like the high enough to realize that the high is better than the hate. Maybe they read a book and it finally speaks to something inside of them and they are able to stop hating for the briefest moment that it takes to discover that there is so much about the world to like and then love and they learn to love. But there are those, like Dr. Covington, who are somehow able to go through their lives building up their hatred over time and, not being violent, are able to exist in that perfect state. I need someone like that because I love Stansbury.

Stansbury is a different kind of town. It really has no right to exist with everything that has happened there over the years. Oh, sure, I could accept a lot of the blame for the things that have happened, but I'll only take the blame if you give me credit for all the good that I have done. There have been so many times that the town could have slipped from the map, given the number of tragic events that have befallen it. For instance, when that busload of young army recruits drafted from the town to fight in Vietnam went to their doom, it could have killed the town. For years, it looked like it was going that way too because people just wouldn't forget about it in any meaningful way. You see, in order for people to move on and get back to their lives, they have to forget about all those bad things that happen. If the people who lived in Stansbury remembered that bus crash in any meaningful way, that kind of darkness would have grown like a cancer and eaten the very heart away from the community. You can't live with that kind of darkness. You just can't and you'll either slowly let it kill you or you'll leave. I knew after that bus crash, much like I've known after many of the other tragedies that have brought the town to the brink of destruction, that I needed to cut out the cancer of those memories.

There always has to be a sacrifice, though. It is something my father taught me. He said for as long as Stansbury had been around, our family was there as well. We were the caretakers who made sure the town survived the blackness that Lord Stansbury cursed it with. The bridge, so beautiful and foul, is an abomination that holds the worst of Lord Stansbury's magic in it and it will eat the town and then other towns beyond it if left unchecked. Stansbury needs to survive if only to protect the world from the bridge. My family, we know the secret of forgetting. It's a powerful spell that keeps the town from thinking on things too much. We are the keepers of it and we are responsible for making sure it is used judiciously. My father told me that we couldn't make them forget every bad thing that happened. Bad things happen and they always will. In

Stansbury, however, bad things happen a whole lot because there is so much bad luck and there is so much bad luck because of the bridge that Lord Stansbury built. My father and his fathers before him tried to destroy the bridge for as long as they had been keeping the town alive. No one knew how to do it, the magic that made the thing being as strong as it was. Sometimes it took unspeakable acts to combat it.

After the bus took all those young men from the town, I was sick with what I knew it would take to make it right and I almost didn't do it. I was very close to letting the town of Stansbury go its merry way because if we all just left it, if we stopped feeding it, then maybe it would die and maybe that would be a good thing. I could go and live and love life without having to be responsible for a battle that, at the time, I didn't have the heart to fight.

Years before that, I asked my father if he knew what had been done to make the bridge, to set the curse. He told me that it was the darkest evil. He looked through the bridge once, saw where it really went, not just to the other side of the lake but to the other side of reality, and knew that only the foulest of creatures could have imagined it into being. There were horrors on the other side that were beyond anything rational men had nightmares to awake screaming from… he couldn't speak of them without turning pale and breaking into a sweat. He told me he knew that if they could ever fully open the passage back across the bridge, they would spread their horror across the world. He was always afraid to try to destroy it because he said the bridge or whatever it was that made it had a way of tricking you. He told me his great-grandfather had been tricked and it drove him mad. Father decided that to be a caretaker was enough. He would keep them all forgetting until I could take over and then he would forget too. He told me that he prayed for the day he would forget.

On that day, the day he forgot, that day he was happy as I had never seen him. He told me that he loved Stansbury and he went out for a walk. That day the bridge took him. Sheriff Jim told me that it was one of those freak accidents that were all too common in Stansbury. My father stopped in at Osno's to pick up some unguent for an infection that had been lingering for a time. On his way out of the pharmacy, he slipped on some ice on the step and cracked his head against the corner of the curb. It happened that quickly. I could only nod at the sheriff as he offered his sympathies. Whatever it was that my father had worked to keep from destroying the town for all those years finally seized upon its opportunity and took him. I expect no less from it when I choose to forget it all. If I choose to forget it all. I am not sure if I deserve to forget all those things I have done in the name of this town. When that bus went down, I knew I would have to do something drastic to keep it all together. But I thought I'd be clever and see if I could take the curse off the town while I was at it. I was still young about this business then and thought I could somehow do more then all those who came before me. Father warned me. But the hubris of youth... I thought with all my studies into the occult and with the accumulated knowledge of the centuries of caretakers that I could somehow break the town of the curse. I knew it would cost us all. But you have to pay, don't you?

Sometimes in life you have to pay dearly. You give up one set of friends for another if there can be some kind of greater happiness in the giving. You give up one lover for another if you think the love will be stronger. I knew the town would have to pay to be rid of the curse of damned Lord Stansbury. And I was sure I knew how to do it. I had read the darkest books of the kind that old sorcerer used. I knew how to do it. I found the counter spells to close his gate that my father and his fathers before knew could never be closed. I would set fire to it all, but I would have to sacrifice the most beautiful of all things to do it.

I had been watching them for years, the same as everyone else. Jenny and John were perfect little children in love, just the kind the spell called for. Innocent only in the way that children who are in love but know nothing of love can be. If I killed just one of them and said the words of forgetting, it would erase the pain of the memory of the awful bus crash from the minds of the town. They lived with it for a few years and I could see it was just starting to eat away at the fabric of the place, but I waited because I knew I could make it all go away if I just waited for Jenny and John to mature almost enough to lose their innocence. They had to be ripe but not rotten. That's what the book said. I thought I was so clever with that damned book. Ripe but not rotten. I was rotten. I could have taken someone else and made the town forget the bus, but I wanted to be more than a caretaker. I wanted to be a hero even though nobody but me would ever know I was the hero. I wanted to be able to leave the town I loved and see the rest of the world knowing the town I loved was safe because I did something heroic and made this horrible sacrifice to save the town. I know that whatever it is that keeps the bridge's power in tact led me to that awful book with that spell. Ripe but not rotten. I had to do it. I was so sure when I took those perfect kids and did those…things. Sacrifice is an awful thing. It is not just the cutting of a throat and a word. Ritual sacrifice is complex and horrible. There are long chants that you have to learn by heart. Chants in forgotten languages that you must remember with deadly precision. Then there's the victims. And the knife. Ripe but not rotten. Oh yes, they were my victims. I cried the whole time as I chanted. I could not just cut John's throat and let his blood do the work. No. That's not how it works. It works because it is a horrible thing to do and it asks for a horrible service. I had to cut John as Jenny watched in horror. I could not stop to explain how they were dying for the greater good. I had to chant and cut. Strips of living flesh. I had to cut Jenny as John cried in agony and horror. I could not tell him that he and his purest love were the real heroes and their death would keep everyone they knew safe from the horror of the bridge. I had to chant and cut and tie. Strips of living flesh extending from one to the other, tied in knots seeming random and insane in design, but perfect to their purpose. Each knot was salted with my tears. As I completed the spell, a spell not intended to destroy this thing but to take the life from these two young… Ripe but not rotten. I could see their very lives sucked from them as the bridge absorbed their essence. I could feel it mocking me for infusing it with power once more. I knew what I had done and I knew I would have to spend the rest of my life paying for it.

Yes, the town forgot about the bus. Hardly anyone gave a thought to it and, when they did, their thoughts were as light as helium and floated away without a care. Most of the town quickly forgot about Jenny and John. Some even denied they existed at all because to remember what I had done to them would have been like a stake through the town's heart. Sheriff Ben remembers, but only because he really wants to remember and if he knew it was me… Well, I think he would kill me as I stand with no regrets. I have toyed with telling him just so he'd do it and I would be done. But I have a responsibility. Gil remembers because Gil never forgets a thing about this town.

And I remember.

I remember cutting Jenny to make the symbol right as the book said I had to. I remember her tears and how she and John never stopped looking at one another as I committed horror upon horror to their flesh. I couldn't tell her how sorry I was and how this was for the town and how I was being a hero because I had to keep chanting. I finished the chant and I finished the spell and then I heard him laughing at me. That laughter echoed through the bridge along with something else. There was a terrible noise, like some unearthly music that nobody was ever meant to hear and it played and when I stand in silence I can still hear it because nobody was ever meant to hear it and the music knows that and it wants to find me. I looked at what I had done to that boy and that girl who were oh so ripe and who would never be rotten and I saw whatever energy it was that kept that bridge from rotting seep back into it from the horror that hides beyond this beautiful place and I knew I had been made to renew that thing I had come to destroy.

I didn't throw in the towel then - and boy, did I spend a few nights with a shotgun in my mouth - because I still had to take care of the town. I still loved Stansbury.

I love Stansbury more than myself, really. My life is no longer about me. I'm not a hero and I don't get to travel around the world knowing I have made it all better. I haven't. I have to keep this place together for the rest of my life. That is my penance. Sometimes, that requires me to do some dark deeds. I am no saint and I am no hero. But I keep it all together.

So I look for the worst people, and there are some pretty bad people out there. There are people like Dr. Dennis Covington who seethe with hatred and who can be counted on to spread their disease to as many people as they can find in order to create a world that hates itself as much as they hate themselves. I try to find those people because I can use them to erase some of the pain the good people of this town feel for a time. That's how this spell works. It's so much simpler. It's just a few words and a twist of a knife and they go and take the most recent cancer with them. Easy. Right now, there's nothing for the town to forget, but I can feel it coming. I've felt it coming for a good long time.

Dr. Covington will find me. I left him an easy trail and he is not a stupid man. He'll come and he'll seek answers and he'll get none. If he comes too soon, he'll wait with me. He may pity himself a bit, but he'll wait with me for the bad thing to happen. If he comes after whatever it is that I need to protect the town from, well… It's just a few words and a twist of the knife and he'll hear the music and he'll understand that the universe has horrors in it. He'll know why he has to join them. He'll see that his death is necessary. He won't care because he doesn't know how. The bad thing is coming soon. When it does, Dr. Covington's life will finally have some value.

I love Stansbury. I love Vermont. I love the United States of America. I even love this world.

I think I'll go for a walk and sit by my bridge. I'll sit by it and admire the skill that made it. I'll sit by it and remember what I did to keep it there. I'll sit by it and listen to that ghastly music that never stops playing. I'll sit by it and suffer for my sins and wait.

V

Shelley waited patiently behind the counter at Osno's Pharmacy for Mr. Lohnegan to slowly pull his wallet from his pocket. Shelley never stopped smiling. She felt it was her job to provide cheer and everyday she practiced being excellent at her job by smiling even when she wanted to scream. Every time Mr. Lohnegan came into the store, she wanted to scream. For one, he was always dressed for winter. Now winter clothes in Vermont are not light clothes. If it's a degree warmer than 1, there's some sweating going on. Shelley's mother used to wrap her to baking when the thermometer dropped below 30. Shelley believed as a native Vermonter that she could wear shorts until it got to around 15 and then she'd start to feel the chill. But, like every dutiful winter soul around her, she'd bundle herself up tight. A layer of long johns, she liked the new silky ones that wicked the sweat away because unless it was a real cold one, she was going to sweat under all those layers and anything she could do to keep it from boiling on her skin was a good thing. She also liked the fact that they were silky. When at all possible, she wore things that were silky or satiny or flowy. Her mom said she was such a girl.

Shelley always wondered at that. Of course she was such a girl. She was a girl! She never understood why girls would dress like guys, all drab and covered in rough cotton. When she went into the big department stores in Burlington, or, when she was feeling wild and went all the way to Boston, she wouldn't hang around the little corner of the store devoted to men's wear. She would wander aimlessly through the three floors of women's clothing. Sometimes she would just wander in between the circle racks and feel the materials. She wished she could climb into the middle of one of the racks of silky nighties and make a nest there and only come out to pee and eat. Her mom used to buy her all these flannel lumberjack shirts like she was going out to cut down trees or something. Heck, the temperature had to drop below 10 before she'd put on a pair of socks. She spent most of her time indoors anyway, so why would she wear shoes for outside? All her shoes were pretty and fun just like all her clothes were pretty and made of fabrics that only girls got to wear. She once bought a black lycra blend t-shirt for Gil from the women's section. The only way you'd know it was a girl's shirt was that the collar was a little bit scooped and the sleeves were a little shorter. She told Gil she just wanted him to wear it for a day, that he could wear it under his flannel lumberjack's shirt of he liked. She just wanted him to feel what he was missing stuck in the men's corner of flannel and rough cotton. It took a while for him to get the courage to wear it, he said. He thought that somehow people would know he was wearing a girl's t-shirt under his flannel lumberjack's shirt. He could have been wearing a corset underneath that old blue lumberjack shirt of his and no one would have been any the wiser. After he finally wore the top she bought him - which he said not to call a top because it was bad enough it was a women's shirt without her having to call it a top...she just laughed at him and asked him if his breasts had grown any now that he had worn a women's shirt. He said that couldn't happen and she laughed some more. She asked him how he liked it. He said he liked it just fine and wondered why he couldn't get a men's shirt like it. Shelley wondered that as well, but didn't wonder too long. It really didn't concern her as she was a girl and could wear just about whatever she wanted and that was fine with her. Perhaps someday men could escape from their little corner, but Shelley was pretty sure that wouldn't be any time soon. They were all too afraid of being comfortable. She didn't know how Mr. Lohnegan could possibly be comfortable all wrapped up for winter when it was over 60 degrees outside. She was wearing a little skirt, a tank and some flip-flops and here he was bundled up for an Antarctic expedition. He was even wearing a muffler over his face, which made it extra hard to hear him, but she was able to translate muffler-English well enough, even when it was spoken with a heavy French-Canadian accent.

"Gmmm mfflg, Smmly."

"Good morning, Mr. Lohnegan. How's the weather out there?" She smiled brightly.

"Uh mfflbffl ilffl fl mf, eh."

Shelley imagined that Mr. Lohnegan was a trapper from the far north. She imagined him out on the tundra staying out of the way of polar bears while he patiently hunted down the rare and priceless arctic fox. But the arctic fox was always too cunning for the old trapper and would foil his schemes. Then Mr. Lohnegan would do a little angry dance and shake his fist and yell out through his muffler, "Iff geff unh, yh rncllffy vmmfl!" and steam would shoot out of his ears, making the ear flaps on his hunter's cap fly up in the air and the little fox would snicker and run back into his den. Shelley smiled at Mr. Lohnegan a lot.

"What can I get you today, Mr. Lohnegan?"

Mr. Lohnegan finally extracted his wallet from inside of his thick down coat. This process was made more difficult because he had to first remove the mittens which were clipped to his sleeves and then the inner gloves that he wore under the thick mittens in case he had to do something with his hands when the weather was 63 above like it was today with the sun shining so brightly that it made the green world around them glow. Now came the process of extracting the wallet from its waterproof lining that, itself, was wrapped in an old woolen sock. To keep the money warm and toasty? Shelley smiled some more.

"Ihl hiffn uhn pffinhimhn uhn ihl nhnn uhm dhnhffl fhnl unh uhm cnf yhrpl. Ihl uhnv unh lhntff cnff cnuhmng, eh."

"Oh, I'm sorry to hear that. The weather has been a little chilly, lately."

Mr. Lohnegan chuckled underneath all the layers. "Uhn nhu nhkn fhn uhf mhn?"

Shelley put on her best serious face as she picked out the items her customer asked her for. "Mr. Lohnegan, I've discovered over the years that people are all built so very differently. Take you and me, for instance. We're not built the same at all. We feel the world differently. I was just thinking about you the other day when I was reading about the temperature in Arizona. You know, my friend, Gil. Of course you know, Gil. Gil Hamilton. He owns the little shop out by the Lakebridge. He told me you come in once and awhile because he's the only place in town you can get a five pound wheel of Cabot cheese and he says you like buying a five pound wheel every once and awhile. He says you come in at just about the right time it would take for someone to eat a five pound wheel without being a glutton about it and he has a lot of respect for you because you must be a man who knows how to appreciate good cheese without overdoing it and gobbling it all down like some tourist who goes into the Cabot gift shop and eats up all the samples just because they're free. He hates people who eat all the free samples they can like just because someone put them on a plate or something you can just come along and eat them all up as if no one else wanted any or anything. Gil says that there should be some kind of social laws that keep people from doing ill-mannered things like eating more than their fair share of free samples. Gil would know because he puts out samples and he says there are people who've come in and polished off a whole plate of sample donuts and then asked him when he was going to put out some more as if he was just going to keep loading that sample plate up for them to eat all of his wares for free. Anyway, Gil spent some time in Arizona and he said it was like living on the surface of the sun and that he couldn't imagine anyone wanting to live in a place that didn't want you to live. Of course, some people say the same for Vermont in wintertime. Not me, because I love the cold. You know that song, California Dreaming, where the preacher likes the cold? I'm the preacher. Anyway, Gil said that that summer he spent in Arizona introduced him to a new kind of hot that he had never thought he would feel. He said after a little bit of standing outside, he stopped caring about living. Here was the sun, this life giving star we've got making us all warm and Gil said the sun was stealing his life from him to give to someone else and Gil thought that perhaps he was just supposed to give up his life so that plants and people in places that weren't in Arizona could thrive. He said a guy he worked with had to drag him inside because he was just going to stand there and burn up otherwise. I'm glad because Gil's my best friend and I don't want him to die, especially from having the sun sap his vital energy or some such thing even if I need that vital energy to live. Let it take the vital energy from people who like it down there is all I'm saying."

"Cuhn Ihn uhv uh mhnny fhns?"

"Oh, sure." She absently grabbed the minty floss for him. Flossing was weird, right? Who thought of it and then decided to cover string with wax to do it? And minty wax at that. Anyway. "So I was looking at the paper where it has the map of all the country and it shows what the temperature is like all over and it uses colors, like the redder it gets, the hotter it is and the bluer it gets, the colder it gets and I was looking at Arizona and it wasn't even red anymore but it was more of a deep purple, like a bruise or something and I thought that it was so hot there that it hurts and I was glad I was up here where it was nice and greenish blue because that's the color of calm, you know? Anyway, I thought that, to some people, greenish blue wasn't a good color for them and they maybe liked the deep purple and, well, that was good for them because they lived there and all. I started to wonder why people would like living there and I started reading more about it and you know what I found out? That besides from it being wicked hot all the time in the summer and occasionally getting what they call monsoons but aren't like the monsoons down in the South Pacific that you think of when you think of monsoons that kill people because of all the rain and wind and islands being flooded and people hanging onto palm trees or they'll be blown away. You know what I mean, right? Well, Arizona has these monsoons where it rains a little bit and there's some thunderstorms and stuff, but nothing really bad happens and I realized that in Arizona, aside from the heat, which you can just go inside to get away from, nothing really bad happens. Everywhere else, really bad things happen. All these other places have floods and fires and earthquakes and tornados and hurricanes and blizzards. Arizona doesn't have any of that. It just has a few months of purple heat. Oh, and killer bees. They have killer bees, too. Anyway, I was thinking about you and thinking that maybe you would like it down there where it didn't get so cold for you. Did you ever think about moving down there or somewhere hot like that?"

"Nhn. Ihn lhnk nh chnl uhn Ihl lhnv Vhmmt, eh. Ihm alhndd ghnhn tn hnh. Ihn dhn nhn uhn pnvhn. Hnhn hnhn!"

Shelley smiled at Mr. Lohnegan. She didn't know what he had done to make him think he was going to hell and she didn't really want to know. Everyone had their secrets and she didn't pry. Sometimes people tried to unburden themselves on her and she didn't want to hear it. She wanted to be able to smile at everyone and give them a little cheer and she couldn't do that if she knew that they were secretly doing really bad things. Gil kept trying to tell her about all the really bad things that happened in Stansbury and she kept telling him that he should take up a new hobby. She was always trying to get Gil to take up new hobbies to get his mind off of all the bad things that had ever happened in Stansbury. Shelley thought that for as long as the town had been around, not that many bad things had really happened. She thought that a guy like Gil who had been to so many other places, big places like New York and Los Angeles and Europe, would see that every place had its share of bad things. She thought if Gil had spent as much time documenting the bad things that happened in Europe against the same time period that Stansbury had been around that he would find that Stansbury wasn't so bad, all things considered. Gil didn't see it like that, though. He said that if a relative number of bad things such as what happened in Stansbury, given the relatively small population and size of the town, happened in Europe, civilization would have collapsed some time ago. She said nothing as bad as the Holocaust had happened in Stansbury, relative size or no, and that nothing as bad as all those people that Stalin killed in Russia had happened in Stansbury, relative size or no. She said she could go on and on and he agreed and agreed that he wouldn't tell her about all the bad things that happened in Stansbury if she would just agree that, compared to, let's say, Middlebury, Stansbury had a much larger history of dark deeds. She thought about that for a moment and told him that she hadn't spent much time in Middlebury and didn't know much about it except that there were a couple of really cute stores off the main road and that she had bought her mother a set of salt and pepper shakers that were supposed to be UFOs according to the guy who made them and she believed that they could be UFOs and that's why she bought them for her mother because he mother loved all things alien. He mother was sure that aliens would land in Vermont someday because, all things considered, Vermont was the best place on earth and there weren't so many people around or Walmarts. Her mother was sure that aliens would hate Walmart. Gil wasn't that interested in salt and pepper shakers. She had bought him a pair as well that were shaped like moose because he was always talking about the moose that wandered around his store. He said he regretted bringing up Middlebury. She said it was his fault and he said he just wasn't going to talk to her anymore about anything, but she knew that was a lie and just smiled at him. He had been threatening not to speak to her for years now, but he had no one else to talk to and no one else would buy him things he didn't need just because they wanted him to smile a little. Shelley just wanted him to smile a little.

"Oh, I need your prescription." Mr. Lohnegan had often assumed that Mr. Osno should just know what he needed. Shelley had learned some time ago that Mr. Osno was the opposite of psychic. Things had to be spelled out precisely to the man or he would get them wrong. Doctors had complained more than once that he made mistakes on patients' prescriptions. Shelley asked them if they were entirely clear as to what it was they wanted their patients to have. Doctors would scribble something on a piece of paper and then assume that the pharmacist was some kind of Svengali or something that could look at the scribble and understand a precise set of instructions from it. Shelley often took the extra time to call the doctor's office to ask them exactly what it was they wanted when they wrote something that looked like a "5" and a "W" on the scrip. More often than not, it was the nurse who she would talk to and the nurse would talk to her like she was less than a person, which she never liked. Shelley never smiled at nurses. The nurse would always ask to speak to Mr. Osno as if Shelley was somehow unable to understand the words that were involved in pharmaceuticals. Shelley would reply that perhaps she should speak directly to the doctor, using a tone that implied that the nurses were somehow less than people and that only doctors were qualified to clarify their prescriptions. At that point, the nurse and Shelley would arrive at a détente of dislike and get on with the business of getting the patient the proper pills. Shelley was sure that she was responsible for saving many lives in Stansbury. Mr. Osno, of course, never said a word about the great works that she did. Mr. Osno, of course, never said a word.

Mr. Lohnegan began to dig through his coat. "Ihn unh inh nhr suhnnuh."

Shelley knew this would take awhile. She also knew that whatever it was, she would have to call for clarification. Mr. Lohnegan saw Dr. Fitzhume up in Montpelier. Shelley flipped open her rolodex and dialed up Karen Beatty, the good doctor's nurse du jour.

"Karen, this is Shelley down in Stansbury." Shelley tried to smile over the phone like Gil told her people could hear.

"This is who now?" Shelley's phone smile faded quickly.

"I'm calling from Osno's Pharmacy about the prescription for Mr. Harold Lohnegan. Could you please clarify the doctor's instructions?"

The nurse took her sweet time, but Shelley made a private bet with herself that the nurse would have the prescription to her before Mr. Lohnegan could extract it from his coat. She usually won these bets, as she did today, but just barely. After she hung up the phone, she compared what the nurse told her to what the prescription said and asked herself once again how anyone was supposed to see the strange hieroglyphic on the scrip and know that it mean that the patient should get his month's supply of hydrocortisone. It didn't make any sense to her. She took her instructions and stapled them to the doctor's scrip. Just as she had been taught to do, she rolled the papers up and inserted them into a small copper tube. Gil told her that arctic explorers would leave their notes to one another in copper tubes buried under large stacks of stones. She asked Gil if he had gone exploring the arctic when he was in Alaska. He said that he didn't have time and, even if he did, he wouldn't because of all the damned polar bears. He said that polar bears weren't cute like in the commercials or the toy stores, although he admitted that toy store and commercial polar bears were exceedingly cute. He said that he heard about polar bear attacks where the damned bears had ripped car doors off to get at the sweet flesh of the polar bear conservationists inside. Once she prepared the tube, she would place it in the slot behind her register and ring the bell. It was an old replica of the Liberty Bell. Once a tourist who came in to buy some aspirin asked he if he could buy it. He said it was an "original" copy of the one in Philadelphia and he would give her a lot of money for it. She asked him how much and wrote the request down. She placed the request in a copper tube and put it in the slot. She rang the bell the customer wanted to buy. A moment later, a copper tube dropped into the hopper and she retrieved it and pulled the note from inside. In Mr. Osno's perfect handwriting was written the words, "Tell the goddamned tourist to fuck off." Shelley smiled brightly at the tourist, if she couldn't sell him the bell, she would give him some cheer. She apologized and said the bell was not for sale. When she first started to work for Mr. Osno, she was more than a little surprised at the tone of his notes.

To be honest, she had always assumed there was some kind of machine behind the wall that somehow read and processed the prescriptions. Her mother thought that Mr. Osno was an alien. Jenny thought that he was the capital "D" Devil. Gil thought if Jenny thought it was Satan back there dispensing medicine then maybe if he agreed with Jenny she'd go out with him so he told her to tell Jenny that he thought Jenny was right about Mr. Osno being the prince of darkness and that he would help her burn the place down if they could call it a date. Shelley said she would tell Jenny no such thing because if she even so much as mentioned the word "date" to Jenny then Jenny would start after her again about how they were meant for one another and that Shelley just had to admit that there was no one better for her and while Shelley thought that Jenny might have a point, she was still holding out for a guy in that she wasn't that attracted to girls and she really wasn't that attracted to Jenny even though Jenny was very pretty in that way that some female cops are really pretty if you look beyond the really tightly pulled hair.

Mr. Osno wasn't a machine and he wasn't an alien and he wasn't the devil. He wasn't even evil as far as Shelley was concerned. He paid her for her work and provided a service to the town and so what if no one could ever remember seeing him or speaking to him. She asked him about it once in a note and placed it in a copper tube and dropped into the slot. His note in reply read, "Go fuck yourself, Counter Girl. I hate people." He always called her Counter Girl. He called all the girls who worked for him Counter Girl because that way he never had to learn a name and it reminded them all that they were easily replaced. Shelley didn't mind. After that, she stopped asking him questions. She had been hired for the job by Denise Harris, who had been Counter Girl for five years. Much like Shelley, Denise always had a smile for everyone who walked in the door. Shelley decided she wanted to be Counter Girl because she always liked Denise's smile and felt that it made her day better to go in and be greeted by it and she wanted to be able to do the same thing for other people. When she went in on the day the "Help Wanted" sign went up in the window to apply for the job and told Denise about her goal to give everyone a little cheer with their pills, Denise told her she had the job, trained her on the spot and never came back. As a matter of fact, no one ever saw or heard from Denise again. Shelley always wondered what happened to her. Gil said it was the curse of the Counter Girl and left it at that. Of course, Gil said the whole town was cursed, so one more curse didn't really matter in the grand scheme of things. Gil said the curse of the Counter Girl was quite real though. He said that every Counter Girl met some kind of horrible end after her time at Osno's. Shelley didn't know what happened to all the Counter Girls and, as no one knew what happened to Denise, no one could rightly say that she came to a horrible end. She might be very happily married with two kids and a dog in Santa Barbara, California, which Shelley heard was quite nice except when they had fires or floods. She assumed it was quite nice because people kept on living there in spite of all the fires and floods. Gil said that if she was happily married out on the West Coast surviving fires and floods, someone would have heard from her. He said it was more likely that she occupied a shallow grave out in the woods somewhere. Shelley told Gil that he could think what he wanted and she would think what she wanted and that would be that. He told her that he hoped she would be Counter Girl for a very long time because when she stopped being Counter Girl, he would be worried. A lot.

Mr. Lohnegan's prescription dropped into the slot. Shelley checked it to make sure Mr. Osno had got it right. She caught his mistakes a few times and, even though it meant a nasty note or two from the back room, she did not shy away from making the corrections. If she could save a life and only receive a few curse words in return, then she counted herself as lucky.

"Here you go, Mr. Lohnegan." Shelley smiled brightly.

"Hnn hun, Hnneh."

Shelley watched her customer slowly put his purchases away into the various pockets of his anorak before replacing his mittens. With a wave he made his way slowly out of the store.

Shelley waved goodbye with a smile. She loved her job.

* * *

Mr. Lohnegan smiled back at Shelley, although she could not see it underneath his muffler. Mr. Lohnegan could have bought his prescriptions and sundry goods elsewhere, but he really liked Shelley because he did not have to repeat himself or undress to speak with her. Plus, she was always so cheerful without being unpleasantly so. He dealt with too many people in his time that smiled because their jobs required it, but behind the smile, there was only menace. He could see it in their eyes and their smiles became shark's teeth that were waiting to rip out his throat and he was scared of them. Shelley didn't scare him so he shopped in Stansbury even though it meant traveling halfway across the state to do so. Of course, halfway across Vermont was not that far in the grand scheme of things and was certainly worth the drive not to have to worry about counter people with vampire smiles who would suck his blood so much as look at him and when then made him remove his muffler to speak with them because they were evil and their smiles grew even wider and hungrier when they saw his face and realized he was frightened of them and recognized that they wanted to devour him. There were times when he thought about removing his muffler for Shelley because she didn't want to eat him and he could smile back at her and not be afraid but he never did because she never asked him to and she smiled at him anyway and he didn't have to be afraid of her.

He got back into his car and turned on the air conditioner. It was awfully hot today. He always made sure to drive just perfectly in Stansbury because the deputy would pull him over if he didn't. There was the deputy up ahead. Normally he would wave at a town deputy but he was afraid to with this one because he didn't know if he could be pulled over for removing his hand from the steering wheel so he just kept his eyes on the road and headed back to Montpelier.

* * *

Deputy Steven Marsters sat in his Stansbury issue police cruiser and watched the freak in the winter suit drive his way out of town. If the freak took even a mittened hand off of his steering wheel to wave at him, he would pull him over. He watched to make sure both brake lights still worked. If the freak so much as had a burnt out brake lamp, he would pull him over. There was just something about the guy Deputy Marsters didn't like and he knew that if he could get him for one thing, he would find all the other things to get him for and maybe he would be able to get him to the office and fingerprint him and run his prints and find out he was some kind of sexual deviant or convict. Deputy Marsters was sure that the freak was some kind of sexual deviant or convict. Of course, Deputy Marsters was fairly sure that everyone who passed him by as they drove through town was on their way to commit a crime of some kind or at least go home and perform some deviant act on their pretty little kitty cat. Deputy Marsters didn't have any pets. People who had pets liked to pet their pets and stroke them and that made them all deviants as far as he was concerned. Of course, he didn't tell anyone about what he thought about them because of what Ben Hamilton had said all those years ago. Until Ben Hamilton threw the election and let that little idiot Tom win the office of sheriff of Stansbury - Deputy Marsters would never call him Sheriff Tom in his mind because in his mind he was just that little idiot who was always doing something stupid like running for sheriff and if Ben Hamilton knew he wasn't going to want to be sheriff anymore then he should have told Deputy Marsters, given him a heads up that maybe it was his time to be sheriff instead of leaving the town in the hands of a little idiot like Tom. Until Ben Hamilton abandoned him and the town, he always felt that Ben Hamilton was the one person he could be sure was not a sexual deviant or some kind of convict. Now he wasn't so sure. Why would he throw the election like that? He never told Deputy Marsters. He just packed up his desk and left. He didn't even say goodbye.

"See you around, Steve." He said as he packed up his desk.

"You're not allowed to call me Steve anymore, citizen Hamilton."

"Okay, Deputy Marsters." Ben Hamilton was always trying to be friendly. Was always trying to give friendly advice. When Ben was Deputy Marsters' boss, he listened because he always looked up to Ben Hamilton. But not anymore. "But listen, just take it easy on Sheriff Tom, okay? And take it easy on the town. I've always told you, these are good people."

"I don't have to listen to you anymore. Have a good day, citizen Hamilton."

Ben Hamilton looked sad at that. He finished packing up his desk without a word and left the office. Deputy Marsters couldn't believe he was gone…couldn't believe Ben Hamilton was gone and that he wasn't Sheriff Steve now. He was supposed to be Sheriff Steve. That was what Ben Hamilton told him all those years ago.

"If you're good to the people," then-Sheriff Ben said all those years ago, "if you uphold the law, but do it with a human touch, let the people know that you are there for them to protect them and to make sure nothing bad will happen to them, but always so they know that you are a real person and can make mistakes, well, they will want you to keep on protecting them. Maybe someday, after I'm gone, they'll want you to be in charge of it all and keep it all safe for them the way I do."

Ben Hamilton gave him the formula for being Sheriff Steve. He allowed them to call him Deputy Steve even though he preferred Deputy Marsters. He looked the other way at all the little infractions that they all committed everyday. The jaywalking. The rolling stops. The parking for over an hour where there was only an hour allowed. He let all the little stuff go and he let them call him Deputy Steve and he smiled at them even though he knew they could see behind his smile and know that he knew that they were all deviants and convicts.

"Deputy Steve? Could you help me with this box?" Charlie at Charlie's grill would say to him. Charlie who always bribed him with a cup of coffee and a donut. What was he hiding that always offered bribes to the local law enforcement? What was in that box that he was helping to move even though it wasn't in his job description to move boxes for the local business people? Did Charlie think coffee and a donut were enough for him to look the other way? Maybe when he was finally sheriff, he would take a closer look at old Charlie. Maybe those boxes labeled with the contents of cans of tomato sauce and freshly frozen cuts of meat were full of sex toys or drugs and Charlie was operating the grill as a front for a druggy bondage house and laughing at Deputy Marsters who moved his boxes of inequity to and fro for a cup of coffee, a powdered donut and a friendly smile. But he moved those boxes and drank the coffee and ate the donuts because then-Sheriff Ben told him to be helpful to the citizenry. He was helpful. At least while he was Deputy Steve.

"Deputy Steve, could you give me a break this time? I was only going a little fast so I could get home in time to feed my boys before their practice." Mrs. Kettleman was always going a little fast for one reason or another and whenever he stopped her for speeding, she always had an excuse and because she was never going any more than a few miles per hour, she was always asking him for a "break this time." While he was Deputy Steve, he always smiled and let her go to meet her secret lover for a tryst while her husband was off hard at work at the dairy collective he helped run. He always smiled at her while she was speeding around trying to meet her pot dealer and get her next fix which she'd go down to the Lakebridge to smoke with her 15 year old lover who was her son's best friend who thought it was a cool thing that he was nailing the biggest MILF in all of Stansbury. He always smiled at her while she was going off to hire a hit man to take out her husband who worked for the dairy collective so she could inherit his insurance money and run off to Montreal with her high school Romeo. Deputy Steve would always smile at her and let her go because he knew she would vote for him for sheriff when the time came but Ben Hamilton had gone and let that little idiot Tom win the election that Deputy Marsters didn't even know was up for grabs. He would always let her get off with a warning to slow down when he was Deputy Steve because that's what Ben Hamilton told him to do. And he always did. At least when he was Deputy Steve.

"Deputy Steve, could you help me figure out this paperwork?" The little idiot didn't want to be sheriff anyway. That's what he told his new subordinate who was ten years older than him and had let him off with countless warnings over the years when he was being nice.

"I'm really sorry, Deputy Steve. Could you take care of this call?" The little idiot never wanted to leave the office and was afraid to wear his gun belt. The little idiot barely had a driver's license and still didn't know how to operate the radio or the controls in the Stansbury issue police cruiser.

"Deputy Steve, I'm going over to Charlie's for a cup of coffee. Hold down the fort." The little idiot was mastering the art of being the typical small town sheriff in that he would go and hang out with the locals and be "present" while having his deputy do all the work. It came to a head after a month of the little idiot playing nice. He told his new boss to call him Deputy Marsters. He told him that everyone was to call him Deputy Marsters from now on and that is how he should be referred to and from now on he was going to enforce every letter of every law because that's what Stansbury needed.

"Okay, Deputy Steve. And I will call you what I want to as I am your boss." *His boss!* "But don't let me get too many complaints that you are overstepping your position or I will fire you. Copy that?"

"Yes, Sheriff." Little idiot got himself some balls.

"Take care of this paperwork, would you? I'm heading over to Charlie's for a cup of coffee."

People in town learned pretty fast that Deputy Steve was closed for business and they were none too happy about it. Charlie didn't offer him coffee or donuts anymore. Mrs. Kettleman learned after her third speeding ticket in as many days that there were no more breaks to be had from Deputy Marsters. Ben Hamilton had tried to intercede on the town's behalf.

"You're not winning any popularity contests here, Deputy Marsters." Ben Hamilton said.

"It's not my job to be popular, Mr. Hamilton. It's my job to protect and keep the peace in Stansbury and enforce the laws of the great state of Vermont. For a long time, I was not doing a very good job of that. I think I was too concerned about winning some kind of popularity contest. But thanks to you, I found out that it is more important to do what's in my heart. You've followed your heart to do whatever it is you have to do. My heart tells me that letting people off for breaking the law just a little or doing little favors for little bribes is no way to keep the peace. It's not my job to be popular. I'll leave that to the sheriff."

Ben Hamilton nodded sagely and went on his way after signing the speeding ticket Deputy Marsters wrote him.

"Deputy Steve?" The little idiot's voice came over the radio. He almost wished he never taught the little idiot to use the radio. He probably had to go and investigate an incident of cow tipping again. There were never any cows tipped, mind you. There were just reports of cows being tipped phoned into the sheriff's office and then he would have to go out and investigate the report that would inevitably be a prank of some kind. The little idiot would remind him that the letter of the law said that there must be an investigation of any incident reported and that since Stansbury's deputy was such a stickler for the law, he would have to go out and do his duty.

"Yes, sheriff." You little idiot.

"Could you go out by the Lakebridge and take a report, please?"

"What is the nature of the incident?" You little idiot.

"I do believe our friend, Mr. Kurtz, has made another attempt to destroy our town's one and only landmark."

"Shall I arrest Mr. Kurtz?" You little idiot.

"If the event warrants it, then you may bring him in. At this time, please take a report. There are witnesses for you to interrogate."

"Don't you mean interview?" You little idiot.

"By all means, interview away, Deputy *Steve*."

"I'm on my way, you little-" Idiot!

* * *

"You little what, Deputy Steve?" Sheriff Tom knew his deputy didn't think much of him and often referred to him behind his back as "the little idiot."

"Pardon me." Deputy Steve's voice on the radio was cold. "I was distracted by Susie Myers' little poodle. She's off her leash again."

Right. "You can write Susie a ticket later, Deputy Steve. I expect a full report on my desk about the bridge incident before you leave today."

"Affirmative. Marsters out."

Poor little Stevie didn't get to be sheriff. Tom used to feel bad for him before Deputy Marsters showed up in place of Deputy Steve. Everyone always thought Deputy

Steve was a bit of a wimp and a kiss ass. But at least he would do what you wanted him to do and he never seemed to suffer the small stuff. Tom and his friends used to get away with murder and Deputy Steve would always let them by, smiling at them with that goofy asshole smile he had before he became dickhead Deputy Marsters with his jock asshole smile. People didn't like being spoken to as if they were trash or had done something worse than park too long or go a few miles per hour too fast. Most of Sheriff Tom's job these days seemed to be undoing all the hard work of Deputy Marsters, who seemed to want the people of Stansbury to live in a police state rather than a nice little town.

Stansbury was a nice little town, all things considered. And Sheriff Tom had been elected sheriff with only three votes - his mom, Sheriff Ben and his girlfriend, Mary Beth. They didn't even want him to win. They just didn't want him to not get any votes. He told them he wasn't even going to vote for himself. He voted for Sheriff Ben. Sheriff Ben was supposed to win the election. Everybody knew that. Tom only filled out the paper because Mary Beth told him that the process of running for a political office would mature him and, for some reason, she wanted him to be more mature. When they started dating, she didn't mind that he lacked maturity. In fact, she loved his comics. He wanted to be an artist for graphic novels. He used to take old Edgar Allen Poe and H. P. Lovecraft stories and draw them out. He always thought he could sell the Poe stuff with no problem. It was public domain. He tried sending the Lovecraft stuff on to the people who owned the rights but strangely they told him his work was a little too graphic and they didn't feel it captured the essential nature of the kind of psychological horror that Lovecraft created. He supposed they were right, but people loved the graphic stuff and he was getting pretty good at it. He went to a couple of comic conventions and some of the big guys in the field were pretty impressed with his work. But, of course, his mother started to get her claws into Mary Beth and started filling her head with ideas about children and the future and how if Tom would just grow up a little he would be a man and how Mary Beth needed a man if she didn't want to be a first grade teacher all her life and even though Mary Beth loved teaching the first grade and loved Tom's comics and told him he was a brilliant artist, she also started talking about the future which she and his mom felt that he needed to grow up and face and that maybe the future would be better if he grew up and did something with his life. For some reason, growing up and doing something with his life led him to filling out the stupid form to run for town sheriff. He found out that apparently you didn't need any experience, that like running for any other elected office, you just needed a few signatures and a filing fee. He collected fifty signatures to get on the ballot and was amazed at just how easy it was. With the exception of his mother, Mary Beth and Sheriff Ben, everyone said that they would be happy to sign, but they were still going to vote for Sheriff Ben. Sheriff Ben signed with a kind of weird smile and told Tom that he would vote for him and that he hoped he would win. What he hadn't told Tom is that he had been waiting for someone to come along and get on the ballot so he could leave the job to go and do whatever it was he said that he needed to do that didn't involve being sheriff. Right up until the day of the election, Ben and Tom had gone along with the charade that it was a real democratic type thing and that Tom could stand a chance of winning. Ben kept stopping in at Tom's "Election H.Q." which was his mom's kitchen and telling him that he better be ready to win this thing what with all the campaigning that was going on. Sheriff Ben said that Danielle, Tom's mom, had convinced him with her cookies to vote for Tom. His mom had signs made and would bake cookies and go door to door in town giving out cookies and telling people what a fine boy he was. Mary Beth had all the kids in her class make signs and go around to all the stores and ask people to put them in their windows and people did because they thought it was funny that someone was running against Sheriff Ben and they all knew they were going to vote for Sheriff Ben so what harm could it do. What the people in the town didn't know, what Deputy Steve didn't know, what Tom didn't know is that Sheriff Ben didn't want to win. In fact, they didn't find out until the day after the election that the day before the election, Ben legally removed his name from the ballot. There was some general outrage, of course, and a lot of anger at both Ben and Tom. People were angry at Ben for not being Sheriff Ben any more and they were angry at Tom for having the nerve to be Sheriff Tom. He was all for not being Sheriff Tom, but his mother and Mary Beth all but moved him into the office. His mom even bought him his uniform and gun. Tom really didn't have a choice in the matter. He went to Ben and begged him to take it all back, but Ben had this look of someone who had been given a new lease on life and did not want to return it. Ben told Tom to take it slow and that people would come around to him being sheriff. He also said that being sheriff wasn't too hard most of the time and that Deputy Steve would probably end up doing most of the work anyway. Deputy Steve tried to get a special election held so that he could be on the ballot against Tom and everyone could vote for the "rightful heir" to Stansbury's badge. That was about the time that people began to warm to the notion of Sheriff Tom. No one really wanted Deputy Steve to be Sheriff Steve. Nobody really liked Deputy Steve all that much and now people pretty much hated Deputy Marsters. When Tom first became sheriff, he kind of hid out in his office, playing on Gil's Playstation and trying not to do anything so he wouldn't do anything wrong. Whenever he had a question, he'd call up Ben and Ben would tell him what to do and pretty soon people started telling him that he was doing the job just as well as Ben ever did. Pretty soon he was down at Charlie's Grill having a coffee and a donut and chatting with the locals. His mom even began to accuse him of growing up and started pushing him to pop the question to Mary Beth. Mary Beth started hinting at the fact that she would like the question to be popped to her. He even called up Ben and asked him what to do and Ben said that he could tell him how to be the best possible Sheriff Tom he could be, but he wouldn't even begin to advise him on the subject of getting married.

Tom sat in his office and thought that he should go out to the bridge and see what Kurtz had done. Tom sat in his office and looked at his notebook in front of him. Lately he had taken to drawing stories about unsolved crimes, especially those with gruesome deaths. He didn't know why his special talent seemed to be capturing death so well, but he was good at it. As his eyes drifted over his notebook, he kept coming back to that little box on his desk. He had gone down to Boston without Mary Beth.

"I have to do some research." Sheriff Tom was not a good liar at all.

"What kind of research, Sheriff Tom?" She loved calling him Sheriff Tom.

"For a case I'm working on." Such a bad liar.

"What case, Sheriff Tom?" She knew and she was just playing with him. "Do you think I could help you with this case? Maybe advise you on it?"

"I think I need to solve this one by myself, Mary Beth." He smiled at her in a way to tell her that if she wanted him to do what she wanted him to do that she should probably just go ahead and let him do it.

"Okay, Sheriff Tom. Good luck with your case. Just remember the number six and one half is an important clue for your case." She winked at him, kissed him, hugged him hard, kissed him again and then left, crying just a little, but he knew from happiness.

He looked down at the box on his desk and knew that he couldn't put it off any longer. His mother was right. He needed to grow up a bit and by filling out that form, by becoming sheriff, he was an adult now and it wasn't so bad at all. He picked up the box and put it in his pocket. School got out in a little bit and he thought he'd try to catch Mary Beth in her room after everyone else had gone and tell her that he had solved his case. He knew more than anything that he loved her and wanted to spend the rest of his life with her.

* * *

As the kids marched out of her room, Mary Beth smiled because she could return her thoughts to Tom, who she loved and knew more than anything she wanted to marry. All day, her friends kept asking if Tom popped the question yet. Tom's mom kept calling to see if he had done it yet. They all knew he was going to ask. After his mysterious trip down to Boston to solve his "case," they all knew he had gone and bought the ring. She even knew where he bought the ring, but she didn't go so far as to find out which one. It was funny, she always knew that Tom was the one. Or, at least, ever since they had started dating and had figured out that they were just about perfect for one another, she knew he was the one. Even when he wasn't Sheriff Tom and just Tom the really talented artist, she knew they would get married. When he ran for sheriff, she thought it was good for a laugh and even played along with his mother that it would help him grow up. To be honest, she didn't care. She loved his comics, gory as they were, and thought it would have been great traveling around to the conventions with him. They were so much fun and she loved meeting all the crazy cool people and going to the events. They went to the big one in San Diego. She was so excited to go to San Diego. It was so beautiful there and even though she was scared to death of earthquakes, she had the best time because as much as she loved Stansbury and Vermont, she loved the beach more and told Tom at the time that they should just stay there and live in a tent on the beach, but he didn't much like the idea of living in a tent on the beach and said that sooner or later California was going to get swallowed up by the Pacific and wouldn't it just be better if they visited the conventions every once and awhile and she said okay. When they were at the big one in San Diego, she met all these writers and artists. She didn't know there were girls who wrote and drew comics, but she met a couple and they were so cool and one of them sold her a purse that she made out of her favorite books. Mary Beth loved that purse and she loved Tom for taking her to meet all of these cool people and she knew that she was going to marry Tom no matter what he did.

When Tom became Sheriff Tom, Mary Beth was happy for him, but didn't want it to be a lifetime thing. She just hoped he would have some fun with it and then get back to the comics. And he did seem to have some fun with it and, sometimes, it seemed to get to him and he took it really seriously, which she guessed he should given that he was sheriff of Stansbury and everything. After a little while, it did seem to go to his head a little and he started talking about how he could be sheriff for a long time if he wanted because the people of the town were really starting to take to him. Mary Beth was pretty sure that most of his reasoning for wanting to be sheriff for a long time was to cheese off Deputy Steve. Deputy Steve was a dick and deserved nothing and Mary Beth just wished Tom would fire him, but Tom kept saying it was so much more fun to send him off to write up reports about cow tippings and such. Sometimes she liked to go out and take pictures of Deputy Steve when he was "on duty." He was such a dick and he didn't realize that he made this dick face when he didn't know people were watching. When he knew people were watching, he would plaster on this weird fake smile that everyone had always known was weird and fake and when he wasn't around, people felt generally better. Mary Beth stopped visiting Tom at work when Steve was around because it was so hard for her not to tell him off and she knew if she told him off, he'd write her up on some weird charge that Tom would just have to make go away the way he made most of Steve's tickets go away. That seemed to be most of Tom's job, but he didn't mind it. He told her it gave him a lot of pleasure undermining the work of Deputy Steve.

Mary Beth asked him if he wanted this to be his career, being a lawman. He kind of hemmed and hawed and finally said that it was what he thought that she wanted him to be, a man with a real job who would give their family a future. She knew that was his mother talking and had gone to talk to his mother about the ideas she was putting into her son's head. Danielle was a great lady and would make a great mother-in-law. Mary Beth loved her and she loved Mary Beth. But Mary Beth loved Tom more and wanted Tom to be happy more than she wanted Danielle to be happy with Tom's life. She and Danielle had even fought about Tom a little bit. Danielle loved to see her son growing up and loved that he and Mary Beth were finally going to get married and she gave credit to Tom being sheriff, which she thought was wonderful and could lead to bigger and better political offices. It took awhile for

Mary Beth to shatter that dream of Danielle's, though. Mary Beth didn't want to be the governor's wife. She didn't want to be the sheriff's wife and worry about her husband getting shot by some weirdo or Deputy Steve. She wanted to marry Tom the brilliant artist and go around to conventions and raise beautiful creative children who would love their grandma as much as she loved them. Mary Beth worked long and hard to make Danielle see Tom through her eyes and realize that he would be so much happier not being Danielle's vision of a grown up and just being Mary Beth's beautiful Tom. Danielle and Mary Beth cried for a while because they realized how much they both loved Tom and, really, each other. Danielle made Mary Beth promise to keep Tom happy and if that meant him not being sheriff, that was okay with her.

Mary Beth waited in her classroom and she knew that today would be one of the happiest days of her life and Tom's life. She was going to say yes to his proposal because he was coming to see her to propose to her with the ring that he spent so much time trying to find for her because he wanted it to be perfect. Then she was going to tell him to quit being Sheriff Tom and she was going to give him the ticket to the upcoming convention in San Diego that she bought for him to match her own and they were going to go and meet cool people and he would maybe get a job working for one of them and then they would be the cool people too. More than anything, though, they would both be happy because they were living their own lives. The people of Stansbury could find themselves a new sheriff to care for them. They never really wanted Tom anyway. Not in the way that she wanted him.

Mary Beth smiled and started writing tomorrow's lessons on the white board in her classroom while she waited.

* * *

He was glad she was smiling. Happy people made him happy. He had been watching her since the kids all left. She was happy with them and she was happy without them. Good. He always tried to find the happy ones. He didn't know why. They just seemed to bring a much better energy to his project. He figured he probably didn't have much time. He knew she was waiting for her lover to come and make her happier still, but he didn't want to risk her being there after that. He knew she had bought tickets to go elsewhere and worried that maybe she wouldn't come back. He really did need her.

For a while, he thought he would take the Counter Girl. He had always taken the Counter Girls before when he could, but when he stumbled onto this Teacher Girl, he knew he had to have her, that she would make a much better addition to his project. She was so happy and so right. The Counter Girl, for as much as she smiled and made other people happy, didn't really have that glow about her that the Counter Girls usually had. He figured it was because of her friends who were so damaged. She was damaged by association.

But the Teacher Girl. She was perfect. She could have been a Counter Girl, really. She was always so joyful, she made all the kids so happy, too. Everyone loved the Teacher Girl. He loved the Teacher Girl. When he loved them, he knew he had to have them.

She wrote on her board. She wrote her numbers and her letters and her handwriting was so neat. He wanted to let her finish so that when they came in the next day and she wasn't there, at least they would have her numbers and her letters. So he waited and watched her. He was in her room and she didn't even notice. She was too happy for her own good, she didn't even feel the danger. He hated that he was her danger because he loved her so much and knew that she could never see how pure that love was. But, finally, she was done. She turned around and saw him and smiled.

* * *

"Oh, hi!" Mary Beth said. "I wasn't expecting you. Tom's on the way. He'll be happy to see you."

"I'm sorry I'll miss him." Mary Beth was confused. Why would he stop by to leave so quickly? "I just want to show you something." He pulled something from his coat pocket and brought it close to Mary Beth so she could see it. There was nothing on the white handkerchief but the smell.

* * *

He caught her as she fell. So much love.

VI

Tod didn't expect a police convention - okay, just two cops and a former cop, but around here that was a large gathering for something as small as attempted homicide on an inanimate object - when he returned to blow the stump of the tree Will Kurtz tried to drop on the bridge. He cleared the tree earlier, so they might not have noticed the stump had it not been for the state chick - she noticed everything. She was right on it and doing some weird CSI thing where she paced the line from the stump to the bridge. She and Deputy Steve were having a bit of an argument while former Sheriff Ben, Gil and a couple of tourists - he knew they were tourists because they were dressed for Miami in winter which was fairly close to Miami in summer which was entirely wrong for Vermont in any season - watched in bemused interest. The female tourist asked Gil to pose with her husband by the bridge and Gil managed to get his father in the shot as well. Tod didn't need photos for memories and didn't understand people who did. It was all up in his head even when he didn't want it there.

Sadly, he lost his moment in time to remove the evidence of Kurtz's "crime." If he went and removed the stump anyway, they would wonder who had come along and removed it and then he might be in something like a pickle if they found out that he had been tampering with crime scenes even if there wasn't a real crime. That still wouldn't stop Deputy Steve from arresting him for something. Deputy Steve had become something of a jackass of late and was terrorizing the town with his strict interpretation of the law. Tod was well schooled in avoiding the law, he made it a point not to cross Deputy Steve's path. They all knew it was Kurtz and that he was pretty harmless for the most part and that even if they went out and talked to him about trying to knock a hole in the old bridge, which had never been damaged before, he wouldn't say anything reasonably sane in return. But he wasn't really a danger to anything but the bridge and wasn't really a danger to that. At least, he had never really been before. Tod did notice something strange, however. Something he had never seen before. The tree had chipped the bridge a little. Just a little. He wondered if Kurtz saw it. He was sure he had. Tod looked down at the stump remover and thought for a moment that when all the attention was elsewhere, perhaps now might be the time to try to destroy the bridge again.

No. It wasn't his job. It could never be his job.

He would stick with stumps... making the world a better place instead of a blighter place. As the stump wasn't going anywhere, he stowed his gear in a shrub out of anyone's way. He thought he would go and kill some time with old Samuel Taylor. Samuel lived out in a shack up in the woods and sometimes Tod would go up and just make sure he was alive. Tod already discovered one or two dead hermits. He didn't like doing it, but he didn't think anyone else was going to. So he headed on out to Samuel's.

The problem with Samuel is that he talked. A lot. Samuel was one of those hermits who was starved for human company but who seemed to think he was so interesting that people should seek him out for wisdom, like some Green Mountain Guru who held office for any truth seekers. And boy, did Samuel have some truth to tell. Samuel knew everything there was to know about Stansbury for some ten generations back or so. Back to the beginning of the place, he told Tod. He said his family had been responsible for keeping the soul of the town from dying.

"And how does one go about doing that?" Tod inquired.

Tod was interested. Once upon a time, Tod had very little interest in Stansbury outside of wanting to see it removed from existence. Even though it pained him to think about it, it was ironic. After all this time, at least he could appreciate that he had become a caretaker of sorts for the town, even if they didn't know it was him. If they knew what he was up to, they would probably be frightened. They probably should be. They only really knew that once upon a time he was deadly.

Tod realized he had a gift for death and destruction at an early age. His father used to take him hunting and Tod could bring down a full-grown bull moose with a single shot from a few hundred yards. When he was young, he learned how to kill and use everything he took and he soon provided his family with a steady supply of meat and leather. He never did keep trophies, though. He always found them to be disgusting. He killed the thing. He didn't need it staring down at him from the wall, asking him why he killed it. He knew that's what the things were asking from their wall mounts. Tod didn't like to answer those questions because he knew that, deep down, he just liked killing things to destroy them.

He always planned on destroying the entire town before he was done. He hated Stansbury from when he was forced to go to the stupid school where they didn't learn anything important. Tod knew how to read. He didn't need anyone to tell him what to read or what the books and stories and poems meant. Yeah, Robert Frost wrote a poem about walls and neighbors and horses in woods and paths and the teachers would sound all self important as they would ask questions that they had the answers to and if your answers were different from their answers they would tell you how wrong and dumb you were for thinking differently…for having a different kind of thought. Tod read those Robert Frost poems and he knew what they meant to him and he knew he was right to think those things no matter what the teachers told him. So one day he went and burned down the school because the path he was choosing was one of destruction of those things that he found offensive. He knew sometimes neighbors would never stay out of your business no matter how good the walls, so he burned the school down because he was right.

Of course, others didn't think his solutions were the right solutions and he was taken and placed in a facility until he turned eighteen. He learned lots of things in the facility. For one, he learned that he was still smarter than the rest of them and that he was right in thinking that it all needed to be destroyed. He believed the world would end in a fire he started. Of course, he stopped sharing what he believed because he had learned that if he was to make a real difference in the world, if he was going to put his stamp on the place in a meaningful manner and not just be another lame traveler stopping to confuse his horse because the snow looked pretty at night, he was going to have to play along. He learned there were places for him to go to learn how to be better at those things he had already shown some skill at and he convinced those in charge of the facility that they could help him be a better citizen if they assisted him in moving on to the military. They weren't stupid, those people. They were much smarter than his teachers back in Stansbury and understood that some people were made for destruction and that those people belonged in a controlled environment like the military. They did everything they could for him to achieve that goal. He took all the right tests and the military was thrilled to have such a savage young killer as Tod had shown himself to be.

After basic, he was sent to one of those secret schools that fiction only hints about for so-called super soldiers. They didn't give him any drugs or do anything more than show him more effective ways to kill and destroy things. They also showed him that where two paths diverge in a forest, scout around a little and you'll find the road that you should always take which is not one indicated by any kind of traffic. It's the one you make for yourself. It's the one that comes from building while you destroy. You build that little space for yourself. While Tod was in the military, he never thought about Stansbury at all. Ever. He was building new roads through places that people in Stansbury never even heard of. He was killing people who he was supposed to kill and sometimes he'd kill people for sport, if they intersected his path.

But as much as the people at the facility and the people at the secret base all thought that Tod was somehow less than human - or more than human, depending on your perspective and need - he was very human, after all. He didn't want to be, but he was. He started having dreams. In his dreams, all those good walls he was building couldn't keep him safe from all that he had done and all those people he destroyed were not being very good neighbors and respecting those walls. He hated those dreams because he was powerless in them. In his dreams, everything he built himself into during his waking life was destroyed by the animals he killed and the people he killed. The only way for him to continue to do what it was he so desperately desired to do, to destroy the world and lay waste to the very foundations of the universe, depended on the kind of perfection of mind that those dreams undid every night. So he had to escape from sleep.

He began to take drugs. Uppers. Anything to keep from sleep. It wasn't too bad at first. He could go days, sometimes weeks, without sleep and so long as he spent some hours everyday in deep meditation and exercise, it did not affect his ability to carry out his assignments. But after awhile, the dreams began to break through when the drugs stopped working so well. He would see his victims staring back at him from the shadows of the corners like ninjas waiting to slit his throat if he turned his back on them. The more drugs he took, the longer he could keep them at bay, but the less effective he was. He started to make mistakes and his handlers started to notice.

They realized right off that he was not meant to be the kind of soldier they tried to make him into. In the movies, they would have sent a group of other super soldiers out to erase him. In the movies, he would have been more super than the rest and he would have killed them before hunting down his handlers and killing all them and, at some point during all of this when he needed some help, some beautiful girl would get caught up in his adventure and help him escape to some far off paradise where he would retire to run some sport fishing business before they needed him again for the sequel. That's what would have happened to him in the movies. Instead, he was sent a retirement notice and a severance check, which he promptly blew on drugs.

When he got that check and that notice, he thought about Stansbury for the first time in many years and thought that before he put a gun to his head to kill all the bad dreams, he would blow up that stupid bridge. He took his toys home with him and built himself a little place up in the woods. For a long time, he planned his assault on the bridge. He had taken a huge amount of the huge amount of the drugs that he spent his severance on. Speed was cheap and they gave him a lot of money. He bought so much of the stuff that he had what the dealer called a small mountain of meth. Every time he would use, he would call it "mountain climbing." The problem was, he was quickly eroding the mountain and he knew that when it was gone, he would eat a bullet. He had to destroy the bridge first.

Then there was that Kurtz kid. Will Kurtz seemed to have a love affair with that stupid bridge. He was out there almost everyday sitting on it and drawing his pictures of it and making his models of it. He seemed to be making a kind of artist's study of the thing that Tod had made of killing. Tod couldn't remember a time when Will Kurtz wasn't haunting the bridge. The kid must have started hanging around it when he was nine or ten and then it was like he lived there. He was there before Tod went off to the facility and was there when Tod came back, only just a little bit older and a little bit stranger. His bridge art had grown in skill and beauty, not that Tod thought much about it at the time. All Tod thought was that Will Kurtz was in the way of his need to destroy the bridge. Tod thought about killing the kid. He thought a lot about killing the kid. He thought that there would be a kind of poetry in killing him along with the bridge. After a month or so with no sleep, Tod started to suspect that Will Kurtz was hiding out in his cabin and stealing his drugs when he wasn't looking so that the kid could spend more waking hours with his precious bridge. It made Tod want to destroy the thing all the more knowing that Will Kurtz loved it so much.

That's why Tod decided not to kill the kid.

He thought it would be better to destroy him utterly. For a while, Tod thought just blowing the damn thing up would ruin the kid's life in a really meaningful way. He had quite a bit of training in psychological warfare and knew that to take away something someone loved could destroy that person. But Tod needed more. Tod needed the satisfaction of making the kid bleed. He needed to feel bones crunching under flesh. Will Kurtz needed to be a bloody ragdoll on the shore…awake. Tod had the drugs for that… for feeling all that physical pain. And then, while the boy wondered why he had been chosen, Tod would add the anguish of knowing that thing he loved more than anything in all the world, that bridge that served no good purpose except to draw tourists to the town like insects to spilled syrup… Will Kurtz would see it all blown all to hell and he wouldn't understand why he had been chosen to witness the death of the thing he loved because he would then witness the death of the man who destroyed him. He would watch Tod put a pistol in his mouth and send a bullet through the top of his skull, erasing any rationale for this mad act.

Tod was good at what he had been trained to do and even though his brain was impaired, he took special care to set all his charges right. Everything in its right place. On that night in November, the woods were snowy. If Tod had thought too much about it, he would not have wanted to destroy the beauty of the night. But he just wanted to destroy, so he didn't think too much about it. He didn't stop to consider anything. He chose this path and it led him to the bridge and to the end of Will Kurtz.

The kid was there. He didn't even notice all of the explosives that were planted at every critical juncture on the structure. He just seemed to be in the weird daze that he always was when he sat on the bridge. He didn't even notice when Tod dropped down from the roof of the structure onto his back. It would have been so easy to snap the kid's neck like they taught him to do… it took a lot of effort not to snap the kid's neck like they taught him to do. But that wasn't how he planned the evening. He knew that he had to limit injuries to the head to make sure the kid stayed conscious, so he concentrated on breaking the body. The legs first so the kid couldn't escape. The knees are especially vulnerable and easy to disable. Tod disabled the kid like they taught him to do… it didn't take a lot of effort. They snapped so easily. The little breaks echoed in the covered bridge and Tod waited for the scream to follow. The scream always followed, but this time it did not. Will Kurtz didn't scream. He just kind of whimpered. Tod looked into his eyes and saw the fear. But the lack of screaming made him see red. He would make this kid scream. Tod broke his arms at the elbows. He could feel the sinews snap as they detached. Jagged broken bones ripped through the kid's skin and blood splashed black and thick in Tod's face. Tod looked into his eyes and saw fear and saw hopelessness. But no screaming. Will Kurtz never screamed, though. He never asked why. He just kind of whimpered. Tod continued destroying the kid's body, bit by bit, the way they taught him to do… a bone here and there was just enough to do it and still keep him awake. Normally Tod knew they were awake because they screamed themselves hoarse and then silent. The kid didn't scream. Tod looked into his eyes and was pretty sure the kid was awake even though much of what had been there now dimmed to a dull reflection of the soft whimper that continued to escape from the kid's mouth. He didn't understand why after all he had inflicted, there was so little. It wasn't the first time that night he wouldn't understand.

Tod pulled out his pistol, a revolver. Automatics fail and for this, he needed something that couldn't fail. He showed it to Will Kurtz's dull stare.

"Not for you."

Tod pulled the kid up to a tree a short distance from the bridge... come to think of it, it was the same tree Kurtz just dropped. Funny thing, that. He sat the kid up against the tree and made sure the eyes were still open, however dull the stare. He would see and he wouldn't know why and he wouldn't understand anything and he would be broken... not like Tod was broken, but worse because Tod would be dead and no one would ever be able to explain to him what had happened or why his life's love had been blown all to little red wooden bits all over him before his tormentor's head was blown all to little red bloody bits all over him. Tod really didn't understand it anymore. He just knew he had to do it. He couldn't even explain it if he wanted to... he didn't want to have to explain it. He just pressed the button on his transmitter and watched it all blow up.

It all exploded all right. Just like they taught him to make it all explode. He pressed the button and it all exploded. Except it didn't. It being the bridge. The explosives went off exactly like were supposed to go off exactly where they were supposed to go off exactly when they were supposed to go off. All the fire and all the smoke exactly like it always had been except it wasn't right because the bridge was still there and it didn't blow up and it didn't burn. Where there should have been fire and debris and destruction, just like he planned, there was nothing at all but the echo of what he did and then the bridge was there like nothing had been done at all. Like Tod hadn't been there at all.

But something had been done. Tod looked down at the kid and knew he destroyed something after all because where there was nothing but a blank stare had now been replaced by something else. Will Kurtz had seen something in all of what Tod did and it had broken him ever so much more than Tod had anticipated. The kid had seen something in the explosion and the fire and the nothing that happened. He had seen the why of it. What Tod did to him, planned on doing to him, was a generic kind of evil. Will Kurtz had seen real evil and Tod could see it in his eyes and hear it in the kid's screams. Seeing the kid and hearing the kid… it destroyed something inside Tod. Tod started crying. He pulled out his pistol and put it in his mouth and looked at Will Kurtz who was not looking at him. Will Kurtz was seeing something Tod could not see and screaming with the kind of fear that Tod could never know. But Tod knew that something he did ricocheted off of the kid and hit him and now he was there and broken and didn't know what happened or why. He only knew he unleashed a deep pain within the two of them. He tried to pull the trigger and end it all for himself. He thought about ending it all for Will Kurtz and then ending it all for himself, but he couldn't pull the trigger. Something was broken inside of him - although some would say something had been fixed - and he knew he couldn't do it anymore. All he ever knew or thought about knowing was the destruction of things and now he couldn't think about destroying anything without hearing the screaming and seeing the fear. Then he was screaming and looking into the abyss of his own soul which was dark and bloody and had accumulated evil beyond repair. He couldn't be that Tod anymore. He couldn't pull the trigger on the gun and he started crying while Will Kurtz screamed and he swore he would do no more and maybe he could make something better.

"How does one go about saving the soul of the town from dying?"

Tod really wanted to know because maybe if he could save the town he could somehow rescue Will Kurtz from whatever it was that still haunted him.

Samuel smiled at him. There was a lot of pain in that smile. A lot of regret. "You have to sacrifice little bits." There wasn't the slightest bit of deceit in Samuel. But there was something else. Something darker. Tod recognized it in people in that he had come to really understand it about himself. He did things in his life that would forever taint him. No good work could ever undo it. Samuel was the same. Tod knew Samuel could never speak about it just as Tod could never speak about it.

"When you grow tired of the job, let me know."

Samuel, knowing that Tod and he were alike in a way they would rather not be, nodded. "Someday, son."

As Tod walked off towards Samuel's place, he looked back at the bridge and still couldn't explain why it was still there when it didn't have any right to be. He saw all those cops and Gil and the tourists and wondered that maybe if they would all stop coming out to see it and paying homage to it and protecting it. Then maybe it would simply fade away from their minds and then it would be able to rot and die like it should have all those years ago.

Then he saw Kurtz. Even from far away, he knew Kurtz saw him. He though about going to him… to tell him about the damage… to tell him how to do it. But Kurtz saw him and there was still fear and pain in him. Tod felt his eyes tear up and quickly turned away.

* * *

The Silver Knight thought about attacking Lord Stansbury's Abomination when he saw that demon walking away from him into the woods. It was that demon that first showed him Lord Stansbury. It was that demon that knighted him and set him upon his quest. But that demon made him pay for his knowledge. That demon confused the Silver Knight the way that demons often do because ever since that night when he had blown open the fabric of space and revealed the dark evil thing that lived beyond the bridge… ever since he left the Silver Knight bent, bloodied and broken by the side of the lake… well, it seems like that demon had been changed himself. He was somehow less… demonic. The Silver Knight was confused by very few things but that demon confounded and perplexed him to the point that he tried not to think about the beast anymore than he had to… which meant only when their paths would cross, which they often seemed to do. That demon would, more often than not, make a quick retreat. The Silver Knight did not think that demon feared him. He did not see how that could be possible given the physical prowess that demon was known to possess. That demon was more likely than not to be of service to the Silver Knight and his quest so he chose to let the beast go on its way once again.

He walked as quickly as possible to his humble keep. He learned that to linger too long after a battle with the dark lord meant answering the inevitable questions from the local constabulary. It was… difficult. He learned early on to mask his speech from those did not possess the fortitude needed to accept the truth. After his first defeat at the hands of Lord Stansbury, he made the mistake of revealing the black knight's identity to one of the King's guardsmen, Officer Paul Godwin. Godwin pretended to understand the nature of the Silver Knight's foe. Godwin said he understood, but Godwin's tone belied his skeptic's heart. Godwin thought him a weak-minded fool and affected his transport to the King's asylum. Upon arrival, Godwin mocked him.

"Good sir knight. May the King's physicians attend to your mind and banish your enemy." Godwin mocked him.

The Knight understood then that others could not see what he saw…could not see how he saw. How could they? They had not been through the trials of the demon and seen through the fire that could not burn. He had been given the gift of true vision. The problem was that the reality of his true vision… the real things he could see and feel and fight… was hidden from most. He had met one or two others, the mystics and hermits and, yes, that demon, who could see it or feel it or know it to be true even if their senses failed them. But most of the people would never see… would never know. Most of those people thought him mad because to them if you could see something they did not or believed something they did not then you were mad and needed to be confined or placed under the influence of foul potions and elixirs that would banish the true vision. Those things did not work on him they way they wanted. They made his head fuzzy and robbed him of his focus and determination. But the true vision was always there. The Black Knight's laughter was loudest when the Silver Knight could not find the will to fight. He did not know how long he spent in the asylum before he learned how to speak to the physicians as William Kurtz, resident of Stansbury, Vermont.

"What is your name, son?"

"Lord William von Kurtz."

Then the pills. The blue one. The pink one. The white one. A cup of juice.

Then the activities. Sitting. Walking. Painting. The puzzle of the covered bridge. 5000 pieces of "The Most Photographed Covered Bridge in the World" which was not Lord Stansbury's Abomination. Gil told him once that a shopkeeper nearby that bridge made the best maple syrup donuts in all of Vermont. The Silver Knight sometimes thought that Gil was obsessed with maple syrup and its products.

"What is your name, son?"

"Lord William von Kurtz."

Then the pills. The blue one. The pink one. The white one. A cup of juice. The Silver Knight never drank juice after he left the asylum. He did not trust it.

Then the activities. Sitting. Walking. Painting. The puzzle of the covered bridge - 1,145 pieces placed.

"What is your name, son?"

"Lord William von Kurtz."

Then the pills. The blue one. The pink one. The white one. A cup of juice. The Silver Knight learned from Gordon Baylor, a thief and sometime bard who had been placed in the asylum to "silence the voices" that it was possible not to take the pills at all. He began with the blue one. He held it under his tongue as the juice washed down the others and then, later on, disposed of it with his physical waste. Gordon did not understand why he would not hoard his pills to trade for tobacco products. The Silver Knight did not believe in polluting his body or the world. His mind cleared somewhat, freed of the blue pill's gauzy dungeon. He could still not focus very well due to the lack of sleep. Part of the blue pill's magic apparently counteracted something in either the pink or white pill and let him sleep. Gordon told him that the voices wanted the Silver Knight to die, that they were afraid of him. He believed the voices were avatars of Lord Stansbury and began to stay on guard against surprise attacks. The Black Knight was obviously frightened that he might escape the asylum and take up the fight once again. Around that time, he stopped taking the pink one.

"What is you name, son?"

"I am uncertain."

"Of your name?"

"Of my existence."

Then the green pill. Then the sleep. Then the shot. Then the blue pill. Then the juice. "Open your mouth, please." Then the pink pill. Then the juice. "Open your mouth, please." Then the white pill. "Open your mouth, please."

Then the activities. Sitting. Walking. Painting Lord Stansbury's Abomination. The puzzle of the covered bridge - 3,723 pieces placed. He started noticing the subtle differences in style between the bridge that had been crafted by human hands and the one built by Lord Stansbury. The Most Photographed Covered Bridge in the World had clean lines that intersected naturally. There did not seem to be any impossible angles or dark runes and symbols integrated into the scrollwork. Also, the Most Photographed Covered Bridge in the World seemed to serve a useful, mundane purpose, crossing a small river that rambled through the road. It did not seem to be a portal through another hellish dimension to a location its creator had been banished from. The Silver Knight could not really be sure, though. After all, he had never visited the Most Photographed Covered Bridge in the World to verify its lack of supernatural purpose and even though Gil had avowed that the maple syrup donuts were "out of this world," the Silver Knight was fairly certain his friend, the squire, spoke in hyperbole and the donuts also contained no supernatural purpose. When he mentioned his belief about the donuts to Gil, there was some disagreement. Gil insisted that the donuts could "raise the dead." The Silver Knight was curious to test that once Lord Stansbury's Abomination had been destroyed and the Black Knight defeated.

"What is your name, son?"

"Lord William von Kurtz."

Then the pills. He avoided them and all his faculties returned after a short while. For some time he went about as if under the spell of the foul poisons.

The activities. Sitting. He hated just sitting but he was supposed to spend time just sitting so he just sat. While he sat, Lord Stansbury had fashioned a weapon out of Gordon. Gordon tried very hard to kill him three times. The first time Gordon tried very hard to smother him with a throw pillow from the couch in the sitting room. The Silver Knight under the spell of the apothecary, sat passively during sitting time and had no volition not to let Gordon try very hard to smother him until a pair of guards pulled Gordon from him.

"Why did he try to kill you, son?"

"His weak mind has been possessed by avatars of Lord Stansbury."

Gordon was placed with the violent "patients" of the asylum for a time. When they finally released him, he came to see the spellbound Silver Knight to apologize for trying to kill him. The trouble was that his apology was in the form of the sitting room pillow trying very hard to smother his face.

"Why did he try to kill you, son?"

"The poor fellow's mind has been tragically altered by the demonic dark magic of Lord Stansbury. I do not hold him responsible for his actions."

The final attempt came after the Silver Knight returned to his right mind, free of the blue, pink and white pills. Again, during sitting time, he sat quietly. He did his best not to draw attention to himself and if they required him to sit, he sat. Gordon, released after months of "treatment" in the violent ward, was led into the room and seated as far from his target as possible. In no time at all, he was running towards the Silver Knight armed with his folding chair. The Silver Knight just sat and waited to be struck. He did not want to draw attention to himself.

"Why did he try to kill you, son?"

"I don't know, doctor. I was just sitting like I was told to do. I'm supposed to sit during sitting time so I sit."

The physician nodded sagely and returned him to the sitting room where he sat. Walking. He tried very hard not to run. He tried very hard to avoid walking next to Gordon. Painting Lord Stansbury's Abomination. For some time, he had been painting around the bridge. Every tree, rock, the lake, a moose… everything but the bridge. One of the physicians commented on the empty space in the painting where the bridge normally corrupted the landscape.

"Didn't there used to be a bridge there, son?"

"Why spoil a perfectly lovely lake with a bridge, sir?"

"Why indeed?"

The physician nodded sagely and went on to the next patient, Lucy Patterson, who had been painting the same "self-portrait" for as long as he had been in the asylum. Her self-portrait was a small blue circle, about the size of a medium orange. She would paint the circle, focusing on "making it perfect." At the end of each session, she would scream.

"It can never be perfect! Fuck it! Fuck it!"

Then she would white wash the canvas and leave.

"It's looking good today, Lucy," commented the wise physician… hopefully.

"I think I might have it today, doctor. I think I might just have it.," replied Lucy…hopefully.

The puzzle of the covered bridge. 4987 pieces placed. No pieces remaining. The Silver Knight was not pleased with the incomplete puzzle. He had been working on the puzzle for so long that he never gave thought to the notion that the Black Knight might try to sabotage even this, the most innocent of projects. It was not even his bridge! It was the Most Photographed Bridge in the World just down the road from Gil's donut heaven and it had nothing to do with Lord Stansbury's Abomination except that once he finished it, he would make his final arrangements to leave the asylum – but he could not leave the asylum until the puzzle was complete and without the missing pieces the puzzle would never be finished and he could never leave. He looked around at the other prisoners. Perhaps one of them had been secretly sneaking pieces away from his table when he was involved in other activities. The guards were supposed to make sure that the puzzles and other works-in-progress went undisturbed, but the guards were lazy and wholly lacking in honor. He had become convinced that Saul Glassman, the guard from Montpelier who had dreamed of taking over his uncle's antique business because it suited his nature, had taken his pieces in the service of the Black Knight. He tried to get Saul to talk about it without giving away that he was not nearly as "cured" as the physicians recently began to suspect. Saul, however, could only talk about how much he wanted to get out of the asylum himself and work at his uncle's store.

"You just sit there on the side of the road sneaking a beer or two from time to time while tourists come in and poke through all your old crap. Occasionally they try to talk you down and occasionally you give them a deal to make them feel better about being so good at negotiating or some such thing but you don't really care because it's mostly just junk anyway and who would ever pay good money for something like a thirty year old 8mm film camera when you can't even buy film for the damned thing and, if you do and get it developed, you're just going to transfer it to video anyway. But some tourist comes in and offers you 15 dollars for the thing marked 20 and you give it to him because the thing was only going to rot in a box anyway and so you get 15 bucks and maybe the guy buys some tourist trinket you got up by the register and you make an extra few bucks because the guy thinks he got a deal. Mostly you just sit there on the side of the road sneaking a beer from time to time watching the cars fly by. That's what I want. So you can't finish your puzzle, huh?"

"No, Saul. I cannot."

"Saul, eh? Not Master Glassman?"

"Is that what you prefer?"

Saul gave him a look and smiled a little. "For a nutter, you're a sly one, you are. But who am I to tell a soul? I don't know where your pieces made their way to. Mr. Hannigan probably ate them, if you ask me. Tell you what, though. You're a crafty guy, your lordship." Wink. "Why don't you just conjure up some pieces? You got a complete picture on the box there. It's that Most Photographed Bridge in the World, isn't it?"

"It is. I hear they have good maple syrup donuts nearby."

"Yeah? Nah." Saul was done with him and chuckled away.

He looked over at Mr. Hannigan. He did not know much about the old man except that he was kind of the scapegoat for everything that happened around the asylum that no one cared enough to care more about. He did not think Mr. Hannigan ate his puzzle pieces. He did not think Mr. Hannigan did any of the things that were blamed on him, like all the missing pies last spring. The cooks in the kitchen always made pies in the summer. Every patient was given their own pie and they would get a piece for eight nights in a row until their pies were gone and then there would be no more pies until the following summer. They were given a choice of apple, cherry, blueberry or strawberry. He always picked blueberry. He did like blueberry pie quite a bit. His parents took him to the Wilton Blueberry Festival in Maine every August when he was a child and he fell in love with blueberries. Even in his darkest hour, a piece of blueberry pie cheered him up. After his parents died, Gil or Sheriff Hamilton brought him fresh blueberry pies whenever they were in season. He loved blueberry pies. They were…happiness. He did not get a blueberry pie last spring because someone stole all the pies. No one knows what happened to them because there was no evidence that anyone could find that they ever existed. He assumed it was the work of the Black Knight who wanted to deprive him of any kind of happiness, even something as simple as a blueberry pie. Everyone assumed it was Mr. Hannigan because everyone was always saying that Mr. Hannigan ate it if something went missing. But the Silver Knight knew it was not Mr. Hannigan. It was never Mr. Hannigan. But Mr. Hannigan did not care if they blamed him. He just sat there, staring out the window and smiling about some little thing he saw out there that was worth smiling about. The Silver Knight realized that there was little he could do to recover the lost pieces. Whatever devious mind had conspired to remove them had long since made sure that they would never be found again. It was a setback, yes, but he was used to setbacks and would not be deterred in his quest to complete the bridge. So he made the missing 13 pieces. He made a template for each piece using the construction paper they gave them for crafts. He carefully cut out the template using a small piece of wood he had sharpened against the floor and kept secreted away where the guards could not find it. He used the cardboard from the puzzle box to craft the pieces themselves and, once he had placed the blanks into the puzzle, he meticulously painted each one so that except under the scrutiny of a trained eye, no one would be able to tell his pieces from the ones that came with the puzzle. And it was done. He tried very hard to hide his hubris at the completion of the Most Photographed Covered Bridge in the World. He failed just a little. Saul came over to look at his completed work.

"Good job, your lordship."

"Thank you."

"Are you done with it now?"

"I suppose so."

"Good."

Saul began to sweep the puzzle back into the box, breaking the pieces apart. Destroying the bridge one snap at a time, a little grin on his face.

"Why are you-"

"Mrs. Patterson up on the third floor has been asking after this puzzle. I told her she'd have her turn once you were done with it. You are done with it, right?"

The Silver Knight watched as the pieces tumbled apart into the box. It was so easy. So easy to destroy a thing...a puzzle...a bridge...a puzzle of a bridge...a bridge. He could leave now.

"I am finished here."

"Good!"

With that, Saul packed up the box and took the puzzle away.

"What is your name, son."

"Will Kurtz, sir."

"Not Lord William von Kurtz?"

"No, sir. Just Will. Sir."

The physicians were skeptical at first. They took some convincing that he no longer believed himself to be the Silver Knight. But he persevered and they finally relented. He now knew how to be Will Kurtz when he needed to be. The demon had taken those pieces away from him that made him Will as well as the Silver Knight. But he fashioned them from whole cloth and now he could be Will again and the physicians believed him. What they did not know, even if they suspected it, was that he was still the Silver Knight. He was still charged with the quest to destroy the Abomination. He now knew that he did not have to tell everyone about it, at least those who could not understand, because if they knew what he did about the demons and evil in the world, they would hide themselves away in asylums and never come out again.

The Silver Knight exited the forest by Lord Stansbury's Abomination near the road closest to where he had to cross to return to his keep. There he could remove and clean his armor and great axe and think. The tree scratched the bridge. The red paint had been scraped away just a little and did not repair itself. This was new to his experience. New was good. Very good. The Black Knight was vulnerable after all.

No, first he would go to see Gil. He needed to tell Gil to stay away.

The Silver Knight was so wrapped up in his new plan of attack that he almost walked in front of Denise Drabos's red truck. He saw Denise smile and wave as she drove by. She was a good lady. She was a friend of his mother and sometimes cared for him when he was younger. Ivy, her Collie dog, barked at him from the passenger seat.

* * *

Ivy barked at the man on the side of the road. He was outside the truck. If he was outside the truck then he was not inside the truck and if he was not inside the truck then Denise had not let him inside the truck and that meant DANGER and she told him that she was ready, willing and able to defend Denise and the truck because she was in charge of taking care of Denise and the inside of the truck when she was inside of the truck. Only people who Denise had let inside of the truck with her gentle voice when they were inside of the truck were not dangerous. When Denise took Ivy out of the truck or out of the house, she was always on the look out for DANGER, but it was harder to spot because they were not inside the truck or inside the house. Denise told her that people were allowed to be outside without "causing such a fuss." But Denise couldn't smell them. They smelled like DANGER sometimes and it was up to Ivy to warn Denise. Denise sometimes got ANGRY with her and told her to SIT or SHUT UP. She always listened to Denise. She LOVED Denise. Denise would give her big hugs and kisses and treats and scraps "even though I'm not supposed to" because Denise LOVED her too.

For now, Denise was SAFE in the truck so Ivy gave her a little kiss and looked back out the window in case there was someone else who needed to know that Ivy was doing her job.

* * *

Denise knew that Ivy was just doing her job, but she still flinched slightly when her bark-alarm went off. It was a good thing Denise was used to her dog barking at just about everything or she might have plowed her truck into a maple or, worse, a moose. People were always hitting moose… or maybe it was the moose that were always hitting people…sometimes it seemed like people got the worse end of those collisions. Ivy was good for a warning when there were moose or people on the side of the road. In this case, Ivy was barking her warning out at Will Kurtz.

"Ivy, you know you don't have to bark at Sir William. He's trying to save us."

Ivy gave her that little Collie smile that said "Yeah, okay, lady. Whatever you say. I'm still going to bark anyway because it's my job." Mark the Breeder told her that Collies always do their job, which is protecting their flock and once you brought a Collie home, you were their flock and they were going to protect you. He got that right. Ivy was always watching over her, making sure nothing bad happened.

There had been a few people along the way who Ivy had not liked not one little bit and Denise knew if Ivy said, "No!" to a person, it was a no go for that person. At least until that person gave Ivy a donut. Ivy was a sucker for donuts. And cheese. And cat poop. Not that people came around handing her dog cat poop, but Ivy somehow always found the litter box in any house with a cat and "helped" the owner by "cleaning" it…Denise did not let Ivy kiss her for a time after her cat box treasure hunts. They say that a dog's mouth is somehow super clean, that a dog's saliva can clean wounds. Denise was having none of that. Dogs eat cat poop. She wouldn't rub cat poop on an open wound. So a dog's mouth? Uh uh. She wasn't buying that. Not one bit. Denise loved Ivy and Ivy loved Denise. That was all that really mattered. Denise thought that was why people love dogs so much. You just know they love you. You just look at them and you can see the love in their eyes and no matter how you are feeling you get to have a little love to keep you sunny even when the storms of life beat against you and try to wash you away.

Denise read a lot of self-help books and tended to think in self-help analogies. She once bought a series of video tapes, back before DVDs… or at least before she had a DVD player, from a friendly guy on the phone who told her that the tapes by this famous TV doctor were the next best thing to having a relationship counselor in your home all the time and that even at two in the morning he would be there for you and would help you when you were crying and blue and eating too much ice cream because the only love you were getting was from your dog and your dog, while unrelenting with her love and warm in bed on a cold night, was not quite the right kind of warm in bed and you would rather something with a little less fur – but not too much less because she liked guys to a have a little fur on them. She didn't understand "manscaping" or whatever the gay guys on TV were trying to get straight guys to buy into. You were born with a thing and you should keep a thing…at least if you were a guy. Guys should just deal with body hair. Girls were supposed to shave it all off because… well… because. She wanted her men manly and not approved by queer eyes.

So she bought the tapes from the nice guy on the phone because she believed him when he said that he found real lasting love because of the tapes and the TV doctor.

And she tried to watch the tapes because she wanted real lasting love and the TV doctor promised his tapes would give her what she really wanted. She tried to watch the tapes.

She put Tape Number One in her VCR. Tape Number One out of the twenty-four tape set she purchased from the nice man on the phone who found real lasting love. She was originally going to buy the first six tapes in the set to see if she liked them but the nice young man said that there was a special for people like her who really wanted real lasting love and that if she bought the whole set she would also get a set of cassette tapes for her car to listen to while she drove around so that she could have the TV doctor with her wherever she went, increasing her chances of finding real lasting love. How could she not find real lasting love with all this help wherever she went? So she put Tape Number One in her VCR and popped her popcorn and sat down on her comfy brown couch and gave Ivy some popcorn because Ivy did that thing where she just stood there next to the couch with her sweet little tri-color head resting on Denise's lap waiting for popcorn to slip into her mouth – real lasting love from Ivy was rewarded with popcorn – and pressed "play" on her remote.

Nothing.

Just the VCR logo on the screen.

She pressed play again.

Nothing again.

She got up and ejected the tape and looked at it as if she knew what she was supposed to be looking at because she had seen other people look at tapes like they knew what they were looking at and then they fiddled with them a little bit and put them back in the VCR and the tapes worked. So she fiddled with the tape, shook it a little, did that thing where you flip the lid up to look at the tape itself and then put the tape back into the VCR.

She sat on the couch. Popcorn. Ivy's head. Pressed play. Nothing.

Just the VCR logo and nothing more.

She thought that perhaps her VCR was somehow defective. Maybe it was a new kind of tape that wouldn't play on her old VCR. So the next day she drove up to Montpelier and bought the latest and greatest VCR. She rushed home with it – but not so fast that she would get stopped by some overzealous trooper or that jerk Deputy Steve who gave her tickets after she didn't go out on a date with him. She knew that he wouldn't give her tickets if they were dating but he was a stupid jerk and she knew that if she could ever watch the TV doctor tapes he would tell her to stay away from jerks like Deputy Steve.

She wanted to listen to the TV doctor's Number One of the six tape series about making your you a better kind of you for you and for your real lasting love partner. But the tape player in her truck ate the tape. When she tried to get Tape Number One out of the player, at first it wouldn't eject. She looked at Ivy and Ivy chuffed a little. Ivy didn't like the cassette player. Not one bit. Denise didn't like it either.

She kept meaning to get a CD player but she had all these mix tapes she made when she was in high school that had all this great music on them and she knew that she would never hear all that music together the way she knew it was supposed to go if she just listened to CDs and she didn't have enough money to get a computer to make mix CDs because she would have to get all the CDs with all the music on the mix tapes and then sit down and make a list of the way each song went on each tape and then make sure that she had the right CD and maybe there wasn't even a CD for that song.

So she kept her old cassette player and her old mix tapes and they played just fine on the player but the TV doctor tape didn't. When she finally got Tape Number One out of the old player it was nothing but a mess of cassette tape spaghetti. She tried to use a pencil to rewind it like she had seen other people do who seemed to know what they were doing but after a few moments it snagged and broke altogether. Holding a mess of broken spaghetti tape, she looked over to Ivy for comfort. Ivy chuffed again and licked her face. Denise had to smile a little even though she had started to cry. Real lasting love, indeed.

She put the tape down and decided that the only real way for the TV doctor to really help her was on the TV. That's where he belonged. Leave the radio to the radio doctors. She never liked them anyway. They were always telling people how stupid they were for doing the things they did and not listening to the problems, which were real and true and needed compassion, not nasty judgmental put downs. That's why she only listened to her mix tapes on the radio.

On her way back from Montpelier, she was listening to her "Travel Mix '86" tape full of cool songs from 1986. She actually made the tape in 1987 so she could make sure she did not leave any of the coolest songs from 1986 off of the tape. Her favorites on that tape were "Broken Wings" by Mr. Mister which was still an awesome song and "Life in a Northern Town" by the Dream Academy. She could play "Life in a Northern Town" over and over again and she would always sing the "Hey ya ya ya" part at the top of her lungs, which mould make Ivy chuff. She put "West End Girls" by the Pet Shop Boys on that tape, but now she didn't know why because it kind of annoyed her. She managed to avoid troopers and jerky Deputy Steve and return home.

She unpacked the fancy new VCR and set it up, following the directions closely. She did everything including setting the time for recording from the TV – something she never did, she liked watching TV live and not on tape. She let the VCR find all the channels. She used the head cleaner that came with the VCR to make sure it was as clean as possible. She put in the test tape that came with the VCR to make sure it worked the way it was supposed to work. She was just a little impressed with herself when it worked the way it was supposed to work. The comedy shows on TV were always making jokes about how only little kids could set up VCRs while the adults just sat around in awe at the new technology. She wasn't so old yet that technology scared her. She could plug in a plug or two. She just had to follow the directions is all. Most people did not want to follow directions. They were too stubborn or something and thought that if the thing didn't set itself up then it must be too hard. She liked directions because if you followed them, they usually worked. And she followed the directions for setting up her fancy new VCR and did all the tests and it worked the way it was supposed to work.

She made a bowl of popcorn and put Tape Number One in the new VCR and sat on her comfy brown couch and gave Ivy her piece of corn. She smiled and pressed "play" on the new remote.

Nothing.

She frowned and pressed the button again and nothing happened again. It was a fancy new VCR and she had tested it and it worked like it was supposed to and still no TV doctor telling her how to have real lasting love. Just to be sure she removed Tape Number One and replaced it with Tape Number Two. Yes, she knew she was cheating. But just the same, she wanted to see if any of the TV doctor's tapes worked at all. She was beginning to feel disappointed in the TV doctor. She did all that she was supposed to do. She bought a new VCR for his tapes. She checked the wires and made sure the whole thing worked because she really wanted real lasting love and the nice man on the phone promised that the tapes would help her get that and she bought the whole set and the cassettes which didn't work in her tape deck and so even though she was skipping ahead she had to see the TV doctor just a little and it was only fair, wasn't it?

She sat back on her couch. This time she was sitting, leaning a little forward so that Ivy could not rest her head on Denise's lap. Ivy didn't mind, though. She had her head in the bowl of popcorn and, as Denise had not yelled at her to stop, she took that as a sign that Denise meant to leave the popcorn for her. Denise closed her eyes tightly and pressed "play" on her new remote.

The VCR made a funny noise. Actually, it wasn't very funny at all. It was more of a crunching noise. At first, Denise thought the noise came from Ivy crunching popcorn, but she soon realized it was far worse and soon replaced by a strange mechanical groan. Before she could act, the groan became a loud SNAP and the VCR turned itself off.

Denise started to cry a little. Just a little. She slowly stood and walked over to the machine and pressed the power button. It didn't do a thing. She unplugged the VCR from the wall and plugged it back in again.

Nothing.

Still trying to maintain a calm center while her emotions stormed around her, she flipped the little flap and peered inside the VCR. She could see pieces of the tape where there shouldn't have been pieces. Somehow the machine had eaten the tape in a way the cassette player in her truck could only dream of cassette consumption. It not only murdered Tape Number Two, it committed suicide as well.

Still maintaining her calm, she carefully put the new dead machine back in its box and plugged her old reliable VCR back in and reconnected it. She put in her well-watched copy of "Mannequin" which she always watched when she was feeling like she was going to fall apart. She loved that movie. The opening credits came on and there was Andrew McCarthy – she loved Andrew McCarthy - and as she slowly leaned back towards her couch, she caught herself. Andrew could wait. She needed to see if any of the Tapes Number Three through Twenty-Four worked at all.

Sadly, she ejected Andrew and Kim from her VCR and put in Tape Number Three. Her heart leapt a little when the TV doctor appeared on her TV. There he was, a little late in the lessons, but ready to give her the secrets to real lasting love, like Andrew and Kim had in Mannequin. After about 30 seconds, however, the picture got all weird, like the signal from the antenna wasn't coming in properly. Without thinking about it, she went to the TV and adjusted the antenna on top for a moment before remembering that it was a tape. The tape wasn't coming in clearly! Suddenly the picture went out and the word "TRACKING" appeared on the screen and never left.

Eject.

Tape Number Four. The sound of rewinding just went on and on and Denise realized that the TV doctor's tapes just weren't going to give her the answers she needed. They were cheap tapes and if the TV doctor sold cheap tapes then his answers were probably cheap too and certainly not going to give her the kind of real lasting love she sought.

So she packed them all up. Tapes Number One through Twenty-Four (what was left of Tape Number Two in any case) and the six cassettes that were hers to keep free but she didn't even want to keep them because they wouldn't play for her and she didn't want any advice from the TV doctor anyhow.

She packed it all up and called the number on the box to ask them how to return the item. The nice man from customer service told her to pack the tapes up and gave her an address and a return number. He said to write the return number on every side of the box. She asked why and he said to trust him and write the number clearly on every side of the box. He also said to use a registered delivery service and not the regular mail. She asked why and he told her to trust him and make sure she used a registered form of delivery so that she could track her package. She thanked him for his time and he asked her if she was interesting in purchasing a set of investment tapes that would help her to be a millionaire investor in the commodities market. He said that the tapes really worked and that the only reason he answered the phone for the company was that, as a millionaire investor himself, he felt a need to talk to other people and help them become millionaire investors too. She asked him what the commodities market had to do with real lasting love and the TV doctor and he said if you were a millionaire investor, it would be much easier to find real lasting love.

She began to suspect that he was not, in fact, a millionaire investor and that the nice man who sold her the TV doctor tapes did not, in fact, have the kind of real lasting love he said the tapes gave him. How could he watch the tapes anyway? They were so crappy! She told him that she wasn't interested in investing today and he asked her if that mean she was not interested in being a millionaire investor in a tone of voice that made her feel stupid for not buying the tapes. She did not think he was very nice anymore and told him to have a nice day and hung up.

She did, however, send the TV doctor's tapes back the way he instructed her to do. And then she waited for her money to be refunded. And waited. And waited. She tracked the package and found out that an A. Martinez in San Fernando, California signed for it. She called the number again and a lady named Judy who had a mean voice answered. She asked when she was going to get her money back and the mean voiced lady asked her if she had proof the package had been returned. Denise told her about A. Martinez in San Fernando and the mean voiced lady said she would put in a refund request and hung up.

She waited for her refund and it did not come and she called and more refund requests were put in until one day when she called and the number had been disconnected and she found out that the company that sent out the TV doctor's tapes had been closed by the government because too many people had been promised that they could become millionaire investors or find real lasting love and no one found love or became a millionaire investor and no one ever got their money back when they returned their tapes even if they followed all the directions.

She realized that she would probably learn more about real lasting love from Kim the Mannequin than any TV doctor and promised herself she would never buy anything from anyone on the phone again, no matter how nice they sounded.

Denise absently scratched Ivy under the chin as she parked in front of Osno's. Lately she started taking sleeping pills and needed to pick up her prescription. As she opened her door, Shelley's voice cried out.

"Ivy!"

Ivy barked once and jumped over Denise and out the door to Shelley. Denise smiled a little. If there was anyone Ivy loved other than her, it was Shelley. Ivy loved Shelley.

* * *

Shelley loved Ivy. Probably not as much as Denise did, but she loved her because she was such a funny fuzzy Collie dog and made her think of Lassie and she loved Lassie. Ivy came running up to her and then flopped down on her side so Shelley could rub her belly. Shelley went down on her knees and obediently rubbed the fuzzy belly and Ivy smiled at her. So cute.

"Hi, Shelley!"

"Hi, Denise. How are things?" Denise used to babysit Shelley a long time ago and they were still what Shelley called "kinda-friends." Kinda-friends were those people who you've known a long time and are all really nice and occasionally you can even talk to them a little about something that you both like and you might even go out to a movie with them if they called you, which they never do because they are waiting for you to call which you never do, and when people ask you about them you always say nice things but you're just not really close or really even friends because when you talk you don't really talk to them the way you do with your real friends.

"Well, you know. Same old same old. Just me and Ivy. I don't know what I'd do without her." Shelley started to tear up a little because as much as she thought that Denise was always so sunny, she could see that there was a lot of sadness building up. Shelley resolved to be more than a kinda-friend to Denise and started by giving her a big hug.

The hug seemed to startle Ivy, who chuffed at Shelley. Shelley knew that Ivy didn't mean anything more than to express her displeasure at the sudden contact with her owner. The hug startled Denise even more. It was obvious to Shelley that no one hugged her for a good long time because Denise began to sob. Not just a little crying, but great, heaving sobs that shook Shelley with their force. Shelley began to cry, too. Whenever someone cried near her, she always joined them, But this was different. This was pain. Shelley had never quite felt this kind of pain before, even when Gil came home after his accident.

"It's okay."

"It's not. It's not. It's not. I'll never be happy. I'll never have anything more than this. I'm alone except for Ivy. I'll always be alone."

Shelley didn't know the words to say to make it better for Denise. Shelley didn't know if the words existed. Anything she said would be a lie or worse, a consolation. Denise spent her whole life being consoled or lied to and Shelley didn't want to continue that. At the same time, she didn't know what to say to make it better and she dearly wanted to make it better for Denise. She pulled away from Denise and, wiping her own tears away, she looked at the woman and, for the first time in a long time, couldn't bring herself to smile. She had always been able to find her smile, but for some reason, something was wrong and the smile wouldn't come.

"I'm sorry, Denise. I really am. I wish I knew what to say to you, but I don't. I wish I had the right words, but I don't. I want to make it all better for you, but I can't. I can be your friend. I want to be your friend. But that is all I can be. I'll watch movies with you and go eat with you and cry with you. But that's all I can do. I know that's not what you're looking for and it isn't enough, but it's something, right?"

Denise grabbed her back into a hug and Shelley knew that somehow she said the right thing for now. "It is something, Shelley. Right now I'll take any something I can get."

Shelley found her smile...just a little. She knew that Denise was grasping at straws and if she could be the straws, well, that would have to make do. She was making a difference and it wasn't like she didn't like Denise. She just never found a reason to be more than a kinda-friend. But Denise needed her and that was enough. She planned on bringing a chicken potpie over to Kurtz after work, but she thought that maybe Denise maybe just needed her a bit more right now. Kurtz could make do with whatever it was that he made do with when she wasn't bringing him something. Sometimes, though, she wasn't sure what that was unless Gil was sneaking him donuts or whatever other garbage he sold out at the store. Maybe Kurtz had a bunch of caring folk who brought him a little something every now and again or maybe he could actually fend for himself. Shelley would have to talk to Gil about it. Gil would know.

"Hey. Space cadet. Hello?" Denise was smiling at Shelley. "Where'd you go?"

Shelley was a little embarrassed. Sometimes she let her thoughts get away from her. "Sorry. I was just thinking about tonight. Listen, I made a fresh chicken potpie this morning. Would you like me to bring it by tonight? Maybe we can watch a movie or something."

"Oh, you don't have to do that. I'm okay." Why did people always think that doing something nice was an imposition? Weird.

"I know I don't have to. I want to. It would be fun." Well, maybe not really fun. But it would be nice.

Denise's smile faded. Shelley felt like she lost her. She could have just been honest and said she thought that Denise needed a friend and that she thought she could be that friend. Denise would have felt the truth of it and would have accepted that kind of generosity. But it was too soon after seeing the woman break down to be claiming any kind of fun would come from eating potpie. "It's okay, Shelley. I'm not feeling all that great anyway and I'd be kind of a pill tonight. Maybe another time?"

"Of course. Anytime you want, just call me, okay?" Shelley meant that and Denise knew it and her smile came back…just a grin, but it was enough for now.

"I will. Of course I will."

They stood there for a moment looking at each other. Shelley was never quite sure what to do in moments like these. She had always been good at ending conversations or leaving when there was nothing more to do or say. But for some reason, there were times when there was uncomfortable pause, as if there was something more but no one could quite figure out what it was. Shelley had seen other people go through it all the time in the store. People came separately to buy things and then ran into each other. They would have these conversations that seemed so wonderful and made Shelley smile to overhear them. Just a bit of gossip or catching up or whatever. They would go on and on and then, suddenly, they would run out of whatever it was they had to say and there would be nothing but the inability to talk combined with the inability to part company. Mainly because they both were in the midst of shopping and still had to occupy the same space but did not care to do it together. They had different things to buy and different days to make their way in and their happenstance meeting was a lovely diversion but did not really figure into their overall plans. It had to be ended and, yet, the first person to say goodbye felt some kind of guilt at instigating the separation, as if they were somehow rude for implying that the day needed getting on with and the plans that were made prior to the encounter needed to be carried out. Sometimes Shelley would butt in and help out, asking if one or the other needed any help finding anything.

Oh.

"Hey, Denise. Do you need any help finding something in the store? You said you're not feeling well, is there something I can get for you?"

Denise looked relieved. Ivy chuffed her approval at the end of the tension. "Yeah. I need to fill my prescription and get some treats for Ivy." Ivy chuffed her approval again.

"Go on into the store. You know where the dog treats are. I'll be there in a second." Shelley held the door for Denise and Ivy. She didn't mind dogs in the store even if Mr. Osno did. If he wanted Ivy to leave, he could come on out and tell her to. All that would happen was a copper tube would drop into the hopper. She would dutifully read the note that would no doubt be full of profanities about Shelley and Denise and Ivy. But, at the end of the day, it really didn't matter. She knew that she would keep on being counter girl until she decided to move on and then Osno would invariably find another local girl to be counter girl and send her little love notes as well. If Shelley didn't like her job as much as she did, if she didn't like being in the middle of things and be able to talk to people, make people smile a little even when they were picking up their medicine which cost too much anyway or when they were finding something to make them feel better, she would leave. She liked to think if they left the store with a smile, if she gave them some good feelings along the way then they would feel better just by having come and seen her that day. So she didn't mind the nasty notes. She was making Denise feel better today and so she felt better.

Before Denise pulled in, Shelley had been on her way out to the mailbox. For some reason, Mr. Osno did not approve of the mailman entering his establishment. He actually did not approve of any government official coming in the store. He saved his most vicious notes for any representative of the government. He felt it a personal affront that they would step foot in his place, as if Osno's Pharmacy was a country and he was its lord and king. She commented to the mayor about this one time when she was away from the store. She wouldn't dream of speaking to the mayor in her boss's presence except to help him as her job requires. She had a little crush on the mayor and felt weird when he spoke to her. For some reason, because he held the title, she thought that she shouldn't just be allowed to go up and talk to him. She couldn't just go up and talk to the governor or the president or something. The mayor was important like them for Stansbury and she always felt a little important when he spoke to her and called her by name. He knew her and that was really cool. Maybe he might even like her a little. He wasn't married and he wasn't that much older than her... or at least she didn't think he was...he could be a lot older but she was an adult now so it really didn't matter if he was older or not because it wasn't like he was gross or something. She daydreamed sometimes about being married to him and being important like the First Lady even if it was just the First Lady of Stansbury which really didn't mean all that much to anyone outside of Stansbury. He hadn't asked her out yet, but he always smiled at her and treated her really nicely. Then again, she always smiled at everyone and treated them really nicely and that didn't mean that she wanted to marry everyone who came through the door.

Did people she smiled at and treated nicely daydream about marrying her? Maybe the mayor was just like her and just wanted people to be happy. If the mayor was just like her, maybe they would make a good couple, making people happy…together. Maybe she would make him a pie sometime. She was sure he liked pie. Who doesn't?

The mayor was very curious as to why the pharmacist was so uptight about his presence.

"It's not just you, Mr. Mayor. He hates everybody."

"Why would you open a store to help people if you hate them so much?" He seemed so earnest with the question. Like it really mattered to him and he really wanted to get to the bottom of things.

"I wouldn't. But I'm not Mr. Osno. There is no knowing him at all. He's just copper tubes in a hopper."

The Mayor shook his head knowingly and even a little sadly. "I guess you could say there's no knowing anyone at all."

Shelley wasn't sure at all if that was true. She thought there were people you could know really well because they wanted to be known. She could talk to Gil forever because they both allowed each other to know each other. They didn't have to make small talk because small talk is what happens between people who have something to hide. Shelley was pretty sure that people liked talking to her because she didn't go out of her way to make small talk. She was always open about who she was and didn't care if people knew the real her because she was totally alright with herself. She wasn't perfect, but nobody was, not even the Mayor, even though he had elements of perfection that could not be ignored. She was fairly certain it would be impossible to ever know Mr. Osno because he didn't even make small talk.

Shelley stood by the mailbox for a moment and imagined the Mayor might come by and say hello to her there if she stood long enough. But she wasn't really destined to be his wife. She knew that. Still, it was fun to think about from time to time. As she got the mail, she laughed at herself for being silly.

A stern Vermonter voice startled the thought from her. "I never could find any humor in mail."

* * *

"Oh, I wasn't laughing at the mail, Mrs. Hirson." Shelley seemed defensive. Nobody seemed to get her humor. Not even Roger after forty years of marriage could get her humor. Perhaps it was in her delivery. Stephanie had been saying humorous things all her life. At least they were to her, but people never got it. All they got was defensive.

"I didn't think you were, dear. I was just making a joke." If you tell someone that what was supposed to be funny was supposed to be funny, would they find it funny after the fact?

"Oh." Shelley seemed to actually think about it for a moment. That's why she liked Shelley. The girl lived in the moment and everything was important in the moment, even an old woman's poor attempt at comedy. "Oh!" The girl actually giggled a little. "That was a good one, Mrs. Hirson."

Not really that good. A good one is got the moment it is told. But Shelley was a good girl for saying so. "You're a good girl for saying so, Shelley."

"Thanks! So are you here to pick up Mr. Hirson's pills or can I get you something else today?" Shelley started walking back towards that accursed store. Over the years the only reason she kept coming to Osno's instead of finding a store a little further away was because the bastard had a good eye for help. The girls he found to smile at the public were always so sunny and warm that she couldn't bring herself to go elsewhere, even if she couldn't stand the man who hired them. Not to say she had ever met him. No one had. That was the problem. She liked to complain from time to time because it was her right and privilege. She survived a whole lot of years on this planet and, as a result, she had a lot of experience to back up her statements of fact. Sometimes those statements of fact came in the form of complaints and those complaints deserved to be aired. If she kept them all inside, it wouldn't be fair to the world. The problem was, she hated to complain to the girls because it wasn't their fault that Osno got her pills wrong or didn't stock the right brands of soap. She tried to convince Shelley to let her slip a note or two in one of those damned copper tubes, but the girl bravely held her ground.

"It's not worth it, Mrs. Hirson. He'll just get nastier."

Which was followed by one of those damned tubes falling into the hopper. The girl dutifully pulled it out and read the note inside. Stephanie could tell from the look on her face that the note was of the unfortunate variety that had fallen into the hopper for as long as she had been coming into the store and complaining.

"What does the old bastard have to say now?" Stephanie knew it wasn't pretty, but she found the notes amusing much the same. Even more amusing was watching the girls, each in their own sweet way, try to disguise the real message with polite rephrasing.

"He says that he understands your concerns and appreciates your business, but he is unable to address your specific needs at this time." Shelley was a dear and very good at her job.

"And what does he really have to say?"

Shelley looked around as if to be sure that no one could hear her, which was amusing and cute as there was no one else in the store. Then she cleared her throat and, in a low whisper, read, "'Tell the old bag that she can fucking take her own ass down to Boston for her special order shit.' I'm really sorry. Um, I added in the part about being really sorry." Shelley tried to smile a little.

Stephanie laughed. It was one of the few times in her life she had laughed as hard as that and for as long as that. Tears streamed down her face as the laughter echoed off the walls and hopefully back through that damned little slot so the bastard in the back would hear her and know that she thought his little petulant profanities were ridiculous. Shelley started to laugh with her, understanding that there was no reason to be afraid of her, that she understood that the man behind the wall was a fool.

Another cylinder dropped into the hopper. Shelley pulled out the note and read it and got quiet for a moment, before her giggles got the best of her and she started laughing even harder.

"What does it say, dear?" Stephanie managed to get the words out.

Shelley wiped her tears away and attempted to compose herself. With her voice unsteady from the laughter behind it ready to explode forth, she read, "I don't pay you to fucking laugh with the peasants, bitch!" And the laughter followed her words quickly.

But Stephanie wasn't laughing this time. She heard the word "peasants" and that got her. Who did this reclusive prick think he was calling his customers peasants? Who would he be without the people of Stansbury coming in to his crappy store because there was nowhere else close by to pick up the pills they needed or a bottle of aspirin? She paid money, dammit, and that had to be worth something more than an insult or a derisive comment. Her family had fought for this country in every damned war back to the Revolution and there was no way she was going to stand by and let this bastard insinuate that he was some kind of goddamned royalty that could command and be obeyed by his customers!

Shelley saw that she had stopped laughing and quickly stopped herself.

"Does he always refer to us as peasants?" The anger in her voice was palpable and sadly misdirected at the girl.

"Not always." Shelley tried to smile a little. "It's actually one of the nicer terms he uses."

And suddenly Stephanie got it. It wasn't about what he had to say. He was never going to say nice things about anyone. It was about these girls. He knew he was a prick and hid himself away as a service to his customers. He hired these beautiful, sweet wonders to stand in for him, take his invective and turn it into something as nice as they were. There was a kind of brilliance in it, really. He obviously had no ability to filter out his integral awfulness as a human being. He protected his customers from himself with a buffer zone of cute and charming girls who made people feel better. And, after all, wasn't it his job to help people feel better? Shelley made her feel better every time she came in the store.

"No, just the pills today. Roger's gone and run out again and he always waits until just before he needs a new batch to send me running. It's a good thing he checked his bottle early today. I remember the one time he waited until after the Leno show to let me know that he could possibly die during the night if he didn't have a refill. Sadly for all of us, he woke up the next morning."

Shelley paused for a moment. Stephanie knew she was trying to figure out if that was a joke. After a moment, the girl laughed. Good for her. Stephanie was happy to take at least one truly honest laugh a month right now. Perhaps it was about time to pursue that career in stand-up. But first, Roger's pills.

As she followed the girl into the store, she noticed Ben Hamilton driving past. Even though she still hadn't forgiven him for abandoning the town to that man-child, she still gave him a polite wave.

* * *

Ben waved back to Stephanie, who was tersely polite even though she would never forgive him. She had been a good friend once, especially after Virginia had died. He spent night after night with her and Roger playing Scrabble. He hated that damned game. All those words. He would sit and stare at the tiles for what seemed like hours. He'd get lost in the combinations. He knew there were words there, but they constantly eluded him. And the ones that he saw would always remind him of Virginia and he would never play those even though he could hear her voice chiding him for losing the good score.

He imagined her ghost sitting over his shoulder sadly sighing as he missed opportunity after opportunity. She was the competitive one and would force him to play all those silly games even when he would rather be focused on his work. She said he needed some good old-fashioned fun and would forcefully sit him down in front of Monopoly. He hated that game above all others...there was no point in it. You just moved your damned shoe or car or whatever around the board and randomly landed on things and paid for them or paid someone else for them until you proved what? That you could roll dice better than anyone else or pick a better card than anyone else? It made no good sense and people just got angry at it because someone rolled the dice better. Virginia hated to lose to him because he didn't really care and she knew it. But she'd still make him play because she loved to win. Of course, any game that involved chance meant that Gil would be banished from the room, if not the house. Whenever she got the bug to play, she might casually make a suggestion to the boy.

"Gil, dear. Do you think you could spend the night over at a friend's?"

"Which friend, mom?"

"Is there a friend you'd like to visit with?"

"Not really."

"What about Will?"

At this point, the boy usually got the picture. If Virginia was willing to send him off to the Kurtz house, then she must really want him gone. "You know, mom. If I'm sitting at the table, only Dad doesn't get good rolls." The boy knew his limitations.

"I'd just prefer to play without your dark power about mucking things up." She called all that bad luck Gil hauled around with him his "dark power" as if he was some kind of medieval wizard from one of his games that he never seemed to do very well at playing. But Ben would never fault his son for not trying to overcome whatever it was that decided to plague him. Gil also had the best humor about it, like it was something that he had to deal with and sulking wasn't going to change it. It's what Ben and Virginia loved most about the boy.

Just as Ben never blamed the boy for his dark power, he didn't blame him for Virginia's death, even though she was surely a victim of it. Something about Gil and cars didn't mix and they really tried very hard never to drive him anywhere. But he did have a tendency to get hurt and they reluctantly would take him to the closest doctor around, except on Sundays, of course, when they'd have to go a bit further on, to Burlington on occasion, to get him to a hospital for his latest break. Most of the time, it was Ben who took the boy. Virginia had a continual prediction that one of these days she'd be taking the boy somewhere and his dark power would finally lash out in her direction and that would be the end of her. When she'd call him, there would always be that bit of fatalism in her voice as she said goodbye and told him she loved him. He never forgot to return the emotion.

"I've got to take Gil off to Burlington. It looks like a sprain, but we need to check it." She was a good mother and always cautious.

"Be careful, dear."

"I will. I love you, Ben." He supposed those were the best last words he could have from his wife.

"I love you, Gin." Those were the best last words he could speak to her.

He didn't know much more than the car crashed and the boy survived and she didn't. Gil said he had no memory of it and Ben never pressed the issue. He didn't need to know every detail of the accident. It didn't matter. All that did was that she was gone and Gil thought it was his fault and Ben had never been able to do anything to change his mind about that. There was no way he could know every little thing, but he did know that he loved his wife and he missed her still and would trade just about anything for one more game of stupid Monopoly with her.

He watched Stephanie make her way into Osno's in his rearview mirror. He worried about Roger. He had been sick for a few years now and the doctors kept trying new pills on him. When he was still a welcome guest, Roger would laughing read over the list of possible side effects of the medications he was taking. He continued to believe that if the mysterious illness, the "Creeping Sick" as Roger called it, didn't kill him, the pills would. He actually started believing that the Creeping Sick was a disease that was fed by the pills, which were constantly changing it and making it evolve into something stranger and, sometimes, worse. Each new pill was a transformative event in the life of the disease, twisting it and reshaping it into an ache or internal bleed or blurred vision. Roger blamed his poor performance at Scrabble on his inability to see the tiles correctly. He said sometimes they would rearrange themselves into demonic messages, but he would never tell Stephanie or Ben what those messages were. He said that the things the Creeping Sick had to tell him were for him alone and it had warned him that if he spilled the beans, the Sick would make him take a different pill to bring about some awful new side effect. Ben had been out of the loop ever since the election, when the invitations for Scrabble no longer came.

"When you come to your right mind and start being Sheriff again, then you can come and play and eat my food. Until then, Ben Hamilton, we'll have none of you." Stephanie had not minced her words.

Ben turned back to the road. Seeing Gil today. Seeing the continued hurt in the boy's life. He knew it was time to talk to him and settle what was between them. If something happened to either of them and he didn't tell Gil how much he loved him, that he didn't have those as his last words with the boy, he'd never forgive himself.

And for some reason he had that awful, twisted up feeling that told him something bad was coming and he didn't know if it was coming for him.

Ben went to the intersection to make a proper U-turn. He didn't give much thought to the ugly old chartreuse Chevrolet sedan driving past.

* * *

He saw the Old Sheriff pass by and then turn around to follow behind the vessel's car…such a pretty shade of green. He heard the vessel's lingering thoughts in his head that it was an ugly color, but this body no longer belonged to the vessel so what he thought did not matter anymore. He had felt the Old Sheriff before and knew he was a good Old Sheriff and that he loved the town. But no one really loved the town as much as he did because no one really knew how to keep the town alive. It required love. It required the will to take that love and turn it into sacrifice. And sacrifice hurt. It hurt him most of all because he always had to sacrifice beauty and perfection for the town.

Beauty and perfection like the Teacher Girl in his trunk. He knew that if the Old Sheriff found her there, he wouldn't see the love. He would just see his own fear and that fear would blind the Old Sheriff to the truth that pain was required. When he had sacrificed the Old Sheriff's wife to make the Black Cloud stronger, the Old Sheriff never tried to understand the way he tried with all the others. He let it be an "Accident" because it was easier to have it be that than to understand that love somehow invited destruction. He loved all those he sacrificed. To the town. To the Black Cloud. He had to love them because it was how he kept it all together. Captain and Tennille sang that love will keep us together and they didn't know that love not only keeps couples together but it keeps towns together.

It was never about him. It never had been. He served the town, much as the Black Cloud served it. Today he needed the Black Cloud for his work. He would go to the little store the Black Cloud kept and move him to his purpose. But the Black Cloud's father, the Old Sheriff, might interfere with his act of love, might interfere with the Black Cloud's purpose. Might interfere with the life of the town. As much as he loved the Old Sheriff and his love of the town, it was time to help him help the town one last time.

He sped up and away from the Old Sheriff towards the Black Cloud. He looked for something off in the woods. Oh, there it was. So beautiful and so loving of beauty. He called to it.

* * *

The Moose thought he heard something call out to him, to come and see. He was fairly sure of it, actually. He was nothing if not polite. If something called to him and asked him to come and see, he would go and see. Perhaps it was something worth seeing and, even if it wasn't, a walk would be nice.

He wandered down his lovely path, fixing little things as he went until he reached the grey hard rock. This is where something called him to visit. It asked him to wait by the side of the rock, but he saw the yellow line there. It was so lovely and none of the smoky beasts were coming. It wouldn't hurt to go and look at it up close for a moment, to admire its perfection.

He carefully walked to the yellow line. It was as lovely as ever. So lovely. He could get lost in it. He thought he might like to follow it for a while. He knew it went on as far as the grey rock did, but he did not know how far that was. For some reason, though he had always known better, he thought that today he might just like to follow it for a time. Not all the way to the end of it, but just for a time. He wasn't even sure if it was his thought. It didn't feel like his thought. But it didn't matter. The line was so lovely.

He was so focused on it as he walked that he didn't hear the smoky beast coming down the grey rock.

* * *

Ben eased his car up to 80. He wasn't in a rush to get to Gil. It was just his speed. Virginia would never let him drive so fast, especially with Gil on board. But he was alone now. She wasn't there to tell him to slow down. So he kept his foot down, thinking about how something bad was definitely going to happen and for some reason he felt like he really needed to talk to Gil about it, like Gil could somehow keep it from happening. He felt certain about that and then he saw the moose standing in the middle of the road and then he swerved the car

and then it began to roll

and then it stopped

and then he stopped feeling

and then he stopped.

* * *

He watched the Old Sheriff's car roll off the road into the tree and he was sad for him. He told the moose that it could go now and it wandered slowly, in that wonderful way those majestic creatures did, off into the forest. He smiled for a moment because he sacrificed something wonderful for the sake of the town. The town would mourn the loss of the Old Sheriff. That was for certain. They loved him and needed him and even though he stopped being Sheriff they never stopped hoping he would start being Sheriff again. But he knew better. He knew the Old Sheriff could never be Sheriff again because he knew that the town needed sacrifices but he did not want to accept it. So the Old Sheriff thought he could discover the nature of the sacrifices and stop them. But to stop the sacrifices would be to stop the town from existing.

He kept the town alive, damn it! Some damned Old Sheriff could never do for the town what he did because the

Old Sheriff was filled with duty and not love. He was filled with love for the town and would do whatever was necessary, even removing the beloved Old Sheriff. For certain, that would make the Black Cloud bigger and darker. It needed to be unleashed so the Teacher Girl could feel his love.

He pulled out his vessel's phone and made a call.

"There has been an accident just north of town."

And that was all it took. And they would come and find the Old Sheriff and they would call the Black Cloud or come and see it in person. It didn't matter. It would be unleashed.

He waited until the sirens were almost there and then he left. He needed to be near the Black Cloud when it learned. He needed to feel its love and its grief, and its grief would be strong because its love was strong, stronger than perhaps it knew. And its grief would be chaotic and its force would shock the town and the town would be on the verge of death and then he would sacrifice the Teacher Girl and the town would come right and then he could wait for another girl to love.

* * *

All Jennifer could think when she saw the car on its back against the tree was, "Aw, Ben. I kept telling you to slow down," because she knew that this was what happened. This was how he was going to end and there he was. She didn't even have to go and check the car to see if there was a chance because she knew from looking that there wasn't. People don't survive that kind of crash. Ben certainly wouldn't have survived it given that he was probably doing 80 like he always was and she was always giving him a ticket for. She should have had his license taken away, but it never seemed the right thing to do even though now it seemed like it would have been right. But it's easy to know the right thing to do after the wrong thing happens. This was wrong. Ben was doing something and now it wouldn't get done and she knew that somehow they would all suffer. She knew that what he was doing was important because it was the reason he stopped being sheriff and now that he was dead he would never be sheriff again. As she got out of her patrol car, the thought escaped her lips. "Aw, Ben, I kept telling you to slow down."

Now she had to be official. Being official meant a lot of things to her, but in the case of an accidental death on the highway, it just about always meant that she would be the one to notify the next of kin. It was something she did at least three times a year and it never got any easier and she remembered each one vividly. If there was ever a reason that she would leave law enforcement, it was telling someone that a loved one (or, quite often loved ones) had died in a less than peaceful way. It was always a long drive and then a longer walk to the door. The last time, it was Fiona Margoles who had fallen asleep at the wheel and drifted in front of a semi. The trucks always win these disputes. But it wasn't just Fiona in the car. Fiona had a three year-old daughter in the back. Her daughter's name was Meaghan. Ken Phipps, who was driving the truck, suffered a broken collarbone and a broken heart. He didn't know the woman or the child and he knew it wasn't his fault, that there was nothing he could do. And there was nothing he could do. And yet he felt the weight of their deaths upon his soul to the point that he took his own life, drunk behind the wheel of a smaller vehicle that lost a battle with a tree. Jennifer didn't catch his death, though. She didn't have to tell his wife and son that their beloved husband and father, who was already dead on the inside, wouldn't be home again. That was left to another trooper.

Jennifer had to take that long drive to see Doug Margoles. Doug Margoles who didn't live so far outside of Woodstock that when people asked him where he lived he would answer Woodstock because he liked the sound of living there. Doug Margoles who worked for years and saved for more to move his wife up to Vermont and away from the more dangerous parts of the country, up to Vermont that they both dreamed about for years and had never stopped dreaming about as being something of a paradise for them, where the seasons announced their changes with aplomb and the world seemed like it was made for people to adapt to live in as opposed a place that people adapted. Doug Margoles who watched her make that long walk up the path from the driveway through the screen door and was swallowed up whole by grief even before she said how sorry she was and that his wife and daughter probably didn't suffer much because they could never suffer as much as he did or as Ken Phipps did. They were done suffering right away, but some kept right on suffering. Some couldn't handle it and drank themselves into a tree. Doug couldn't imagine Vermont without Fiona. He couldn't imagine life without her and Meaghan. And not too long after he saw to their funerals and blankly received the condolences of people who may have suffered their own losses but could never really quite understand his pain and lack of understanding that after everything he had done to make the world beautiful and safe for his family that they could be ripped from his life without so much as a "Goodbye" and "I love you." And not too long after he watched the food that people brought him to eat rot on the counter because he didn't care if food rotted because rot was all that was left in the world for him. Not too long after that, he wandered out into this place that he dreamed of that ended up a nightmare and ended his life there.

Jennifer knew Ben's next of kin all too well and wished that she was not the first there who would have to tell Gil his father was dead. She also knew it would be unfair to ask anyone else to do it because she knew him all too well and he would need something like a friendly face because he would blame himself in that way that he blamed himself for every bad thing that happened to those around him and the world around him. Gil wouldn't be like Doug Margoles, though. He expected the worst and when it came, it only served to cement his beliefs about himself. Strangely, even in all that darkness, he was still always a bit cheerful in his pained kind of way, as if even all of the bad things that seemed to happen around him and to him were just things that happened and there was no reason to get to down about them. She knew that Gil would blame himself for Ben's death, but he would also survive it. There were others in town who would take it much worse because they had been so hopeful that Ben would come to his senses and take his rightful place in Sheriff Tom's overbig shoes. Jennifer was one of those. So was Gil. She was sure that Gil would mourn the work his father did not finish and most likely feel some kind of filial obligation to take up his father's sword and fight his fight. Or he might just record it as part of the town's long history of tragic events that he kept in his head or some set of journals some place. Gil would take the death well because it was no less than he expected. Still and all, Jennifer had no desire to deliver the news. But, then again, she never did and did anyway.

She approached Ben's car. Although she was certain of what she would find there, she had to officially look and make her report. She heard another car approach and hoped it would be Sheriff Tom but knew it would be Deputy Steve and that would make this worse. She tried not to look up and instead looked in the car and saw what she expected to see which confirmed the worst and also that Ben probably didn't suffer much. She heard the footsteps approaching and knew it was Deputy Steve who could never fail to make a bad day worse.

* * *

As Deputy Marsters approached the State Trooper who stood at the accident scene, he thought this day had just become a whole lot worse.. He had a very bad feeling. Some said he had no real instincts… that he just kind of held on to the book and went by it and couldn't "intuit." But he had bad feelings and as a cop, he respected them. He had a bad feeling when he got the call and seeing her face, he knew his bad feeling was more than that now. For all of the problems he had with Sheriff Ben as of late, he couldn't believe he was gone. It wasn't right.

Verify. "Is it…"

The Trooper looked up at him. She never gave him the time of day unless it was official. She was working hard to stay official so she wouldn't have to share even a moment of sympathetic loss with him. Bitch.

"Deputy Marsters, could you secure the scene? I need to go tell Gil…I mean the next of kin." There was almost a crack in there somewhere where she was maybe able to see him as human. She was on the verge of crying and he thought he might offer a shoulder but then didn't. She didn't want it of him and wouldn't accept it if he did. At the very least, she was the only one who didn't call him Deputy Steve and treated him like a cop, so he would do what she wanted.

"Yeah. You go and do that, Officer Kennisaw. I'll handle things here." She nodded and headed toward her cruiser. He turned back to Ben's car. He hated that Ben was dead, but maybe now that he was gone, people would stop thinking of that little idiot as a placeholder until Ben found his right mind and became sheriff again. Maybe they'd can the little idiot and ask Steven to be sheriff the way he should have been after Ben left.

He smiled a little bit at that. Just a little.

* * *

As Jennifer got into her cruiser, she checked the mirror and she could have sworn she saw that asshole deputy prick smiling as he looked at the wreck. Asshole prick must be thinking about how he can be sheriff now. Everything you ever wanted. Right, Deputy? She even considered that he had something to do with it but he loved the idea of being a cop so much that if he even thought of committing a crime, he'd arrest himself. She knew that even if Sheriff Tom stepped down, the people of Stansbury would take a good hard look around for anyone other than Deputy Steven Marsters to be their new sheriff. People just didn't like the guy. They didn't have to and he could be good at his job, but no one wanted the asshole who was good at his job to be the guy in charge.

Still out loud and now with the kind of feeling she didn't like to show while she was wearing a uniform. "Aw, Ben, I kept telling you to slow down."

She pulled out of sight of the accident and then stopped her car in the road and wept for the loss of the man she wished was her father. But she knew she had to visit Ben's real child. As much as she needed to simply sit and cry for Ben, her needs would have to wait until she could sit somewhere quietly off-duty and get good and sloppy drunk. Her needs could wait until then so she stopped crying and reminded herself that she had a job that Ben would have wanted her before any others to do and put the car back in gear.

Gil's shop wasn't too far from the accident, which made it worse because she somehow knew that Ben was on his way to see his son. Still, the drive was far too long for such a short distance. She parked her cruiser in front of the store and looked inside. Gil was in there fiddling with his little toy and talking to Will Kurtz. He had that weird combination of comfortable and melancholy that made you sad for him in some way even when he was smiling at you and joking with you. She looked up in the mirror at herself and saw an unkempt girl with eyes swollen red from crying and knew that he would know before she even walked the long walk to his door. Somehow, they always knew.

* * *

Gil knew something was off with the world for a little bit now, but he put it aside. Something was always off somewhere and he couldn't take responsibility for all of it. Instead, he'd just keep on trying to figure out why the stupid trebuchet wouldn't work right. "So for some reason, no matter what adjustments I make, the thing won't hit that one stupid model. I'm pretty much done with the whole campaign at this point."

Kurtz shook his head slowly and stared that intense stare. Gil looked away for a moment and caught his little moose sentry giving him the same stare. Et tu, Moose? Et tu? Back to Kurtz, who had this strange little smile on his face. Something Gil hadn't seen in a very long time, since before the attack in any case. Since then, his friend had not been what one might call inclined towards levity.

"What is it, Will?"

"I scratched him today. He is wounded. He can be wounded." Kurtz looked back towards the broken old model that stood despite Gil's best efforts. "'Tis time, Gil. I know 'tis time." For some reason, Kurtz almost looked sane.

"Are you sure? I've never seen so much as a chip off that thing."

"I am certain, Gil. So....I need to make a request of thee." Here it comes.

"Of course." And…

"Could you see fit to travel to another domain this evening?" There it was. Kurtz understood Gil's luck and wanted it nowhere near the bridge tonight if there was even a possibility that it was somehow vulnerable. As much as Gil would love to be there to see it go down, he also knew that he would definitely prove a liability for his friendly knight.

"As you wish, Sir William." He bowed a little towards his friend just as State Trooper Jennifer Julia Kennisaw graced his store with her presence. He was about to make a snide comment to her, just something playful enough to get a rise, but then he saw her eyes. Something there that wasn't normally there. Sadness? Pain. The worst. "Dad?" The word slipped from his mouth and he knew.

She nodded and he knew if she had to say anything her careful mask would crack even more than it already had.

"Jen…how?" But he knew. Dad drove too fast. "Dad drove too fast?"

She nodded again. "He's just down the road if…you…want…"

He went to her and held her not because he needed it but because she did. If there was one person who loved his father without question, it was Jennifer. His father reciprocated in his own way. There was certainly more of a bond between them than there ever was with Gil. All they had together was their obsessions with Stansbury's curse. Beyond that, they had barely spoken about much since Gil got back from Alaska. "It's okay, Jen. I don't need to see. It wouldn't do him or me any good."

He always had issues with the old man and knew that at some point the speed would get him. He told his father on more than one occasion that the speed would get him but his dad would always repeat his little mantra, "A good car wants to go 80. Who am I to keep it from what it wants?" And then he would laugh at himself because he knew what an idiot he was. It was like he was chasing Gil's mother and hoping that one day he would find her on the road somewhere.

"I hope he found her." Gil smiled a little at the thought. It was a good thought and he would keep it.

"Who?" He looked up at Jen.

"Mom."

"Oh. Okay then." She signaled that the hug was over and he let her go. "Well...Gil. Let me know if there's anything I can do for you, okay?"

"How about date sometime?" He tried to laugh but it hurt a little too much.

She tried to laugh as well, but it didn't come out right. "Um, I don't think so, Gil. I'll go and let Shelley know." And she left and she wasn't quite as sad and neither was he.

"I am very sorry to hear of your father's death, Gil. He was always good to me." Kurtz. Gil turned back to the knight and saw his old friend for the first time in a long time. There was Will, crying those tears that hadn't come to Gil yet. Gil didn't know if they would ever come that way. Maybe it hadn't sunk in yet or maybe he spent so long waiting for it to come that now that it was real, that his dad was gone...it just felt so damned inevitable that Gil wanted to scream at the universe that good people like his father should have better lives and quieter deaths. For all of the good his father seemingly did, did he really do anything other than maintain the town? Did he make it better or did he just keep it from getting worse? Did he even do that? The town always seemed to do a pretty damned good job of keeping itself together even before his dad came along to stand his watch. People felt better maybe when he was in charge, but what did that really matter in the end when tragedy would keep hitting and then people would keep moving on with their lives. So old Sheriff Ben had gone and quit and left the town watch to Tom because he knew that in the end it didn't matter who watched the little things come and go. The big things kept on happening and he thought that he could change that. But he couldn't. It wasn't in him and he knew it and he kept on driving like a bat out of hell maybe hoping that he would crash and die and not have to be so damned responsible for everyone and everything. He did this to himself and Gil couldn't cry for him just yet even though his crazy delusional friend could stop being crazy and delusional for a moment to feel the death and mourn it.

"Yeah, Will. I'm sorry, too." Was he?

Will left the building and there was the knight again. "Your father was an excellent constable and he will be missed. He would also understand that the enemy is at hand and he is weakened and it is time to strike. When I go into battle tonight, I will carry a token of his to deliver to the dread lord. I am sorry to repeat the request after this news, but the chances for success still depend upon you not being here."

Of course. "As you wish, Sir William. I think I'll close up shop and get the hell out of dodge right now. Can't say if I'll be back anytime soon, you know?"

"You must wander as you will. You have my thanks." And with that, Kurtz turned and left the shop, walking with a purpose that Gil found admirable considering that it was a doomed quest. Even if the bridge was damaged or destroyed or nothing happened at all, it would all still just keep on happening and happening. At this moment, Gil didn't have a bit of romantic thought in him. It had been spent at 80 miles per hour and then a stop too soon.

Gil opened the register and took what little money was there. Enough to gas up the tank a couple of times and maybe spend some time in Buffalo or Albany making some more and moving on from there. Whatever. As much as he loved Stansbury, he couldn't stay right now, the way he always had to go away for a time because all that love just made the pain of knowing everything he knew all that much worse. It wasn't going to stop. It wasn't going to stop. It wasn't going to stop. He knew this at the core of his being and he knew the signs that something bad was coming and he didn't want to be there when it did. It could go and get horrible without his witnessing it and recording it in his book of all the shitty things that had happened to Stansbury. He didn't even take a second look at the messed up bridge. He just grabbed his keys and left, leaving that little sign in the window that let people know the shop wouldn't be open to sell apple cider donuts and maple syrup that day, locking the door and not looking back.

* * *

He could see the Black Cloud locking up to leave from where he parked the vessel's car just beyond the Black Cloud's little store in that little spot in the woods he always used that always seemed to be there just for him and always seemed to go away when he was gone. He loved that nature opened up for him and bent to his purpose. It told him that he was doing the work as was meant to be...that his love for the town and all his sacrifices were good and right and he was blessed. He lost track of how long he had been doing this. It wasn't important really. He knew of time as the seasons passed and days became nights. And he knew when he was needed and when to wait and watch.

He watched the Police Girl go into the Black Cloud's little store and he watched her leave and he watched the Strange One leave and then he watched the Black Cloud leave.

And there it was. Now the spring was wound up tight and all he had to do was let it uncoil itself.

He got out of the car and opened the trunk and looked at the Teacher Girl and wished she could be as happy as she had been before. He knew that the Counter Girls and now this Teacher girl could never be as happy serving the town as they were before the town called him to them. He thought he understood for a moment and then that moment passed. He told them how they were part of something wonderful and yet they never found the joy in it that they should have. To contribute to the life of the town, it was their last best gift. And now it was the Teacher Girl's turn.

He looked down at her and smiled.

* * *

Mary Beth looked up at John and saw that strange smile on his face that he never smiled before and knew that he was going to kill her. She could struggle or scream, but no one would hear through the gag and she was bound up too tightly to move. She was going to be killed by this monster that she never knew was a monster and she didn't know why except that victims of monsters never really knew why. He told her in a voice that wasn't his that she should be joyous, that her glory would be the town's salvation. But he was a monster and he was going to kill her and she didn't understand how her death would mean anything other than the end of her life. It didn't make any sense to her.

That's what really bothered her, even more than the fact that she was going to die. She always worked to make sense of the world, to see the way things worked and she loved teaching because she thought she understood something about the world and when she could give that understanding to someone else, it was like another light going on and she turned it on, which gave her a purpose that seemed far more valuable than to be the victim of some monster. The one thing she was never able to grasp was why there had to be monsters. Not like the ones in movies. She didn't need those because she knew that there were real ones out there who did so much evil on the earth and people saw them doing this evil and some stood by and watched and others helped and others were too afraid to stop it. And those were the monsters with public faces and she thought there might be a reason for them that she could sort out just a little but her mind wasn't twisted enough to make those connections and she was glad of that. The ones that nobody knew about until it was too late, like this one that was going to kill her, she couldn't even begin to understand. He could tell her everything and every reason and still he would be unknowable because it could never occur to her to take someone from their lives, their happy lives, her happy life and take her from her love and take her and…she was going to die and she didn't understand.

For a moment, she saw the road through the trees and saw Gil there by his car. If only he could see her he would at least know the monster had her. But she knew he wouldn't. She couldn't move, couldn't make a sound and the monster had her and she was going to die. All she could do was try to send Gil a mental message. "Look at me!" She yelled it in her head and even though she didn't really believe it would work, she hoped that it actually might and that he would turn his head just for a second and see her.

* * *

Gil turned for a moment and he would have looked out towards the bridge as he always did, but he was on autopilot set for out of town. He told his body to get in the car and go and he didn't want to think about anything, not even the leaving. He was aware that he was in the car and that he was driving…that he was leaving. But he didn't want to think about anything else right now. Years before, when he had been travelling, he learned this trick of entering a kind of meditative state where there was just the physical act of driving and the noise of the road and nothing more, nothing in his head to contemplate because if he thought too hard about everything that was going on, he might lose that perfect focus on the driving that he allowed his body to have. He thought of it as becoming one with the machine, that he was just the thing that helped it to go and he would play his part and he and the machine would get to where he needed to be and when he got there he could find some job that allowed him to become a part of some other machine and not think about anything while his body did that. It was only when he stopped doing something that his brain would come alive and he would think. Right now he couldn't afford to think because then he wouldn't be able to do anything else.

He wondered if his father needed the speed to set his mind in motion and he thought of his father and his mind drifted from driving to death and he knew his father was going to die and he was waiting for his father to die and there was no good reason for that because his father was healthy and took care of himself and removed himself from the stress of the Job and of the expectations of the town and no one but Gil knew what he was doing and so he could do it without anyone butting in or asking how he was doing or wondering why it was taking him so long to do it and then he would feel all that stress all over again and he would start to drink or eat too much or drink too much coffee and that would have killed him just as quickly because his father couldn't stand to not be doing the right thing because it was what he was born to do and Gil knew that he died doing something important and something noble which was something that Gil could never quite do or never quite be because no matter what he did it always came out badly and even though he liked people and he was a good person it didn't matter because he was cursed and his curse hit people like a ton of bricks and even though they might survive his presence they could never really be successful in what they were doing around him and maybe if he had always stayed away from Stansbury his dad wouldn't have crashed into the tree because his dad had been so close to the store and to him and it must have been his curse that killed his dad and anyone else that died in the town while he was there was probably his victim too and he should probably just find a mountain somewhere and build a cabin and live there and not see people anymore and that way no one would ever die because of him again but he loved to be around people too much and he loved to hear their stories because there was life in them and not everyone he met was hurt or killed or suffered he hoped because there were so many people he had met along the way who were really wonderful and didn't deserve to be a victim of this thing that followed him and he could never get rid of and maybe it was because of the town and the bridge and maybe it was something worse but he never knew except to know that it was a real thing and it was a part of him and he wished he could make it go away…

Gil barely noticed as his car rammed into the phone tower.

* * *

Denise barely noticed the crash outside of her house. She had been thinking about going down to Charlie's Grill to see if Danny Smith was tending bar. He sometimes worked the bar there when Charlie was out and even though Charlie wasn't out that often, when Danny was there, he was always really nice to her. He would pour her a sloe gin fizz. She started drinking sloe gin fizzes when she heard the name of the drink in a movie and thought that it sounded like just about the best thing ever and even though it wasn't the best thing, it was still kind of sweet and fizzy, like a soda with some kick. So she decided that it would be her thing, her drink, because it made her smile just to say it. Danny would tell her how nice she looked or pay her some other compliment. She knew Danny didn't have a thing for her, but he was nice and nice to her, so that was good enough sometimes. Maybe some other guy would see Danny being nice to her and paying her a compliment and think that she was worth being nice to and paying a compliment or even just being a little bit interested in and might ask her out or just want to sit and talk. Right now, all she really wanted to do was have a nice conversation with someone who was a man and just a little bit interested in her. She wouldn't even think about their wedding right away.

When the cell phone tower that looked like a pine tree crashed through the roof of her house, Denise barely had time to stop thinking about her wedding to the nice young man who she was going to meet tonight at Charlie's. She barely had time to look up as her ceiling caved in on her. She hoped that Ivy was outside and would be okay. She loved Ivy.

* * *

Ivy LOVED Denise and it was her job to PROTECT her. Ivy looked up from scouting the perimeter of Denise's property when she heard the loud noise. DANGER! She starting shouting as loudly as she could as she quickly bolted back to the house, back through her door to Denise who she LOVED and who LOVED her. She could smell SMOKE which meant FIRE and it was not where it was supposed to be it its place but it was coming from Denise's place which meant that DENISE WAS IN DANGER! She shouted even louder as she ran to Denise's door which was closed. She pawed and scratched at the door to get to Denise, to make Denise open the door so Ivy could save her from the DANGER. But Denise didn't come and Ivy could smell Denise in the room and could smell the SMOKE in the room which meant there was FIRE in the room and she could smell Denise's BLOOD in the room but she could not hear Denise breathing and she knew that Denise was in DANGER and something was WRONG and she LOVED Denise and couldn't save her and she started crying and scratching at the door because maybe Denise would wake up and come and open the door or maybe she could scratch her way through the door and she had to keep trying because she LOVED her.

She shouted even louder.

* * *

The dog's barking broke through Gil's stupor. Gil had been somewhat stunned by the sudden appearance of the airbag in his face. It took a moment for him to realize that it had deployed after he rammed his car into the tree that was not a tree and another moment to realize that he had knocked it over onto the house that the barking was coming from...not only barking but smoke.

"It's all me."

And he was out of his car and running into the house because it was his fault and there was someone in there and even if they lost their house because of him he hoped that would be all they lost. But he knew it would be more than that. He tried to get out of town before he could do anymore. He tried and failed and that did not surprise him and he didn't even know why he was trying to get into the house because he could not succeed at saving anyone in there. His world just didn't work that way and yet he went into the house because there was nothing else to do and if he died doing it at least he wouldn't be there to destroy people's lives anymore.

There was a lot of smoke in the house and it was hard to see and even harder to breath. He hated smoke and knew it was a bad idea for him of all people to go charging into a house full of it. But he followed the dog's whimpering and found her...it was Ivy and that meant this was Denise's house and he could feel the heat burning through the door from the room that Denise must be in given the claw marks on the door and Ivy still struggling despite the smoke to get to her owner. Gil knew that there was no way for him to get to Denise and there was no way she was going to make it out of that room. He also knew that the one thing she loved more than anything else in the world was her dog and if he could at least save the dog he would have done something for her. So as hard as it was, he got his good arm around the dog, who was barely conscious enough to give a protest whimper, and tried to wrap his damned prosthetic around her as well, but that didn't do much at all. And he stopped thinking and he started dragging the dog as best he could. He couldn't see anything and didn't even know if he was going in the right direction, but he just kept telling his body to go and to get Ivy out of the house that was coming down all around him. He wished there wasn't all this smoke. He hated the smell of smoke.

* * *

Roger smelled smoke, but he thought it was another side effect of all his damned pills. He hated taking all these damned pills his damned doctor kept prescribing and that damned pharmacist kept filling and his damned wife kept picking up and putting in the little days and nights of the week pill machine dispenser that would ring its damned chime every twelve hours rain or shine to tell him that it was time to take all the damned pills that supposedly kept him alive but had so many damned side effects that life didn't hardly seem worth living. His mouth was always dry no matter how much damned water he drank. His damned joints always ached. His damned food tasted like ash. He was either constipated or had diarrhea all the damned time. He had gas both damned ways and his damned gout was constantly flaring up even though he took all those damned pills to keep the damned gout from flaring up. It just wasn't worth it anymore.

"Damn it all to hell, Stephanie! It's just not worth it anymore!"

She wasn't listening to him. She was sticking her face in the window and talking on the damned phone and not paying him any attention. She never paid him any damned attention except to make him take the damned pills. He wondered why she even bothered to keep him alive because she never wanted to hear what he had to say or cared about what he wanted to do. Their whole damned existence together had come down to her not so gentle damned reminders to take his damned pills. It didn't make any sense. She didn't even really talk to him anymore. She used to talk to him. Now she talked at him. She ordered him around like a five year old and punished him like a five year old when he tried to act like a 75 year old which, to her, was not that far off a damned five year old when it came to how he should be treated.

"What's out the damned window that's so damned important, Stephanie?" Because if he said her name enough, maybe she turn her damned head around to answer him.

"Shush up, Roger. I'm trying to call the fire department. Denise Drabos' house is on fire and Gil Hamilton just went on in like a one-armed fool to save her and the cell phone isn't getting any kind of signal."

"Oh."

He would have brought up that it was her damned fool idea to get rid of the old house phone and just rely on that damned cell phone that she took with her when she went into town leaving him with no damned way to call anyone if he had a damned problem like a heart attack or a stroke or any one of the damned side effects of the medication. He would have brought it up but she probably would punish him in some little way for backtalking her so he didn't bring it up.

He also didn't let her know that he wasn't going to sit by and let a couple of good folks burn without seeing if he could do something about it. It wasn't neighborly. So while she kept pushing the damned buttons on a phone that obviously wasn't going to work because the damned tower tree thing had crashed down on the house, he ran across the street to do something. As he opened the front door of the house, smoke came pouring out at him and he realized that this was a damned fool idea. But he was going to do this because he had to do something, because someone had to do something and no one else was around to do it. And he was tired of doing nothing. For years he had done nothing but take pills to stay alive in a life that had become a series of days doing nothing waiting to die. In any case, he figured he was taking at least one damned pill to protect him from all the damned smoke. Everything tasted like ash anyway.

Roger let the smoke pour out as he went into the house.

* * *

Stephanie looked up from her phone and out the window and saw the smoke engulf Roger as he went into the house.

"Oh. Roger, no." It came out of her mouth without sound because she was unable to breath as she watched the house collapse into smoke and flames. She tried to catch her breath, but it was lost to her. She thought about trying to catch it again and realized that she didn't want it anymore and she let it go as she let go.

* * *

Gil did not let go of Ivy even as the heat wave from the collapse of the house knocked him over. Not that he needed much help. All things considered, the fact that he actually made it out of the house alive seemed to go against all reason. Even more unreasonable was that he managed to drag a 60-pound Collie dog with him and she still seemed to be alive, if barely. If it weren't for the fact that he was responsible for the situation, he might have felt a little pride at his heroism and the fact that he didn't lose another limb in the process. At least his father wouldn't be there to chide him for chasing danger. Some benefit.

"You're an ass, Gil."

And there was nothing but the blaze and smoke and the dog's shallow breathing and nothing more. No sirens. He felt like there should be more going on. He wondered where all the people were because usually people came to see a fire. But it had hardly burned long enough to draw a crowd and it wasn't like this was the most populated area. Still, Stephanie Hirson lived across the street and while she wasn't a busybody, at the very least she would have called someone to come. He had to assume that she would call someone. He had to get the dog back to town. It was all he could do for Denise to make sure that Ivy was okay.

After a moment, he got up and went over to her old red truck. He knew Denise kept a hide-a-key under her back fender and sure enough, there it was. After struggling to get Ivy into the truck, he got in. He wasn't supposed to be in town because Kurtz needed him out but he was responsible for what happened to Ivy and it wasn't like Kurtz could really do more than act out one of his fantasies anyway and nothing would come of it. The bridge would still be there and Kurtz would still be crazy. Saving the dog was more important. Right now, it was all he had to hold onto because he was on the edge of not wanting to hold onto anything anymore.

This time he started the car and began driving back into town on autopilot. He had done about as much thinking as possible and he needed to rest his mind before it broke completely and he ended up like Kurtz. So he let his mind go and let his body become part of the truck and he headed back into town.

* * *

The Silver Knight saw Denise Drabos' red truck heading back into town as he crossed the road. After he left Gil with instructions to leave town, he went back to his keep to pick up his arms and do battle with the Black Knight this one last time. He recognized the distress on Lord Stansbury's Abomination and knew that there was only this one moment in time to finish it. If he was not successful, he would be lost and evil will have won the day. In his heart he could not believe that evil would prevail in this battle. He did not believe in that kind of world. In his world, good must overcome many hardships but in the end, it would reign victorious. He knew himself to be an avatar of goodness and he had been picked to fight this battle. He had been picked to do battle. He had been given the ability to know the evil's true form and he was firm in his belief that his righteous victory was at hand.

So one last time he made his way through the forest towards the bridge. Armed with his axe and one hundred pounds of black powder and nothing more, not even his armor for if his victory was at hand, it did not matter if he survived and if it was not, no armor could protect him. He saw the bridge ahead and it seemed strangely calm, as if it was just a bridge and nothing more and it was just a lake and nothing more. But he knew better. He just hoped that the dark lord's weakness was enough for this last campaign as he pulled his deadly cargo down to the lake.

* * *

As he slipped down into the water of the lake with the Teacher Girl in tow, he caught a glimpse of the Strange One coming towards the bridge with what must have been some kind of weapon. He might have worried about the Strange One and his explosives if he did not sense the Black Cloud returning to Stansbury. Oh, the joy of things moving with purpose and the love he felt knowing he moved with his. The love of the bridge and of the town and he knew that even this Strange One who felt the love of the bridge and mistook it for darkness would come to see the joy of this day.

He swam quietly under the bridge with the Teacher Girl floating behind him. Oh the joy she would feel when she took her place at the heart of the bridge and the heart of the town. Her pure love would overflow and protect Stansbury until it was time to for her to be replaced as she now replaced the last Counter Girl. He swam under the bridge until he found that Special Place that his creator made. He felt the symbols carved into the wood and moved his hand along them as he chanted the words he had so many times before with so many different voices, so many vessels who gave up their flesh so that he could protect the town. He could not remember the last time let alone the first. He felt the wood grow warm beneath his hand as the Special Place began to open. What love was left from the last Counter Girl spilled over him and it was ecstasy and he remembered this feeling from the last time or the time before or the time before and it was the love draining away and he knew that he must complete his work and set the Teacher Girl in place because even as the love from the last Counter Girl faded and even though the Black Cloud loomed over Stansbury, the bridge was without love and the town was without love and at this moment it was still possible that somehow the Strange One could destroy everything. Even now, as the Special Place opened, he heard him overhead and felt worry for the very first time. That amused him.

* * *

Tod was a little amused by Kurtz. "You're doing it the wrong way." He kind of smirked when he said it.

Kurtz looked up at him and fear crept through his eyes. There was something wrong with the kid today. He didn't quite have that way about him. But it didn't really matter. He was going to kill himself with all that black powder and Tod couldn't sit by and watch and even though he swore not to destroy anything ever again, he knew that if Will killed himself and he stood by and let him, it would be worse. They could always build a new damned bridge if they wanted one over this lake so badly. They couldn't put the kid back together again if he blew himself all to hell. So when Tod saw him carting all that black powder down to the lake, he took a good hard look at his oath and realized that it only served him. If he could help Will Kurtz blow the bridge, maybe it would help him heal and then maybe Tod could heal as well. He decided that he wasn't really destroying anything at all. He was helping. He was rebuilding. He could live with that. So he went back to his cabin and gathered his blasting supplies.

"If you do it that way, you'll kill yourself and the bridge will still be here. Why don't you let me help?"

Kurtz nodded and smiled grimly.

* * *

He smiled a bit as the Special Place was fully open now. It was always joyous as he watched the shell of the last Counter Girl dissolve away into the waters of the lake. The town would miss her love, but he felt the love from the Teacher Girl the way you feel the warmth from the sun after a long cold rain and knew the town would thrive with her at its heart. He began to chant the words quietly. They did not need to be loud. They just needed to be right and there was no one who knew them as he did and no one who could say them with his joy in service. He never stopped chanting as he carefully moved the Teacher Girl into the place where she would truly live.

* * *

Mary Beth knew that this cold dark place under the bridge was where she would die. She heard him say the last of his words. She could tell they were the last of his words by the strange satisfaction that he voiced with the last one, as if he was breathing life into something that only he knew. As the last word faded, she felt a pull from deep within herself, as if somehow his words actually meant something more than the crazy mutterings of a madman.

"You are the new love." He spoke to her as he cut her throat. "You are the new heart."

As the world closed around her, she felt something worse than death. She wished she could scream this one last time as she understood utterly and terribly that she would not die, not just yet and she wished she would. But there was nothing but silence as she felt the love that was not love that would slowly devour her soul.

* * *

The Silver Knight watched in silence as that demon…this person, Tod, finished his work. This was now their work. The Evil wounded the both of them in some way and although the quest was his, he was not greedy and he did not need glory. Victory, honorable and shared, was victory still.

But something seemed wrong. Not with Tod. But something else. He knew how this place felt and he knew its magic and he worried that something had happened, that the moment had slipped away from him and the Abomination was no longer vulnerable.

"Tod... I mean, Squire Tod. I believe we have lost our advantage. I believe we must retreat." Not cowardly. A good knight knows when to pull back and reassess.

"But Will...Sir William. I know my business here. I've done it right this time and there's no way this thing will stand." He seemed confident, but Will had seen such confidence before, had possessed such confidence before and had met defeat at the hands of the Black Knight. This was no longer the time.

"I'm afraid it will."

"Oh, yes. You can feel it, too, can't you, Strange One? You can feel the *love*." It was not the voice of the Black Knight. It was someone he knew but not that someone somehow. And the way he said *love* made it sound like a plague. He turned around and saw the figure there at the other end of the bridge.

"Let's get some distance and blow this thing, Will." Tod sounded scared and Will didn't blame him. All at once he needed to be somewhere else, but he could not move. All at once, it seemed like all those thoughts he had about quests and chivalry and being the Silver Knight vanished into the ether and he was just Will Kurtz again, stuck on the bridge and haunted by the demons there. All those stories that Gil told about Lord Stansbury and the black arts and his curse and here he was and there was a real demon staring back at him out of the eyes of his friend, John. He had to get out of here now.

The John-figure chuckled. "The *love* surrounds us now and it's spreading back to the town. You can feel it, can't you, Will? Teacher Girl had so much *love* to give."

Will turned and ran.

* * *

Tod watched Will become himself as he ran away. He didn't understand much of what was happening, but he felt the power of this place before and it left him empty and now he felt that power again and he would not run and he was not afraid of that person at the other end of the bridge. Will was running away, but Tod would stay and take this person down.

He drew his 9mm pistol and sighted carefully. He was always a good shot. He had been trained how to take this shot and he would do his duty.

The figure chuckled and he didn't give it a chance to speak and he fired his weapon like he had been taught to do.

Maybe the wind shifted…

Just a bit of bad luck…

He missed his mark ever so slightly and set it all off.

VII

Jennifer sat in her squad car and drank her coffee as she filled out a request to be transferred to another location. She couldn't do Stansbury duty anymore. She had been doing it because she felt like it was her town and she was helping to protect it but she couldn't protect it. Nobody could protect it. Ben couldn't protect it. He tried and tried for his whole life almost and then he died and all the others died and it kept on happening and now she was supposed to what? To be like Ben? To carry on and try and try only to see another bit of tragedy rock the town and all that you do and that you've done means nothing when in just brief moments it all comes undone. She couldn't keep it safe. She couldn't keep people sane. And it was worse here because these were her people and this was her town and she had always known them all and she knew that if she stuck around they would start looking to her for comfort and safety and she couldn't really do anything at all for them. She couldn't be like Ben and put on a smile and pretend that everything was under control with people she knew.

She could do it with strangers, though. They didn't need to know much more than she was Officer Kennisaw.

Swanton looked promising. It was a beautiful country town with the culture and charm of Vermont. At least that's what their website said and in some ways it sounded like Stansbury except that it was way up north away from Stansbury and as far as she knew there were no haunted covered bridges or history of tragic events. She put Swanton down on her form as the center of an area she would like to patrol. It was a little closer to Burlington and just over the border not too far from Montreal where she knew a girl who she liked to see from time to time and maybe she could see her a little more often than that.

She just wanted to protect people and know it meant something at the end of the day. At the end of yesterday, nothing seemed to matter. It was all just chaos and entropy and it would always be that way here no matter what anyone did. Maybe it was time for people to just stop pretending that it was all okay and pack up shop and go. There was one shop that needed packing up more than any and as much as she thought that in all the madness of the last day no one would bat an eye if that damned pharmacy went up in flames and that reclusive vampire bastard inside went up with it, it just wasn't in her to do it. She could never prove anything she ever thought and to deliver a death sentence to someone just because you thought he was a cancerous life-sucking fiend was just not something she could do. But she wished someone would. She would gladly toast marshmallows over his corpse.

But the town. The damned town. It would go on. All these old towns up here went on. Swanton was going on and she hoped she could keep it safer because she couldn't do anything for Stansbury anymore.

Jennifer put her car in gear and headed back to her station, slowing down a little as she passed the Winnebago to send the nice couple inside the all the good fortune she could offer. She hoped they would find a friendlier destination for their next stop.

* * *

Marisol paused for a moment to watch the State Police car pass by and then looked back to her map of New England to see where she wanted to go next before she programmed the GPS with their destination. She never liked maps that extended beyond a region because they gave her too many things to think about, too many places she might want to visit all at once. She used to have a map of the world on the wall of her cubicle at her job managing the offices of a small group of attorneys in Miami who shared the offices but were not really a firm. They just found it convenient and cheaper to have one office with two secretaries and one office manager that they occasionally forgot was an office manager and treated like a secretary and sometimes like a cleaning lady and always like someone who was somehow a lesser being than themselves because she only had an associate's degree in accounting from Miami Dade College and didn't attend some high and mighty state school like the U of F which was mostly notable for inventing Gatorade as far as she was concerned. She was sure they did other useful things aside from inventing tasty sports drinks and playing sports well, but she wasn't really all that interested in it or in the people she worked for because they were mostly not very interested in her except for the things she was paid to do for them and the things they could get her to do that she was not specifically paid to do but did anyway to make sure that she kept her job. However, they would all take the most wonderful vacations all over the world and when they would come back, she would ask them about where they had visited and then place a tack on her map of the world with a color based on whether or not she would also like to go there. Henry Dominguez, who practiced a kind of personal injury law where people would come to him if they hurt themselves at their job and he would help them make even more money for not working even if they didn't hurt themselves all that badly, liked to go on "adventures" as he called them. To him, the idea of driving around or seeing sights was, as he called it, "like death." So he went on adventures to places like Costa Rica, which seemed like a really beautiful place to go with lots of things to do and see, and he wouldn't sit on a beach and enjoy the wonder of the water. He would be off in the jungles on some kind of flying rope so that he could see the ground from the air going 35 miles per hour, which to Marisol seemed less about seeing the jungles and nature and more about flying around on a rope at 35 miles per hour and she knew there were places in the U.S. where you could do that too so she didn't understand why he would need to go all the way to Costa Rica to fly around except so he could brag about going on an adventure to someplace exotic to Marisol. She would smile and enjoy the story and think about the places he went to and ask herself if they were worthwhile aside from the adventure parts. If it was a place like Costa Rica, which seemed a nice place to drive around and see sights, she would put a green tack on it as someplace she might bring up with Rick someday. If it was ice climbing in Banff, which Henry could never seem to pronounce properly even though he had been there, that seemed like an activity in a place that was awfully cold and uncomfortable and not much fun unless you liked being awfully cold and uncomfortable, she would give it a red tack as somewhere in the world she did not have any desire to visit. She knew her limitations and, more importantly, she knew Rick's.

Rick was pretty clear after yesterday that Vermont was maybe a little too dangerous for them and if they wanted to be in the line of fire there were plenty of areas of Dade County that would do just fine for that. He didn't need to drive a few thousand miles to feel like he could be the next one to go. And she didn't disagree with him. All those poor people who died, people they met with and laughed with and made the kind of good connections she liked to think lingered on in the memories of everyone long after they were gone so that someday they might think of Miami or see a Winnebago drive by and think of Marisol and Rick and smile. But now people like that nice clerk, Gil, would think of them and remember the horrible day they drove into town and brought a hurricane with them.

So she looked at her map of New England and thought that they might avoid Salem, Massachusetts, even though she had a green tack for that one after hearing about all the fun and cheesy museums there. So many bad things had happened there and it would make her think of Stansbury and she really needed to not think of Stansbury as much as possible right now. She looked up at Maine and thought it might be nice go and look at the ocean because it was the same ocean she saw at home and she and Rick could have a lobster because he talked about eating a Maine lobster in Maine. He had this idea that they should visit places famous for their food and eat their food there so it would be authentic...he dreamed of eating arroz con pollo in Havana. That seemed like a nice thing to do. They might even look at a lighthouse or two, so long as they weren't haunted.

She didn't need any ghost stories right now either. She thought about Henry Dominguez and how he would have seen the last day as an adventure and if he had been through it all and come back to report it to her before asking her to fetch him a cup of coffee and run some copies. She would have probably put a red tack on Stansbury. She and Rick didn't need adventures. They just wanted to drive around and see things that seemed worth seeing. So she programmed the GPS for Kennebunkport because one of the presidents lived there and if they were lucky they could see him.

"It's time to go, honey."

Rick looked up from his book. "Figured out where the next stop is?"

"Kennebunkport, Maine."

"Doesn't the first Bush live there?"

"I think so. Maybe we might see him."

"Okay. So long as it's the first one. I liked him and his wife with the necklace. I'd like to take a picture with them maybe."

Rick made his production about setting himself up in his "Captain's Chair" and making all his adjustments to all of the fancy gadgets and whatnots that this machine came with that Rick had gone on and on about how much they needed every last one of them when they bought it even though she knew it was all a show and he really would have been happy without any of it - except maybe his CB…he loved yelling into that box. He started it up and the GPS gave its first instruction, which would take them out of town past the little shop and the bridge and all those places where all those people had died. He started to reprogram it for an alternate route.

"Rick. Can we…" She was looking at those little damaged bridge models that the poor dead boy made. "I think I need to give those back to Gil. I can't have... those and I don't feel right throwing them away."

He looked up at her and she could tell he really wanted to get out of town without revisiting all that pain. But he nodded anyway and left the machine alone. He pulled out of the rest area where they had parked for the night and headed back towards Gil's shop. Aside from the one deputy sitting in his squad car, there was no one else out and about. It seemed like the entire town stayed inside wishing yesterday away.

Rick sighed quietly. "I've never seen a ghost town with people still living in it."

With no more to comment on, there was only the sound of the GPS calling out where to turn and how close they were to the turn and then the turn and then how far to go before the next turn. And then the town was gone and then they saw the remains of the accident where the nice old sheriff had passed. There was nothing left there now but some caution tape wrapped around a tree and some flare scars on the road. Rick slowed down just a little to pay his respects, as he always did when they passed an accident scene. Then she could see the little shop up ahead and Gil sitting out front. There was a dog lying next to him and he scratched its head absently. Looking at him, she suddenly felt the sadness of the world and wished that they left town the other way and not looked back.

* * *

Gil just sat wishing he could have left town yesterday. He barely even noticed as Rick and Marisol pulled up. He hardly breathed a word of thank you to her condolences or in acceptance of the bridge models she laid gently next to him. He didn't think on the fact that Rick never even left the Winnebago and before it occurred to him to say something more, Marisol was gone and he had no idea how long it had been since she had come and gone. It didn't matter really and it only crossed his mind because he thought to worry for a moment that they were able to make it out of the town alive. They had come close to him and that wasn't working out very well for people. He was pretty sure he had 6 deaths on his head right now. Not that it was really his fault, but it was his curse and if he just kept his mind focused on driving then he could have made it out of town and even though Kurtz failed at least he and Tod wouldn't have died and he wouldn't have hit the tower and killed Denise and the Hirsons and it wasn't his fault really. The shit that happened to him and around him wasn't his fault and he knew that and his parents and friends always told him that and yet it always felt like it was his fault because he knew that his simple presence made things worse and he knew that if he had somehow managed to get out of town, if he had never come back to the town, things might have happened but they wouldn't have been so messy. But there was always that thing that kept him here or sucked him back. The last time he came home it was because of his arm and he thought once he figured out how to use the prosthetic he could find his way back out into the world. But that never happened like it should have.

 He looked down at the piece of plastic strapped to what was left of his arm. His dad said it served him right for being fool enough to lose it and Gil should be grateful that it was him and not someone next to him like it had been up in Alaska. Gil's dad understood that he was a walking time bomb waiting to go off on himself, but more often on someone else. He never said it, but Gil knew his dad blamed him for his mom's death. No more so than Gil, though. That was a pain that never went away. Not like his arm. He hardly thought about the pain of that anymore.

He didn't even feel it when his arm was ripped off at the elbow. That's what he always told people when they asked him if it hurt. They always assumed that it was this incredibly painful experience and they wanted to hear about the pain. Sometimes he would appease them and tell them

"Yeah, it hurt. The worst pain ever. I don't like to think about it and I still wake up screaming, it hurt so bad."

They would nod, awed, like he was some kind of hero for having suffered. They always asked if he lost his arm in The War. They wanted his loss to have meaning and losing a limb in The War seemed to be the most meaningful way to suffer such a thing. While he thought it might be easier to just say, "Yeah, I was in The War." He believed that would be a dishonor to real vets who suffered for more than a side of beef.

What they didn't want to hear. What he told them anyway, because they asked - and, really, most people didn't ask... most people tried real hard to ignore his prosthetic or just pretend it was a real arm - was the truth. He was another victim, along with millions of cows, of the slaughterhouse machine.

Gil drifted into Milwaukee. Something weird about Milwaukee – if you stand in the middle of it, you can smell the breweries and the chocolate factory and the slaughterhouses. Gil didn't know why he followed the scent of blood. At the time, he believed he would find some kind of answer in all the blood. It was a gut feeling more than anything. Plus, he heard the jobs there were easy to come by and he needed to make enough money to move to New Zealand. He believed that there was no place on the planet he would rather be than New Zealand except Stansbury – but at the time he couldn't think of going back there... as much as he loved it, loved Vermont, there was too much pain in knowing. It just seemed…peaceful. He needed peace and green grass and mountains and New Zealand had those to spare. Sure enough, he had no problem securing a job. It didn't pay well, but he was used to that. He would stick with it until he made enough to save enough for airfare. Feed Kill Chain. That was his title. Feed Kill Chain. He tried not to think about the fact that he never had a job with a more horrifying title. The job, however, was more horrifying. After the cow was knocked out by a hydraulic bolt to the head, he would quickly chain its hind legs up so a conveyor could take it to the next phase of its death where its throat would be cut. He never really had time to think about his job while he was doing it. The cows came fast. The chain came fast. He had to keep the whole thing moving and it kept moving 14 hours a day. He stopped seeing the cows as living things. He called them widgets and it was his job to keep the widgets moving. It was a factory that made meat from widgets. When he was done for the day he found a bed and slept and woke up the next day and went back to his place in the machine making meat from widgets.

On the day he lost his arm, he figured he had probably been working for 10 hours or so before it happened, before his arm became a widget for the machine to grind up and spit back out as meat. One second he was chaining the cow's hind legs for the sticker and then… nothing. No pain. He floated up over his body. Actually, floated is not really correct. He climbed a ladder and sat on a rafter over his body. He sat down and looked down on the commotion beneath him. There was so much blood it was hard to separate what was his with what was cows'. There was a small group of people gathered around him. They automatically moved him out of the way so a replacement could keep the machine running… keep processing the widgets.

A woman's voice spoke next to him. "Think they'll try to get you your arm back?"

He looked away from the crowd around his body and was somewhat unsurprised to see an angel sitting on the rafter. She was somewhat cherubic…had a halo, wings, white robe. The whole deal. Her blue eyes glowed a little, but that might have just been a reflection from her golden halo.

"Not really," he replied. "I'm sure it's been processed by now. They move pretty fast around here and no one really thinks about what it is they are butchering."

"Hell isn't this bad." She glared at Gil. "Hell is not this bad. It's a good thing you have to stop."

"Why do I have to stop?"

"You've only got one arm now."

Gil looked down and made sure this was true. He thought he should be in some kind of pain. "I should be in some kind of pain."

"I'm keeping you from it. You have enough suffering in your life. You will have more. You don't need this."

"What do I need?"

"You need to go home." She glared at him again. There was something about her eyes. "You have to go home."

Gil did not know why she was making this demand. He would accept all the pain in the world before going back to Stansbury.

"You don't have a choice. Go." Something about her eyes.

"Mr. Hamilton?" Gil woke up and looked up at the doctor.

"Yes?"

"I'm afraid we couldn't find your arm."

"I know."

And so he went home and it seemed the whole reason he had to come home was to be there so people could suffer around him and die around him and he could be there to witness it all and record it all. And to what end? To what end? So that when people came to town he could be the friendly ghoul and they would get a good scary story about some bastard warlock who had made this terrible thing and ever since the people of the town had been trapped in this cycle of death and uneasy amnesia? Was he there to warn off folks who upon seeing this seemingly ideal small Vermont town might think that it is a good place to call home and be sucked into the grip of this horrible cursed place?

He looked down at Kurtz's little busted up models and a laugh came out of him. Ivy looked up at him weakly and chuffed. Chiding him for his inappropriate mirth? She whined a little and went back to sleep. Despite her close proximity to Gil, she survived. Perhaps she was immune to his plague of misfortune. He hoped so because she was his charge now. They wanted to take her from him but he would have none of it and, strangely, neither would the dog. They said she would probably have a little lasting damage from the smoke and so she would never be whole either. For better or worse, she bound herself to him and they would suffer together.

"What do you think, Ivy? Should we go and see?"

She looked up at him as if to say, "You go and see. I'll just stay here if it's okay with you." Collie girl was smarter than him.

As he got up, he grabbed one of the models Marisol had left behind. For some reason he thought he'd bring it down to the lake and then he held it for a moment before a wave of nausea washed over him. It was all he could do not to vomit on the dog as bile and what little liquid was in his stomach poured out of him. He wasn't sure how long he dry heaved the nothing in his belly because when he was done and there was nothing left of the nothing, a second wave hit him. This was the sadness and the fear and the anger and the all of the negative everything and it came all at once as a scream. He had no words but just this sound that contained the whole of his pain and he could not stop even as what was left of his voice was stripped from his throat. Every bit of it and he kept on almost silently, hoarse air worked to fill the silence as it emptied from his lungs and he kept on until his eyes were swollen and no more tears could flow and then he collapsed and found himself standing over himself.

A woman's voice chuckled next to him and then spoke. "Did that help?"

He turned and there was his angel. "Why did I have to come back? For this?"

She smiled and her chuckle became a laugh that chilled him. "Yes, my darling Cloud. Without you, the love in this place would vanish and it would all come undone. The town needed you, Gil, and you were perfect." And the laugh again, only this time it was so very wrong and he tried to really look at her but there were her eyes again and they were wrong and he didn't understand.

And Ivy was licking his face and whining and chuffing. He tried to say something to her but nothing came. He just pulled the dog to him and hugged her and she didn't try to escape from him because she needed to be held and to know that he was okay and not leaving her.

For some reason, he still felt like he needed to go down to the lake and see. He had been told what happened there, but he needed to go and see. He weakly pulled himself up to his feet and looked down at Ivy.

"I'm going down there, okay?" It was more croak than words, but she seemed to understand and resumed her place on his porch. "Stay." She stayed. "Good dog." He made his way across the road to the path.

For no good reason, the forest was beautiful and serene in a way it had no right to be and as he spotted the bridge, it somehow seemed brighter and redder than before, as if it had been built all over again. He saw Shelley sitting by the bank and staring at this insane thing that spanned a lake for no good reason and he suddenly believed in it all, every last bit of it.

"I'm so stupid."

* * *

Something like a voice croaked behind her. She didn't want to turn and look because she thought it might be a recently evacuated spirit. Maybe Kurtz still fighting his crazy stupid fight from beyond. But she could never help but to look and was only a little relieved to see Gil there because he was bound to be the most broken person in a town full of them and she didn't know if she had it in her to hold him together. But he was one of her only real friends left and she needed him even if he was just barely there.

She patted the ground next to her. "Come. Sit."

He smiled a little as he plopped down next to her. As best as she could make out, he said, "I think that's what I just told the dog."

Dog? Oh. "You have Ivy then?"

He nodded and gestured back to his store.

"What happened to your voice?"

He looked around the lake…at how the bridge stood shining and new while all the trees on either end of it were broken and charred and the ground black from the blast. It didn't make any kind of sense except if you believed Kurtz after all or believed even a little part of Gil's town history.

"It was just too much to take and it all came out at once."

And she understood that even though it was barely there. When Jenny came to tell her that Ben died, she had rushed back to Gil's store, but he was gone and she expected that he would be gone for a good long time. For as long as she had known him, when something really traumatic happened, he would vanish without so much as a goodbye. Then she would start getting his post cards. Wherever he would land until he moved on, he would send her a card that simply said, "I'm alive and here. Love you." She kept his cards in a little album at home, but never looked at it. She was like that with so many things in her life. She would collect things, organize them, put them away neatly and then not think about them. She somehow believed that someone, someday perhaps in the far future when people were collecting things from the past to figure out what things were like, would come across her neatly cataloged life and write a book about her that people would read and know this time in history through her preserved collections. She believed that it was her ticket to immortality because she believed if they recreated her life in the future in that way, they might be interested enough in her to find some way to reconstruct her through DNA in her collection or maybe even use a time machine to come back and get her right before she died and bring her to the future where they could make her young again and then she could live forever there. So what she did was important because that could happen and she wasn't going to risk not doing everything she could for that future. But she also wanted to live her whole life now as well. That was important because she loved the people here now and she was needed now, especially after what had happened. Gil wouldn't leave this time. He would simply fade away and that would be worse because there would be no post cards and he wouldn't really be alive.

She took his hand and looked at him with her most severe, but caring and loving look, which she had practiced in the mirror so she knew it was what she thought it was and not to be mistaken for some other strange look…people thought they were giving looks that meant one thing and they actually meant something else and then they were confused when they were misunderstood.

"I thought I was going to have to go home and wait for another post card for my collection. But then there you were with the dog and I wish you weren't there and I wish you weren't here. I think you'd be better off out in the world right now. This is not a good place and you don't belong here. Please take Ivy and go, Gil. Go somewhere beautiful and peaceful…like New Zealand."

Gil laughed silently but his face showed so much pain and she started crying because he had lost hope.

"I can't leave, Shelley. If I went to New Zealand, it would be swallowed up into the Pacific, but somehow I'd float and float and float and end up back here. Why go out in the world and cause all that misery and pain when I can stay here where people are used to it?"

"It's not your damned fault, you asshole! Yes, you are as cursed as this fucking bridge! But you didn't ask for it and you didn't make it. How can it be your fault if it was just something you were born with? Are you supposed to go hide in a cave or kill yourself to save the rest of us from you? Would that make you noble somehow? Oh, sure. We'd all, and at this point I just mean me and Jenny because there's no one else to talk to around here about this crap, we'd go on and on about what a decent guy you always were and how hard you had it and how your bad luck fucked everything up. And we'd miss you because most of the time when nothing bad was happening around you, you're an amazing person and an amazing friend and…and…and… I have all these post cards that say that you're alive and you love me and no one else ever tells me anything like that because I'm just this fucking girl at a counter."

He picked up a stick and drew a little box in the dirt. In the box, he wrote, "I'm alive and here. Love you." Then he gave her a hug and walked over to the bridge. He didn't walk on it. For as long as she knew him, he never walked on it. He would look in it and through it, looking to see where it was supposed to go. But he could never bring himself to walk through it because he said he was afraid that he might not make it out the other side…that he would find where it was meant to go and that could not be a good place. She tried to imagine all the things Gil would tell her about like she tried to imagine Kurtz's world.

But Kurtz was not alive and he was not here. All that time when she and Gil would laugh at what Kurtz was up to and admire his little bridges and all the effort he put into his world, they never really thought anything could happen to him. It didn't really seem possible. She always thought that if someone suffered as much as he had, he would be done with it and could move on beyond it. But Kurtz never really moved on from it. He was always kind of suffering from that attack and they all just played along. What she didn't get was what he was doing here with Tod Logan and John Patrick. It didn't make any sense. As far as she knew, Kurtz had a restraining order against Tod and every time she had seen Tod in town, he had always been so meek, not like before he attacked Kurtz when he had been a lunatic. She really tried very hard not to talk about him or to him or think about him at all because he would always be the one who broke Kurtz and she would never forgive him for it. Now she thought he must have been the one who killed her friend, but at least he had blown himself up for good measure. There was some kind of justice in that, but she wasn't sure what because Kurtz never really hurt anyone at all and his fantasy was harmless because he had never done anything to the bridge either, not that anything could apparently be done to the bridge being that there had been explosions on either side of it and they apparently missed the whole damned thing and it didn't make any sense unless you believed what Gil said and then it made even less sense and then maybe the explosions had been on the bridge like it really seemed which was the only way this made any sense at all. But it didn't matter. It didn't matter because Kurtz died here and Tod and John, too.

John made no sense at all. Everyone thought he was away at Colby College up in Maine studying English Literature. Shelley never saw John without a book of some kind in his hands and he wasn't like the other kids reading stuff just because the teachers made them or reading some popular thing that everyone else was because if you didn't read that popular book or series of books and tell everyone how amazing they were or even if you liked them - because popular books are sometimes popular for a reason - you would trash them to your friends to show how cool and above all that you were but you read them just so you could speak with authority about how awful they were. But John didn't read like that. He just read all the time and read everything. She never saw him with the same book and she knew he wasn't trying to show off or anything. So when he went off to Colby to study books, she kind of laughed because as far as she was concerned, all he ever did was study books and why did he need some college professor to help him do what he always did so well anyway. But she supposed people went off to college not just to learn things they already knew, but to talk to other people who loved the kinds of things they loved as much as they did and share their love. John had a lot of love to share. Sheriff Tom said he talked to him just a few days ago and he was loving life up there and thought he'd stay the summer instead of coming home. A few people had seen him around town yesterday in that stinky old green Chevy Caprice he bought at a police auction up in Burlington and bragged about paying only 200 dollars for and no one doubted for a second, but he never stopped in to talk to anyone like he should have and then they found his car up off the road and found his body blown out into the woods.

They found Kurtz on the other side along with what was left of Tod and she had seen all that because she had been up with Jenny where Ben had died when they heard the explosion just after Gil came back with Ivy almost dead from the fire that killed Denise and Stephanie and Roger and she maybe wondered if she had some of Gil's bad luck because she had just seen Denise and Stephanie right before they died and if it had just been one or the other than it might have been coincidence but it was the both of them and sure they lived right across the street from one another and so the fact that both of them came in at the same time was an even bigger coincidence to the point that with everything else that happened that day it didn't seem possible that it was a coincidence which meant that she was somehow responsible in some small way for what happened because if she just insisted that Denise spend the night with her then Roger wouldn't have been there. No one knew what he was doing there but he would have only been in the house of Denise was there. And if she was with Denise, he wouldn't have been there and he could have called someone when Stephanie collapsed and she knew she wasn't really responsible but that didn't change how she felt and maybe that was how Gil was feeling right now. Shelley stared at Gil and wondered how he made it through days like these.

* * *

Gil stared into the bridge. None of this was his fault. Shelley was right. This thing or whatever was behind this thing had done it to him just like it had killed his father. It had been waiting to kill his father for years just as it had been waiting to kill all those people and it used him. He just had to be there. It needed him in Stansbury and so it kept pushing him back. When the boat went down in Alaska, he came home and when he didn't stay it took his arm and sent him home and even though he knew well enough that he shouldn't be here he stayed because whatever he did, it was going to suck him back in and use him and he couldn't do anything about it except blame himself and he wasn't going to do that anymore. It won and he couldn't do anything about it. He wasn't going to try to figure it out anymore. He wasn't going to worry about it anymore. He wasn't even going to come down and see it anymore. It was here and it was going to be here no matter what he did. He knew leaving Stansbury wasn't really an option, so he wasn't even going to try. What he really hoped was that somehow he would forget it all the way everyone else seemed to. He could see Shelley was starting to figure things out and ask the questions that everyone started to ask and then one day she would just wake up and all this would be there, something she remembered as a bad time but not something that made her ask why and how and she would just go on about her business because that's what always happened and he wished desperately that he could do that to, that he could just open his store and sell his syrup and donuts and moose dolls and not have to know about any of it because it was the knowing that was destroying him the way it destroyed his father and Tod and Will and everyone else who ever somehow kept on understanding even when everyone else just stopped.

Gil turned around and went back to Shelley.

"I'm done."

"Done?"

"Come on."

He took her hand and started walking away from the lake.

* * *

Shelley let Gil lead her for a moment and then stopped. He was her friend, not her boyfriend. She didn't have to come just because he said come. She still needed to figure this out, to try to see what they all saw because it was all wrong and somehow she knew it had always been all wrong and she didn't understand why she had never seen it before.

"Wait."

He stopped and looked at her. "It's not worth it, Shelley. Don't think about it too much and in a little while it'll all just fade away like it always does."

"What are you talking about?" He didn't make any kind of sense.

"It wants me to be like Will. It wants me to go crazy and stare at it all the time and feed it and I'm not going to. I'm just going to go away and I'm going to mourn the loss of my father and my friend and just try to live until it decides to kill me. And then I'll die. It's not my concern and it's not my job. I don't have to solve it or kill it or anything. I just have to wait until it's my turn." He let her hand go and started walking away. "If you want to feed it, go ahead. Just don't talk to me about it."

And then he was gone. She let him go and turned back and sat down by the side of the lake again and watched the water. Nobody ever did anything in this lake. Nobody ever swam in it or fished in it or just went out in a little boat on it. People just came and looked at the bridge and left. It didn't make any sense. She decided to go swimming and started to get undressed. Suddenly she stopped and decided not to go swimming and sat down and looked at the water and wondered why nobody ever went swimming. It didn't make any sense.

Made in the USA
San Bernardino, CA
04 September 2014